'Why were you seeking me, my lord?'

Conscious of just the two of them, the intimate aura permeating the room, Elena sought for calm reason. She swallowed and said in a slightly tremulous voice, 'I know it was not to say—er—say what you have just said.'

Stephan sighed, as if unwilling to leave the intimate scene. 'I came to tell you that we shall be sailing at dawn tomorrow and that I shall be coming to collect you, Elena.'

'I'm an early riser, my lord. I'll be waiting for you.'

He raised a brow. 'You will?'

'I will.'

He laughed, and brought her hand to his mouth and murmured, 'That sounded as if you were taking marriage vows.' He kissed the back of her hand, gazing at it, smoothing the soft skin with his thumb. Then, brusquely, he said, 'I'll see you in the early hours, *mevrouw*. Don't change your mind.'

With slow reluctance he released her hand and unexpectedly Elena felt bereft. 'I shan't, my lord.'

'Good. I am pleased to know that there are some women who try to keep their word.'

Yvonne Purves was born in India and attended boarding school in the Himalayas. Alas, being deaf, she finished at the bottom of the class. Even so, she has always been an avid reader, and can't remember ever learning to read; it came naturally. She was at college in Delhi when Gandhi was assassinated and watched his funeral go by from India Gate. She came to Britain and married here. She has three grown up children and acquired a dog through the RSPCA.

She has been writing since 1980 and has now had five historical novels published, three of which are Masquerade Historical Romances.

Previous Titles

THE DIAMOND COBRA
THE BURNING QUEST

With much appreciation to
Senior Editor Elizabeth Johnson and
Editorial Assistant Vivian Leger.
Also to the people of Shotgate.

NOBLE
BUCCANEER

Yvonne Purves

*First published in Great Britain 1990
by Mills & Boon Limited*

© Yvonne Purves 1990

*Australian copyright 1990
Philippine copyright 1990
This edition 1990*

ISBN 0 263 77006 0

*Masquerade is a trademark published by
Mills & Boon Limited, Eton House,
18–24 Paradise Road, Richmond, Surrey, TW9 1SR.*

*Set in Times Roman 10½ on 12 pt.
04-9011-70148 C*

Made and printed in Great Britain

CHAPTER ONE

RAIN bore down like steel rods on this grey August afternoon and tossed the East Indiaman, *Eastern Command*, as it berthed at the docks of George Town on the eastern seaboard of The Prince of Wales Island.

Standing beneath the awning on deck with her companion beside their luggage, Elena Drew anxiously scanned the dockyard where dark stevedores, wearing conical hats woven from palm fronds, and stripped to the waist, toiled to load crates of cargo. Probably spices, from the strong smell wafting to Elena's nostrils. While they laboured in the downpour, the workers chanted or yelled orders. Not a single European could she see anywhere, let alone the Englishman whose miniature portrait she carried in her locket, and whom she had crossed several seas to meet and live with. Her gaze rested for a while on men carrying huge umbrellas of straw, bustling about on the quay, some in jewel-coloured silks and ornately embellished turbans. She assumed these people were rich merchants.

'Have w-we arrived at the right port, do you think, ma'am?' the middle-aged chaperon asked worriedly, shifting her plump weight, clad in black, from one foot to the other and mopping her bright pink face with a large handkerchief.

'Of course, Aggie. Captain Copeland talked of little else at lunch,' Elena answered, sounding confident, but feeling uneasy. She had been placed at the cap-

tain's table as an honoured passenger and Aggie had
been relegated to another table with the petty officers
when she was well enough to be present at meals. 'He
informed us that this island became a British possession twelve years past in 1786, and that it was orig-
inally called Penang but the British renamed it the
Prince of Wales Island after Prince George.'

Beyond the wharf, Elena beheld a towering structure
which she believed was Fort Cornwallis. The captain
had given his table guests a brief history of the island
and informed them that the fort housed the settlement of the British East India Company.

'There seems to be little but jungle behind that tall
building, ma'am.'

Elena narrowed her eyes, straining to peer through
the relentless downpour. She silently agreed with
Aggie. Indeed, apart from the quayside and Fort
Cornwallis, there appeared to be unending forests that
stretched up the hilly interior.

'Never knew it could be so hot with all that rain,
ma'am.'

As she sweltered in the humid atmosphere, Elena
found no reason to argue, but it would not do to start
complaining of the climate and distressing Aggie
further.

''Struth, this be a wild land. I'd not have come had
I known. Look at them peoples: so dark, with strange
slanting eyes. And then there be no Mr Drew to meet
us . . .'

'Enough, Aggie! You should be used to dark people
since the crew of this ship consists mainly of lascars.
Pray, what would you have done if Father had not
appointed you my chaperon?' Elena did not wish to
remind Aggie of her straitened circumstances, but the

woman's whining jarred on her nerves, adding to her own misgivings over her unorthodox marriage.

Aggie Davis had been one of her father's seamstresses whom he had reluctantly dismissed, to economise. But now that Elena had married, by proxy, the wealthy son of her father's creditor, she had immediately appointed the destitute Aggie to act as chaperon-cum-maid on the long voyage to the Far East where Anthony Drew, the husband she had never seen, dwelt. He worked as a trader for the lucrative British East India Company.

'Look, ma'am, I think a gentleman is coming up here,' Aggie pointed out excitedly. 'Can't see 'is face, 'cause of the umbrella, but his garments are what our gentlemen at home wear.'

Elena spotted a tall figure moving with easy strides up the gangway. When he reached the top he spoke to one of the crew standing sentinel, there to see that no strangers boarded ship.

The crewman pointed towards the captain's cabin and the gentleman handed his umbrella to a small dark man following behind, who, she surmised, was a servant.

Elena noticed that the European with his back to her was dressed in the height of fashion. A green cutaway coat of watered silk covered his broad back and sat snugly on wide shoulders. Tight pantaloons displayed shapely legs partly covered by polished boots. A black tricorn covered his head but she glimpsed fair hair gathered in a wide green bow at his nape, before he disappeared from view. She had no idea what his face was like as he had not glanced her way. Even so, she felt her heart quickening; he might be her husband come to enquire about her from the captain.

She congratulated herself on her careful choice of
dress. Nervously she smoothed the high-waisted creation cut in lilac sheer silk that her perspiration caused
to cling closely to her slim body. The colour suited
her large violet eyes. However, while she had dressed
earlier, the mirror in her cabin had reflected her face
pale and drawn, making her look what she considered
far from her best, effected by the trials she had endured on the voyage.

Because of nausea caused by the rough sea, both
she and Aggie had been confined to their bunks for
the first few days of sailing. Elena had recovered first
but had spent most of the remainder of the voyage
tending her chaperon who had suffered severe bouts
of seasickness.

The vessel gave a sudden lurch and she heard Aggie
groan. 'Why don't you sit on one of our portman-
teaux, Aggie? It shouldn't be long before Mr Drew
arrives.'

But the chaperon suddenly forgot her queasiness.
'The cap'n and the gentleman be coming now, ma'am.'

Elena swung her gaze in the direction Aggie indicated and watched the two men approach. In less
strained conditions she would have considered the pair
comical: the short, stout captain, his chest thrust out,
and his tall, elegant companion.

She had no time to make further comparisons since
the two men now stood in front of her. The tall
stranger took her breath away. If he was her husband
then she had married someone who could compete
favourably in looks and stature with a Greek god. She
touched the locket suspended from a gold chain round
her neck and knew that the miniature portrait of her
husband hidden within, which she had studied daily,

did not in the least resemble the stunning individual who stood a few feet from her; but portraits could be misleading.

'Mrs Drew, why are you standing out here when you two ladies could be sitting in comfort in your cabin?' the captain asked with some concern.

To Elena's annoyance she felt her cheeks glow, aware of the younger man's probing brown eyes sweeping over her in swift appraisal. She had to swallow to enable her to speak at all. 'It was stifling down there, Captain. We decided it would be more comfortable up here. And indeed it has been entertaining for us, watching the activity on the docks.'

'Quite, madam,' the captain agreed, scratching the side of his nose. 'Allow me to introduce you to Lord Stephan Van Coen, of the Dutch East India Company, who is here to speak to you on behalf of your husband. My Lord, this is Mrs Drew and her companion Miss Davis.'

Van Coen's straight masculine lips parted in a smile that dazzled her a little and showed a set of immaculate strong teeth. He caught her small white hand, encased in a lace, elbow-length mitten, and bowed over it while she held her breath for no reason she could account for. 'Enchanted, *mevrouw*.' The hint of an accent affected the deep timbre of his voice and this convinced her that he was in truth Dutch. Never before had she met a foreigner and she had no idea how to act. Her confusion grew.

She inclined her head graciously, conscious of the warmth of his strong, sun-browned hand and the rapid beat of her heart. 'How do you do, my lord?'

All too soon his long fingers released hers and, turning a little, he bowed politely to Aggie. Unlike

Elena, Aggie made no attempt to conceal her admiration. She turned bright scarlet and bobbed in a quick curtsy. 'Pleased ter meet yer, m'lord.'

'We cannot talk here, *mevrouw*,' he addressed Elena. 'What I have to say must be said in private.' He then spoke to the captain. 'Kapitein Copeland, could you please arrange for the ladies' luggage to be brought ashore where my men will take care of it?'

'Of course, my lord. Anything else?'

'*Ja*, Mejuffrouw Davis will need an umbrella. I'm afraid I cannot shelter both ladies beneath mine.'

Captain Copeland gave quick instructions to one of the sentinels and the man handed Aggie his own black cloth umbrella.

The two ladies said their goodbyes and thanks to the captain. Lord Van Coen offered his arm to Elena and held the umbrella over her with his other hand, as they concentrated on negotiating the wet and slippery gangway till they stepped on to the teeming docks. To her surprise he guided her a short way to where another ship was berthed.

Once they reached the bottom of the gangway Elena removed her hand from his arm and stepped back, eyeing him with suspicion, anxiety gnawing at her. 'Is my husband on board, my lord? And is he ill that he could not meet me?'

He gave her an enigmatic look, but said nothing. Taking her elbow in a light grip, he propelled her a mite too firmly up the gangway. 'Your husband is not here, *mevrouw*, but I have been bidden to take you to the island he—er—is on.'

Too late she realised she had not thought to ask this man for proof that he had come from Anthony. She glanced at his features and noticed the determined set of his mouth and strongly etched jaw. The brown eyes, with their daunting flecks of red, stared straight ahead, their inscrutability filling her with dismay.

From the deck of Van Coen's vessel, she looked back and down at the docks but could see no sign of Aggie in the milling crowd. If she shouted, her voice would be lost in the general din below. Moreover, she felt averse to creating a scene. 'I—I do not see my chaperon.'

He cast her a sidelong glance. 'She'll be here soon.'

She regretted her gullibility in trusting this man who was probably laughing at her.

He must have sensed her fear for he said calmly, 'Don't be alarmed, *mevrouw*, I won't harm you.'

The ship swarmed with a motley crew of European and Asiatic seamen all busy on the rigging. It did not take her long to assume that the vessel was being readied to sail.

Elena believed too late that she could be a victim of kidnapping and had stepped unwittingly into a trap. She prayed that it was mere conjecture on her part, a trick of her imagination; except this did little to provide her with consolation.

The vessel itself was not as large as the *Eastern Command* and the cabin Lord Stephan escorted her to was small and plain. Only after he had shut the door did he relinquish his hold on her arm.

Pointing to one of the two chairs near a table, he invited, 'Please sit down, *mevrouw*.'

She could do little else but comply, but did it with aplomb to impress upon him that she felt no fear.

From a sideboard, he lifted a cut glass goblet and a couple of tumblers and placed them on the table.

'This is fine Madeira, ma'am. Would you care to try some?'

'No, thank you, my lord.' She yearned to dispense with time-wasting courtesy and demand to know where her husband was, and why Van Coen had brought her to this brigantine. Except she knew better. Years of dealing with her father's customers had schooled her in the art of patience; a quiet brain worked efficiently.

'Mind if I do?' he asked, raising a thick dark brow.

She shook her head and watched his strong, tanned hands as he poured the drink for himself. Then he removed the tricorn hat.

Elena had been brought up to regard staring as uncouth, but she could not help herself. Without his hat he looked devastating, the gold of his wavy hair highlighted by pale, almost silver streaks, presumably bleached by the tropical sun. He finished his drink and caught her gazing at him. Elena calmly lowered her lids and looked absently at her hands clutching her reticule, but she knew the high colour in her cheeks betrayed her embarrassment.

'Why don't you remove your hat, *mevrouw*? Make yourself comfortable. But it is becoming dark in here. I'll light the lantern.'

He moved with smoothness from one subject to another in a relaxed voice that helped to put her at ease. While he rose and lit the lamp hooked to the bulkhead, she eased off her ostrich-feathered hat with a sigh of relief, placed it next to his on the table, lightly fluffed up her dark red hair dampened with perspiration and made sure the purple ribbon still secured the heavy curls on the crown of her head.

She looked up to find him back in his seat and blatantly staring at her. 'Anthony did not own a portrait of you, so neither of us had any inkling how beautiful you are.'

'Thank you, my lord,' she said and rushed on, fearing that if she gave him a chance he would resort to mild flirtation, totally inappropriate in this serious situation. 'Where *is* my husband?'

He half filled a tumbler with wine and pushed it towards her. 'I think you're going to need this, *mevrouw*.'

A prickling sensation worried her nape and she knew it had nothing to do with the steady trickle of perspiration. 'Is—is Anthony ill?'

The softening of his eyes in pity was more like a blow from an axe as the truth hit her. 'No, *mevrouw*.'

Colour went out of her face. 'Is he—is he . . .?'

Stephan nodded gravely. 'You have been a widow for nigh on six months.'

In the stunned silence that followed she heard the shouting of the tars and felt the roll of the brigantine as it ploughed out to sea.

She did not feel grief. How could she sorrow for a man she did not know, had never seen? Even so, the shock of learning of his death when she had hoped and prayed for a happy life with him was traumatic. Moreover, the ramifications of hers and her father's future brought on by this tragedy threw a black cloak of despair over her. 'How—how did Anthony die?'

'Take a sip of that wine, *mevrouw*.'

With a trembling hand Elena lifted the glass to her mouth and without thinking drained every drop of the Madeira. She did not even splutter nor taste the liquid, so benumbed was her throat.

'He died of a tropical disease. Unfortunately one has to have a robust constitution to survive the maladies rampant in the East. I fear Anthony lacked physical stamina and suffered constant ill health. He is buried on the island we're sailing to.'

The wine appeared to stimulate her frozen mind. 'There seems little point in my going there, my lord, if only to place flowers on his grave. I never knew him and the most logical action to take would be for you to return Aggie and myself immediately to England.'

'I disagree, *mevrouw*. The sensible course you can take, for the moment, is to get some sleep. The wine should help.'

He came round and assisted her to her feet. Just as well since her legs wobbled. 'Your chaperon must now be in the adjoining cabin where you are to sleep. A light supper has been ordered for both of you.'

He handed over her hat, led her to a side door in his cabin and opened it. 'There's Mejuffrouw Davis awaiting you. Goodnight.' He bowed over her hand, stepped back into his cabin, and shut the communicating door.

Aggie lay on a bunk and moaned with every roll of the ship. Elena for once ignored her chaperon's condition and informed her of Anthony's death.

Aggie shot up, her seasickness forgotten, and wrung her hands. 'Mercy! What is to become of us, ma'am?'

'Do what my lord Stephan Van Coen advises. Let us go to sleep and when we are refreshed in the morning we will be in a better frame of mind to tackle the problem.'

*   *   *

The two women were ready for the summons to disembark which came early next day via a series of rapid knocks. Despite the humidity Elena had managed to snatch some sleep.

Stephan Van Coen conducted them on to a wooden jetty instead of the proper stone quayside which Elena had expected. The rain had stopped and the sun blazed down fiercely from an azure sky. The ostrich-feathered hat, which she had considered an encumbrance yesterday, now proved a boon, its wide brim shading her face. Elena found the walk on the long jetty a little enervating; it made her feel as if it were floating away from under her unsteady feet. And only Van Coen's strong arm, to which she clung, gave her the support she needed to keep a straight course.

At last they reached the shore of silver sand where onlookers, comprising a medley of races, crowded. Stephan Van Coen startled her by sweeping her up in his arms. 'What are you doing, my lord?' she demanded indignantly, clutching at her hat.

'You'll have hot sand in your delicate silk slippers, *mevrouw*, if you attempt to cross the beach. I can assure you that burning sand on your skin can be as searing as the touch of a naked flame.'

She stared down at the unshod feet of the spectators. 'But these people are barefoot.'

'They're used to it, lady,' he said drily.

Elena looked over his shoulder to see Aggie happily ensconced in the arms of a burly crewman who returned her rapt smile with a sour grimace.

Someone in the throng asked a question in a foreign language and Stephan Van Coen shouted back a reply in the same tongue. Roars of laughter filled the hot air. Elena kept her eyes lowered, not knowing whether he had cracked a bawdy joke at her expense. She would only make a fool of herself if she upbraided him over it. Anyway she decided to rise above the trifling of a *risqué* jest when she had more pressing decisions to make regarding her future once Stephan installed her wherever he intended to install her.

They finally arrived beyond the beach on a road shaded by towering palms. Waiting, patiently chewing the cud, were brown oxen yoked to a covered cart. Once the women and Stephan were seated inside the conveyance it set off at an ambling pace, wheels creaking, with the driver serenading the animals. Elena picked up a palm-woven fan from among the few lying on the cloth-covered floor and fluttered it near her face, enjoying the manufactured breeze.

She wished she were the singer, who did not seem to have a care in the world. Indeed his melody appeared to have a lulling effect, not only on Aggie, who nodded off to sleep, but on Stephan also. He stretched out his long legs, folded his arms, pulled his tricorn forwards and dropped his head on his wide chest.

The back flap of the cart had been rolled up to enable air to pass through the stifling interior, she supposed. Elena saw another similar vehicle some distance behind and assumed it carried their luggage. On the land opposite to the beach were flooded fields in which people were busily planting what she later discovered was paddy. Despite standing in water and being constantly bent over in the burning sunshine, those employed in this back-breaking work sang happily as they toiled.

Beyond the fields flourished thick jungle, green and lush. The air abounded with the refreshing smell of rain-washed foliage. Then the cart trundled through villages, their neat huts propped on stilts. Pigs and chickens rummaged and scratched around in the space beneath.

Though she found the scenery with its happy people fascinating, Elena suffered inner tension, wondering what this Dutch nobleman Stephan Van Coen planned for her.

She rested back against a cotton-covered cushion and let out her breath in a tired sigh.

'We'll be there soon, *mevrouw*.' His voice, though low, startled her slightly. 'You look pale. Do you not feel well?'

Glancing with surprise at him, she marvelled that he could see her through the hat covering his face. 'Perhaps a little shaken, my lord, especially in my legs. But I expect that's due to the long voyage.'

He pushed back his hat and smiled at her. It brought a peculiar spasm to her heart. 'True. For a start you have to find your land legs. The walk along the jetty proved that. It's nothing untoward. We seasoned sea-dogs find a little difficulty too in adjusting to the steadiness of land after a long spell on the ocean waves. You'll soon be fine again. By the way, may I congratulate you on conducting yourself like a true *tuan*'s wife?'

Elena leaned forward, her dark brow elegantly raised in query. 'Sorry? You said *tuan*'s wife. What kind of wife is that?'

'A person of some stature or a white man who behaves with dignity is known as *tuan*. It could also be interpreted as master, governor or boss.'

'And I, as Anthony's wife, would be addressed as . . . ?'

'You would be called *mem*, probably derived from the Indian *memsahib* meaning mistress. And you'll be considered the lady of the house.'

If I stay that long, Elena responded silently.

The driver of the bullock cart drew aside the front flap and spoke rapidly to Stephan, addressing him as *tuan*.

'Ahmed says we have arrived. Welcome to Besar Rumah. It means Big House.'

'Did it belong to Anthony?' she asked.

'No, *mevrouw*,' he replied, but he did not expand on that while assisting her and Aggie to descend.

The two women stood on the long driveway gaping at the vast marble building ahead of them. To Elena it could be termed a palace, exotic and beautiful with its scalloped archways, gilt domes and towers rising into the azure sky clear of clouds.

'Ooh, ma'am!' gasped Aggie, her eyes wide in awe. 'Never saw no building like that at home.'

Elena looked indulgently at her companion and smiled sadly. To Aggie this island must be like fairyland despite the heat. Little did she know that her stay here was transient, like a dream. They would soon be embarking for home since Elena had no business here with Anthony dead.

Stephan pressed a couple of coins into the cart driver's palm and beckoned to Elena and Aggie to follow him.

Only when Aggie tottered did he come between the two women and offer them his arms for support. They staggered up marble steps to scalloped arcades surrounding garden courtyards filled with exotic flowers Elena had never seen before. He brought them to large, high-ceilinged chambers with meshed doors and silk-draped walls. 'I'll leave you to relax here. There are two suites of rooms so choose one each for yourselves.'

'My lord,' Elena called quickly before he could take his leave. 'I need to speak urgently to you.'

He pinched the bridge of his nose and sighed. 'There's no hurry for that. Give yourself time to recover from your voyage. In a few days, perhaps.'

'No, my lord. I shall not be able to rest till I have spoken to you.'

'Very well, speak and be done.'

'Not here. Is there nowhere private we can discuss the matter?'

His thick brows rose in surprise. 'Alone with me?'

'Yes.' She suddenly realised what she had said and turned quickly to Aggie. 'No offence to you, Aggie. I will explain later.'

Aggie did not look too pleased; even so, she replied politely, 'I'm not offended, ma'am. I'll see to the luggage and unpack.'

'Thank you, Aggie,' she said, following Stephan out.

They passed through more arcades and exotic gardens where parakeets screeched and silver fountains chuckled, till they arrived at the entrance of what she assumed was another suite. 'These are the Sultan's chambers. But he doesn't reside here any more. Now I have the use of them.' They continued along a corridor with doors on either side. Stephan stopped and opened one of ebony and ushered her in. 'This is the library, where I generally do my paperwork.'

The high chamber had shelves of leather-bound volumes from floor to ceiling against its four walls. In the centre was a large teak desk, and there were

several gilt chairs with brocaded seats spaced round
the room. He drew out two, offered Elena one and,
taking the other, placed it near the desk before he sat
down.

'Now, my lord. I want to know what your plans
are for me. Why have you persisted in bringing Aggie
and me here when it would be more convenient for
you to hand us over to the British East India Company
who would arrange for our passages home?'

'I fear that is not possible, *mevrouw.*'

She could feel a tingling on her skin that augured
ill. 'Why not, sir?'

The red flecks in his brown eyes seemed alight as
he studied her face thoughtfully. 'It is as well you are
sitting, *mevrouw.* You will understand why I advised
you to relax for a few days to prepare your body for
the blow it is to receive.'

'I assure you, my lord, that I am not the type ad-
dicted to the vapours. My life has not been pampered
and cushioned from the knocks fate cares to deliver.
Therefore, I would appreciate frankness.'

He shrugged his wide shoulders, lifted his brows
and spread his hands. 'So be it, *mevrouw.* Anthony
made a will.'

An unnerving excitement ran in her veins. She had
to clasp her hands tightly to stop them from shaking.
'Yes? And?'

'And he willed—*you* to *me.*'

CHAPTER TWO

A CLANGING echoed in Elena's head like iron ringing from the blow of a hammer. She stared at him dumbfounded.

Lord Stephan Van Coen took the opportunity to study this woman who seemed unconscious of her stunning beauty. Those eyes of hers were a vivid shade of violet that remained the same colour day and night, unlike most eyes that appeared dark at night. And they were like a cat's: all iris and very little white at the corners. She blinked and he noticed the phenomenal length of her lashes, which curled slightly and were tipped with wine-red, the same shade as her hair.

He disliked the sympathy he felt for her; he disdained women of quality whom he regarded as scions of selfishness and capriciousness, obsessed with fashion and gaiety like his own mother had been. He had assumed Elena was of that type and had looked forward to apprising her of the shocking contents of Anthony's will. Alas, this girl had proved herself in a unique class—one hitherto unknown to him. 'I warned you, *mevrouw*, that you would be surprised. Perhaps a drop of claret will help?'

She ignored his offer. 'Surely, my lord, you do not intend carrying out so barbarous a wish? This will of Anthony's treats me as an inanimate possession.'

'Before I continue to state the full terms of the will, *mevrouw*, I must verify that you are indeed Anthony's wife.'

The little colour in Elena's cheeks vanished. Slowly she rose to her feet. 'How can you doubt it? In truth, sir, I am not given to such evil practices!'

'Sit down, *mevrouw*, if we are to have a sensible discussion.' He waited till she complied and was astonished when she did. 'Now, you will agree that I know nothing about you...''

'But Captain Copeland performed the necessary introductions. Is that not enough proof?'

'No. The real Mevrouw Drew might have taken ill and died at a hostelry and you as her companion-nurse could have taken her place. As an impostor you would have known that Anthony was a very wealthy man.'

'How could I know that, my lord?'

'Easily, from papers the dead woman carried which would proclaim Anthony a nabob. If I knew him, he would have been sure his bride was informed of this.'

'I have a baptism certificate to prove who I am.'

'A baptism certificate could have been stolen. But there were some things an impostor wouldn't know.'

'And that is?'

'The information his father sent him about his real wife. It isn't much, but it is vital proof.'

'My lord, I care not whether you believe I am Anthony's wife or not. As I have said before all I ask is that you return Miss Davis and myself home. There was no point at all in your bringing us to this island.'

'You will need money for the two return passages. Do you have it?'

She had a few gold coins in her reticule which had been intended to tide her over till she met Anthony. Her father-in-law had not entrusted her with hers and Aggie's passage money out here but had paid it directly to the East India Company offices at Leadenhall Street, London. She avoided Stephan's eyes and looked up at the red embroidered screen punkah cooling the room. It wafted back and forth, manipulated by ropes passed through a skylight and operated by some unseen servant beyond. 'No, I do not have enough money.'

Stephan gave an impatient sigh. 'If you can prove you are Anthony's wife, then you will be an heiress. Does that mean anything to you?'

She hesitated. With her inherited wealth she could send money home and give her father a life of ease in his declining years. He would no longer be beholden to Anthony's parents, or need to work late into the night to please an exacting client. He could have a cottage built with a large garden. He had always enjoyed growing plants and could indulge himself and employ a servant to cook and keep house for him. 'Then, ask your questions, sir. I have nothing to fear.'

He leaned forward, elbows on the desk, and observed her keenly. 'Your maiden name, *mevrouw*?'

'Elena Worth. But if I am an impostor, I would have studied that from the baptism certificate,' she remarked cynically.

'Just answer the questions, *mevrouw*.' She rolled her eyes to the ceiling and turned her pink mouth down in mock patience, but said nothing. He smiled a little sardonically and went on, 'Tell me briefly about your life and how you came to be married by proxy.'

'You mean Anthony did not tell you, my lord?'

'Anthony told me everything during a lucid moment. He would have questioned you in the same way as I am doing to verify your identity. If you must know, *mevrouw*, though there have been few imposters it is best to take precautions. Now, if you please . . .'

Elena thought carefully that she must shed her indignation if she were to benefit by Anthony's will and so help her father. And her in-laws could do nothing about it.

'I was born in Maldon, in the county of Essex. My father is Thomas Worth and my mother was Anne.'

'*Was* Anne?'

She nodded. 'She's dead. My father had an outfitter's shop which he ran successfully and this enabled him to pay for me to have quite a good education. Alas, when I grew up, my mother fell ill and I took her place in the shop. But as time passed her condition became worse and the physician's bills mounted. My father was compelled to dismiss his employees—one of whom was Aggie—to economise. But the bills kept mounting and he borrowed money from Anthony's father, who is a wealthy landowner. Eventually my mother died.' Here she paused, recalling her grief and glanced down at her hands. Then, swallowing, she continued. 'My father's business began to slide because without his employees he could not meet the delivery dates. I helped. We both worked late into the night, but it wasn't enough. Father was heavily in debt to Mr Drew, Anthony's father. The interest alone could not be met. The debtor's prison stared Papa in the face.' She remembered that terrible moment of despair when she had hugged her father and they had both sobbed. If it had not been for her, he had said, he would have taken a knife to his wrists. She had pleaded with him to have faith in the Almighty. Something would turn up. It had, but in a way that she could not have foretold.

'Go on.' Stephan's cool voice brought her back to the present.

She blinked, straightened her shoulders, and continued, 'Then Mr Drew sent for Papa and me, over the lapsed payments, of course. He astonished us both by promising to cancel the debt and to help Papa in his business if I agreed to marry his son, Anthony, by proxy. I love my father too much to see him languish in a debtor's prison, my lord. So—so here I am.'

Elena's heart filled with bitterness because she had been forced to reveal the most hurtful and humiliating period of her life, when she had been compelled to marry a man she had not seen. Even so, the sacrifice was worth it if it meant her father could enjoy security and peace of mind till the end of his days.

'And Aggie? Why did she not stay behind and return to working for your father?'

'She preferred to come with me.'

'In the hopes of finding a husband?'

She raised her chin and looked down her small narrow nose at him. 'You will have to ask Aggie that, my lord.'

'There is just one more question, a crucial one. Describe Anthony's parents and the furniture in their parlour.'

She did so without hesitation but she had to shut her eyes and try and recall the furniture. She had been too afraid and shocked to notice her surroundings. However, after deep concentration, she at last remembered picking agitatedly at the gold fringe edging the red brocaded upholstery of her chair, when Mr Drew stated his proposal. Breathlessly she told Stephan.

He smiled in relieved approval. 'Good. Now could I have a specimen of your handwriting?' He passed her a sheet of paper and a quill dipped in ink.

She reflected there was little point in refusing and scribbled a couple of lines stating that she and her companion had voyaged to the Prince of Wales Island on the Indiaman *Eastern Command*.

Stephan opened his desk, withdrew an envelope, and compared the script with a sheet inside. It must have been the letter introducing herself to Anthony which had been dispatched a month before she sailed. She held her breath while he checked the writing. At the time she had written that letter she had been meticulous, to impress Anthony. Would the neat calligraphy match the hasty scrawl she had just scratched?

Elena let her breath out quietly so as not to exhibit the relief she experienced when he looked across at her and smiled. 'I believe,' he said simply.

'What are the terms of the will, my lord?'

He wondered if she was like his mother, greedy for gold. All that rigmarole about her only wanting to return home could have been a blind shielding her true avarice. She had forgotten that Anthony had put her completely in his power. 'Perhaps it has escaped your memory, lady, that Anthony willed you to me.'

'What exactly is meant by that, sir?' she asked diffidently.

'Anthony was aware he was dying and felt worried about you, because he knew it was too late to prevent you from coming out here. Else you could have had the marriage annulled. You still can, of course, but you lose all claim to the remaining terms of the will.' He paused, perhaps to let his words sink in. 'Anthony wished me to take care of you.'

'Oh, you mean, you will be my protector, while I am out here?'

'In a more intimate way.'

She could feel her heart increase its beat as her mind grasped his meaning. She rose and drew herself up to her full height which was tall for a woman. 'I will be no man's mistress, my lord. I will work for you in any other capacity that does not entail loss of virtue or honour.'

He fingered his chin while his brown eyes boldly dropped to her full breasts, clearly defined by the sweat-dampened dress. 'And that is?'

'I can help settle Anthony's private accounts. As a wealthy man, he must have had a number of assets, land, et cetera, which need methodical listing. I am qualified because I did my father's bookkeeping for him.'

'You're right, *mevrouw*, Anthony had much property not only here but in England. However, his accounts have all been taken care of. And even if they hadn't, you would not consider such work honourable.'

'May I know why, sir?'

'You may indeed, lady. You would be promoting piracy.'

Elena frowned down at him, her large violet eyes quizzical. 'I fear I do not understand.'

'To put it bluntly, Anthony was a pirate.'

*   *   *

Elena groped behind her like a blind person, looking for the seat of her chair, and slumped down on it. Silence hung, stretched and screamed in the vast chamber.

'Did you need to tell me that, my lord?'

'I fear that I had to. I think you'd better know something about Anthony's life here.'

She nodded dismally, her dream of building a cottage for her father fading by the moment.

'When he died he was still officially employed by the East India Company. They did not know that he was supplementing his wages with the lucrative gains of piracy.'

'And he willed this fortune to me?'

'No, he willed it to me along with you.'

'Then what was that proof of identity charade about?'

His straight lips curved with mockery. 'To make sure I acquired the right woman.'

She had not missed the slight stress on the word 'right'. There was little she did miss in the company of this compelling man; he kept her brain and senses in a high state of alertness.

'Aren't you going to ask me how I met Anthony, *mevrouw*?'

'Does it matter, my lord?'

'It certainly does.'

'How?'

'Anthony desired that I—er——' he scratched the whiskers on the left side of his face '—take care of you.' He paused to give her time to absorb what he'd said, but she could only gape at him speechlessly. 'We met when I captured the East Indiaman on which he was sailing to the Prince of Wales Island, where he had been employed as a trader for the East India Company. I——'

She leaned forward in her seat. 'Excuse me, my lord, you said you *captured* the East Indiaman?'

'That is correct,' he replied smoothly, leaning back in his chair, but never allowing his gaze to wander from her.

'Is Holland at war with us?'

'The Dutch and British are not the best of friends out here in the East, and they have forged an uneasy alliance—but no, *mevrouw*, our countries are not in conflict.'

'Then—then I am baffled that you should *capture* a British ship. Such practices occur only during wars...'

'And piracy.'

Elena gave a loud gasp and shot to her feet, her colour ebbing and flowing with a turbulence that matched the tide on the Essex shore.

He clicked his tongue in mock admonishment. 'Really, ma'am. If you keep bobbing up and down I fear I'll develop a nasty squint.'

She ignored the quip which she deemed ill-timed. Nevertheless, she unconsciously did as he bade and sat down abruptly, not because she feared he would acquire a squint but because her legs were on the verge of collapsing. 'Have I been brought to a nest of pirates? And how long have you plied this nefarious trade, my lord?'

'A goodly number of years,' he said with bland satisfaction.

'Do you—you not consider it appalling? Or perhaps you have given the practice up now?' she asked hopefully.

Her hope died when in answer his laughter rang with incredulity. Slowly she realised that she herself was a captive.

'This island ... Who does it belong to, my lord?'

'Me.'

Astounded, she could scarcely believe anyone could be so shameless, act as if they did not possess a conscience.

'Let me assure you *mevrouw*, that I did not acquire this island through mayhem and bloodshed, but quite legally...'

She laughed shakily, disconcerting him momentarily as he admired the evenness and whiteness of her teeth. 'In truth, I would have thought that the word "legal" and its variations did not hold meaning for you.'

Nevertheless he carried on as if she had not interrupted. 'It previously belonged to the Sultan of Kedah and he awarded it to me for safeguarding his ships from foreign pirates. Ironical, isn't it? But then life is a paradox.'

Her smooth brow puckered in a quizzical frown. 'But I remember Captain Copeland introducing you as a member of the Dutch East India Company.'

'It's perfectly true. I hold shares in it and from the profits, everyone assumes, I purchased this palace. But you know differently.'

'Are you not afraid I will put it about that you are a pirate?' she asked, hoping to jolt him out of his complacency.

He lifted his broad shoulders in a nonchalant shrug and grinned easily. Except his words were underscored with a trace of steel. 'Everyone here knows that—we are all pirates in arms. And you cannot spread the word elsewhere since you are not likely to leave this island except in my company or at my behest.'

Elena began twisting her hands agitatedly in her lap. 'Sorry, my lord, I must insist that you return Aggie and myself home. It is against my principles to live among the lawless.'

'I regret, *mevrouw*, that I refuse to honour your insistence,' he said in a soft courteous voice as if he were paying her a compliment. 'You are here to remain. And you would not be living among the lawless, but the righteous. My principles may not be conventional; however to me they are just and I and all on this island abide by them.'

'I—I—— Could I have a glass of water, my lord? I fear I find this—this discussion somewhat—er—fatiguing.' Heaven help her! She prayed she was not about to submit to the vapours.

'Why, certainly.' He strode to the door and pulled a long cord by its side.

'I think we should revert to the topic of Anthony's life, my lord. You were saying you captured the Indiaman he was on.'

'*Ja,*' he agreed, nodding as he returned to his chair. 'We, of course, divested the ship of its valuable commodities which were being exported from India. We imprisoned the ship's crew and merchants in the hold. Late that night, Anthony asked one of my men if he could speak with me. I consented and we immediately struck up a rapport. Anthony confided that he felt too restricted working for the East India Company. He asked to join me. But I persuaded him to stay with the Company to use it as a screen to safeguard his reputation, and join me occasionally on raids. As he was a senior trader, he did not have to account for his every movement, so long as he could show healthy profits on his sheets. He also supplied me with vital information about the shipment of valuable commodities. Alas, he contracted a terrible sickness.' He spread his hands. 'And you know the rest.'

A knock sounded on the door and Stephan called out something in the local tongue. A small man in white livery entered with a glass of water on a silver salver. Stephan directed him to Elena. He drew up a small ebony fretwork table, and placed the tray on it. She smiled at the servant and took the water. 'Thank you.'

'That's Abdul. He's been my personal valet for years.'

'And he's a pirate?'

'Of course.'

Elena drained the glass, inhaled deeply, and set it down on the salver. She extracted a dainty lace-edged handkerchief from her reticule and dabbed her mouth. 'That's better,' she remarked, and went straight on to say, 'What did you do with the prisoners?'

'Not what you think,' he said, chuckling. 'We did not force them to walk the plank; on the contrary, we allowed them to continue their voyage but less the commodities.'

With some distaste she said, 'You are obviously proud of what you do, my lord. Rather an unusual occupation for an aristocrat.'

'*Ja*, and, whether you approve or not, I consider my brand of piracy to be right,' he reiterated. And to confirm his commitment he brought his fist down with a light thump on the arm of his chair.

'How did you come to be a . . . what you are?'

He laughed softly at her hesitation. 'I assure you, *mevrouw*, I do not take offence at being called a pirate. My true designation is buccaneer captain—I command the brigantine I brought you here on. It is known as the *Stephan*—my father's gift to me. I hasten to add he knows nothing of my so-called lawlessness. He is a director of the Dutch East India Company. But after a couple of runs between Rotterdam and Malacca, I decided I could be of more use to people that mattered by opting for piracy.' He abruptly changed the subject. 'But I brought you here not to relate my life story but to discuss your future, *mevrouw*.'

'Precisely, sir. What do you intend doing with me?'

'I thought you might have guessed by now.'

She sighed impatiently. 'I fear I am not blessed with the sight.'

'I intend to comply with Anthony's request.'

Elena tried to quiet the pounding in her head. She supposed he would offer either to be her legal guardian or—proposition her to become his mistress. Without hesitation she intended refusing the latter. For him to propose marriage to her would be definitely out of the question since he, being a Dutch aristocrat, would naturally choose a partner of his own class and nationality. It mattered little that he had opted for a degrading life. He could toss it aside tomorrow with no loss of face or fortune. Such was the luck of the rich upper classes. 'And Anthony's request is?'

He looked at her with lazy speculation through the mesh of his dark lashes, a faint smile playing round his mouth. 'To make you my bride.'

She had to wait several seconds before she found her voice, and he appeared in no hurry to hear her speak. 'But—but that's impossible.'

Stephan shook his head and laughed cynically. 'You're not making sense, *mevrouw*.'

Of course she wasn't making sense, she thought vaguely. How could she with her mind whirling in confusion?

'You marry a man by proxy and take a gruelling voyage which spans eighteen months to be with him. *That* you consider possible. But when *I* propose to you it entails no ordeals; the opposite in fact. You will enjoy all the comforts befitting the mistress of this palace. And you turn round and say it's impossible. Or am I so repulsive to behold?'

'No, of course not; you are pleasing to look on, my lord,' she said, and he laughed. Elena could feel the heat climbing from her neck to her face. 'When I agreed to marry Anthony I had no notion he was involved in piracy and I doubt whether his parents are aware of that.'

'*Mevrouw*, I believe you would have married a murderer to save your father from a debtor's prison.'

He had judged her correctly, she reflected miserably. She probably would have married anyone to save her beloved father. 'My lord, I have received so many shocks this morning that I cannot reason sensibly. I ask for time to think over your proposal.'

He bowed his head graciously. 'You have all the time in the world, lady. Even so, it would pay you to bear in mind that your refusal would mean the loss of a considerable fortune. Not only you but your father, Aggie, and your father's employees would face dire consequences.'

Elena stood up. 'My lord . . .'

A long clock in the corner of the room chimed the noon hour.

'I'm sorry to have kept you here so long, *mevrouw*.' He offered her his arm which she took diffidently. 'Luncheon will be served in an hour. I'll come and fetch you.'

'I am not hungry, my lord. Perhaps if you could have a cool drink brought to my chambers, I would be most grateful.'

He escorted her to the entrance of her suite. '*Mevrouw*, it is inadvisable to do without nourishment in this climate. You must keep up your strength to fight the numerous infections that afflict the East. I'll call for you.' He bowed briefly and strode away.

She felt lost as she passed from one spacious chamber to the next: all luxuriously decorated with pink, satin-draped walls and furnished with wide divans covered with the same material as the drapes and liberally heaped with silk and satin cushions in every hue. She stood on a deep-pile blue carpet in one of the rooms and called, 'Aggie, where are you?'

Voices echoed somewhere beyond the chamber and Aggie entered through a door hidden behind a curtain. 'Ah, ma'am, I am relieved to see you! Can't make head nor tail of what them servants are saying.'

'Where have you put my luggage? I see no signs of it anywhere. All these rooms look alike. Which one is the bedroom? And I fear I cannot find the bathroom. I need to take a wash before my lord Stephan Van Coen returns to escort us to lunch.'

'It took me a fair bit of time finding the bathroom, what with them wall drapes covering the doors. Come, ma'am.' Aggie led Elena out of the chamber and passed through a couple of others, then drew back a curtain and pushed open a door. 'There you are, ma'am. I dare confess the sight of the bathroom fair shook me.'

It shook Elena as well. The bath was like one of those sunken pools she had passed in the courtyard, but this one was of marble, round and scalloped. Water gushed in to the bath from a gold tiger's head, and scalloped channels took care of the overflow.

She twirled her hands in the cool depths, its invitation too potent to resist. 'I'll take a bath. Where have you put my clothes, Aggie?'

The chaperon beckoned her to an antechamber where there were two wide and tall cupboards with intricate designs of birds and animals carved on their doors. Inside were her clothes, neatly stacked. Elena selected a lemon day-dress of fine muslin with a pale green sash. Anthony's mother had accompanied her on a shopping spree and had generously paid for and allowed Elena to choose her own clothes for her trousseau, as her mother-in-law called it. 'Mind you buy good quality clothes, lass. Don't want Anthony to think Mr Drew and I have chosen a drab yokel of a bride for him.'

Elena and her mother-in-law had travelled to London where they were directed to several modistes. She had chosen the one with an elegant but simple dress displayed in her window. As the Prince of Wales Island was reputed to be hot with no winters, she had ordered three light dresses with necessary accessories, bonnets, hats and sunshades to suit and an elaborate ball gown.

Feeling refreshed from the cool bath in the pool, she was pleased with herself in the muslin creation which she saw reflected in the tall dome-shaped mirror framed in gilt. 'You look beautiful, ma'am,' Aggie said. 'My lord will be besotted.'

'Aggie, I haven't dressed to charm him. I just wish to make myself presentable. And you, Aggie, have you none other to wear than that black thing?'

'No, ma'am, I have but two dresses and both are black.'

'I wish mine fitted you . . .'

Aggie chuckled. 'We'd have to sew two of yours together side by side to fit me, ma'am. But surely I do not have to accompany you to lunch with my lord?'

'You are my chaperon, Aggie. I need you to be with me most times.'

Aggie pursed her lips in disapproval. 'Ah, but you were alone with my lord for the best part of an hour. That don't seem proper like. It don't seem to signify in this here uncivilised land.'

'It was necessary for me to speak to my lord alone. Uncivilised, did you say? I wouldn't call a palace like this uncivilised!'

'No, ma'am.'

A tap sounded far off and Aggie rushed to answer its summon. 'That'll be my lord, ma'am.'

Elena followed Aggie through a series of chambers and waited in the last one as the chaperon opened the door and bobbed. 'Afternoon, m'lord.'

'Good afternoon, Aggie.' He looked beyond her to Elena, and the red flecks in his brown eyes appeared to light up. 'Ah, it is a delight to see a lady actually awaiting her escort.'

She smiled and bowed her head courteously. 'We are ready, my lord.'

'We? I intend taking just you to lunch. There is no need for your duenna since you are to be my bride.'

CHAPTER THREE

AGGIE looked crestfallen and a little hurt that Elena had not mentioned his lordship's intention to marry her. She stepped back into the room. 'As your lordship wishes,' she said huffily.

Elena heard Aggie faintly, her ears buzzing from the shock of Stephan's blatant announcement that she was to be his bride. 'But I have not given you my consent yet.'

'We'll talk of that later, *mevrouw*. Discussing matters outside apartment doors I find reprehensible,' he said drily and offered her his arm. 'Shall we go?' Elena did not take it.

She summoned enough equilibrium to say coldly, 'And where do you suppose Aggie is to eat, my lord? You cannot expect her to be confined to these chambers.'

He bowed a little to the chaperon, who turned scarlet. 'My fervent apologies, *mejuffrouw*. My British midshipman, Mynheer Russell, and his lady wife—she is half Malayan and half Dutch—will be calling on you to partake of lunch at their premises. I think you will feel at home with them.'

Aggie seemed a mite abashed; nevertheless, she gave a quick curtsy and said, 'Thank you, m'lord.'

He turned to Elena. 'I hope that satisfies you, *mevrouw*.' Again he held out his arm.

This time she took it, but glanced back anxiously at Aggie. 'You'll be all right, my dear?'

The chaperon perked up. 'To be sure, ma'am. I can hold my own,' she asserted with a sniff, shutting the door of the suite.

Stephan and Elena reached the vast dining-chamber without saying anything. What she noticed first was that there were three men and a woman seated at the long banqueting table. The three men rose as the couple entered. Stephan immediately made the introductions. 'This is Kapitein Vans Paul and his lady wife. Then there's Captain Porrot, a compatriot of yours and a friend of Anthony's, and Monsieur le Capitaine Fourier. Gentlemen, meet Mevrouw Drew, the late Anthony's wife.'

Elena let out a quiet breath of relief that he had not announced that she was to be his bride. But he might yet do so during the meal, she thought suddenly, and immediately tensed.

All three men and the woman came forward to greet Elena. She noticed they were all dressed in the height of fashion favoured by the upper classes at home, and secretly commended herself for taking pains with her toilet. Confidently she smiled and responded to the introductions, aware that the men's eyes were studying her, not with admiration, but with barely concealed animosity. Why, she wondered, did they disapprove of her?

Then she was distracted as Stephan pulled out a crimson brocaded chair on the right side at the top of the table for her and took the seat at the head. She sat opposite Mevrouw Vans Paul, aware that she was under keen scrutiny from the woman's blue eyes. But there was no such hostility in them as she had observed in the men.

Servants with a mongoloid cast to their features, smart in peacock-green liveries of wide calf-length trousers, hip-length shirts gathered in with wide crimson sashes, to match the wall drapes, and printed cloths wrapped round their heads, poured drinks and served sections of marsh melon as the first course. It was delicious and Elena realised the extent of her hunger.

'We are sorry that you were not able to meet your husband, Mevrouw Drew,' Mevrouw Vans Paul said in a mellow voice. 'Anthony was exceedingly popular—isn't that so, Stephan?'

'Indeed, *mevrouw*, but I don't think Mevrouw Drew wishes to be reminded of her loss,' Stephan remarked coolly, and Elena wondered if he disliked the Dutch girl.

The lady addressed turned a delicate pink and, to save her from further embarrassment, Elena hastily said, 'It doesn't matter, madam—I didn't know Anthony so I consider him a stranger. However, I do not wish to give the impression that I am callous; his death was a shock to me and I feel sorrow for him as I would for anyone who loses their life.'

'Let us not dwell on so gloomy a subject. And I beg you not to stand on ceremony, my dear—do call me Lucy. And you are...?'

'Elena.'

'What a pretty name, just like its owner.'

'Thank you, Lucy. If I may return the compliment, you are a comely lady yourself.' Of a certainty Lucy Vans Paul could have been moulded from translucent china, so delicate was her complexion and so ideally suited to the fine pale gold of her hair.

Lucy dabbed her small mouth daintily with a napkin, her bright blue eyes glittering with laughter. 'Why, thank you, my dear. I wish Mynheer Vans Paul was as generous as you,' she said drily, sweeping her husband a disdainful glance. But he appeared to be engrossed in what Captain Fourier and Captain Porrot were saying.

There came a lull in the conversation as the servants changed the plates and brought round the main course. Elena eyed the thin sticks with meat skewered on to one end of them, and raised her shapely brow enquiringly at Stephan.

'That's called satay—you should dip it in that separate bowl of peanut sauce supplied. Try it, *mevrouw*.'

All eyes watched Elena as she tentatively dipped the satay in the reddish sauce and nibbled. Indeed she had never in her life eaten anything so full of flavour. 'Mm . . . it's piquantly delicious.'

'What a boon for the cook! He'll be grateful that here's one palate that does not need educating,' Stephan remarked, laughing, and the others chuckled politely with him.

'When did you leave England, *madame*?' Captain Fourier asked Elena, his handsome dark eyes resting— again with that hint of hostility—on her. He was soberly dressed in a black cut-away coat over a snowy shirt and cravat.

'Eighteen months past, Captain.'

He put his deeply tanned hand on his straight black hair, which was tied back in a broad ribbon, and thought for a while. 'That would be in March 1797. A month after the sea battle between your country and mine. I fear our nations have been in conflict ever since the revolution. Is that not so, Monsieur Porrot?'

'Assuredly, sir,' the grey-haired Englishman said and added with pride, 'Our great commander, Horatio Nelson, defeated the French in the battle of St Vincent.' He then looked across at Elena with alert but cold grey eyes and addressed her, 'Did you not hear about it, ma'am?'

Was he implying that she would be too ignorant to know of major events occurring in the world? she wondered, discomfited. She adopted his cool demeanour and said, 'Yes, there was some talk of it on our ship, but my companion and I were too ill from seasickness to worry about wars. And our worthy captain was too preoccupied in—er—endeavouring to reach his destination intact.' She almost said that the captain was more concerned with keeping clear of pirates, but just stopped herself in time.

Captain Fourier's long face creased in a smile. 'Your Horatio Nelson may be the English hero, but Napoleon Bonaparte is every Frenchman's idol. *La!* but that makes little difference to us out here on Pulau Mutiara, for we disregard each others' nationality and are united in a single cause. You could call us comrades in—er——'

'Comrades in arms? Is that what you mean, *mynheer*?' Stephan cut in smoothly.

The Frenchman rubbed his clean-shaven chin and lifted his shoulders in a Gallic shrug. 'As you say, *monsieur*.'

Elena found it amusing that, though these men professed unity under one banner, they insisted on preserving their national identity by making use of their language in addressing people. She had an uneasy feeling that Fourier had meant to say 'comrades in crime'. She felt dismayed that these four men with their impeccable grooming and faultless display of good manners were none other than buccaneers. Slanting Lucy a quick glance, she wondered if this beautiful, elegant woman knew that her thin, tall husband with his fiery hair and immaculate clothes was a notorious outlaw? Of course she must, though she probably regarded him as a romantic hero. Elena tried to shrug off the sensation that none of Stephan's captains liked her. Did they regard her as an intruder? Perhaps that was the reason for their hostility.

As the dessert of fresh fruit was passed round in a shallow wicker basket, Stephan named each of its contents. Elena thanked him and selected a slice of papaya. Simultaneously she asked Lucy, 'Have you been here long?'

Lucy cut a side off a large mango and expertly scooped out the golden flesh with a small silver spoon. 'About a year on Pulau Mutiara, but I was in Malacca for a couple of years before coming here.'

'Have you been married long?'

Lucy hesitated and glanced at her husband, but he appeared to be oblivious to the conversation, apparently wholly absorbed in relishing his bite of guava. 'I—I met Jan at Malacca and we have been—er—marrried nigh on fourteen months.'

A telling pause ensued and Elena mused whether she had committed a *faux pas* by asking an awkward question.

Stephan came to the rescue. 'Anyone for more wine?' He beckoned to a servant to refill the glasses. 'Let us drink a toast to welcome Elena and wish her every happiness on Pulau Mutiara, which, incidentally, means Island of Pearls.'

She blinked at him, surprised by the toast; he appeared confident that she would stay here permanently. Even so, she breathed easier that he had not mentioned his wish to make her his bride. She would have been compelled to argue and consequently embarrass everyone. Elena acknowledged the toast with a smile and a thank you.

After that the atmosphere relaxed and the men began discussing the weather and the best time for sailing. They would probably be on a piracy mission, Elena speculated. Perhaps they intended to set sail tonight. Were these men independent pirate captains owning their own vessels? If so she could appeal to one of them to take her to the British possession, the Prince of Wales Island, where she could persuade the governor to send her and Aggie home. Once there she could put in a claim for Anthony's property. As his legitimate wife she must be entitled to it.

But what if these buccaneers were working in conjunction with Stephan? She yearned to be alone with him so that she could learn more about these other captains.

Her chance came when he took her back to her apartment. 'Would you care to come in for a while, my lord? I have a number of questions to ask.'

His unique eyes skimmed appreciatively over her for a while, a faint smile playing about his masculine lips. He looked superb in a pale blue cut-away coat that contrasted pleasantly with his smooth-fitting buff pantaloons and hessian boots. All was designed to show off his magnificent physique. What a pity that he functioned on the wrong side of the law. She astounded herself by abruptly and irrelevantly musing on what it would feel like being kissed by him. The thought brought a slow burn to her face, intensified by his unwavering look. Desperately Elena began searching for something to say, when, at last, he spoke.

'First, *mevrouw*, I must laud you on your excellent conduct at lunch. I believe everyone present was as impressed by your beauty and manners as I was. Regrettably, however, I cannot tarry and hear what you wish to discuss. But, I promise you, tonight after we have dined I'll be able to give you my full attention. Meanwhile, I suggest you take a siesta. You must still be tired from your long voyage.' He lifted her hand and pressed his mouth to the back of it without taking his eyes off her face. The kiss caused an uncontrollable yet pleasant shiver to streak up her arm. 'Till dinnertime, *au revoir, mevrouw.*'

There was no sign of Aggie, as Elena closed the door on Stephan's departure and made her way through the rooms. She assumed her companion was either still dining with her new-found friends or had retired to her own suite where she was enjoying a siesta.

She noticed the coolness of the bedchamber as soon as she reached it and shortly discovered the source. Frames of wet grass placed over the two large windows not only kept out the glare, but the wind blowing through them cooled the room.

Taking out a silk night-robe from the cupboard in the antechamber, Elena discarded her high-waisted dress and slipped into the comfortable loose garment.

With a sigh of pleasure she sank on to the soft divan and, eliminating all troublesome thoughts, forced herself to relax.

* * *

Elena was already awake when a smiling female servant brought in a tray with a silver teapot, steam curling from the spout, cutlery, china cups and saucers and a plate of biscuits. The tiny woman was dressed in the same colour as her male counterparts but the style was different: the shirt she wore fitted her tiny waist and fell to her knees, over a skirt consisting of a single length of material wrapped round the waist to fall in soft folds to the ankles. The servant smiled, nodding her head and saying something. Elena presumed it was a greeting and smiled back. She rose and took the salver, placed it on one of the ornate tables which stood against the draped walls, and gestured politely to the servant that she could go.

I must learn the local tongue, she told herself, because I have an uncanny feeling that I shall be on this island for some time, and unless I wish to remain isolated from the islanders it will be necessary for me to master their language. Perhaps this knowledge will come in handy at some time.

Thus musing, Elena poured out a cup of tea, which was hot and refreshing. The first time she had tasted the drink was on the *Eastern Command* at Captain Copeland's table. At home only the rich could afford to buy China tea and there she had drunk the popular and cheaper hot chocolate.

While she enjoyed a second cup she pondered on what had happened to Aggie. She knew a reluctance to go in search of her suite for fear of getting lost, and had not as yet investigated the whole of her own apartment. Draining her cup, Elena was about to move to the bathroom to bathe and dress for the evening when Aggie came bustling in, looking excessively pleased with herself—and no wonder!

Elena's eyes widened. 'Why, Aggie! Where did you get that beautiful dress? I declare I have not set eyes on such pretty floral material. Is it cotton?'

Aggie glided mock-regally to where Elena sat and held out her skirt for the girl to feel. 'Yes, ma'am. I had it made,' she said smugly.

'Pray, when?' Elena asked astonished. 'You haven't been on this island for a full day yet. Are you having a game with me? I dare say your dinner companion gave it to you.'

The chaperon laughed shrilly. 'Ma'am, if you saw Mrs Russell you too would laugh. She is a wee lady if ever I saw one. In no way would any of her clothes fit you, least of all me.'

Elena spread her hands helplessly. 'Then how...?'

'Well, now, ma'am; I suppose I'd best start from the beginning. Mind if I sit down?'

Elena gestured to a small divan and both settled down on it, Aggie smoothing her skirts carefully like a young girl in her first party dress.

'Mr and Mrs Russell called for me just as my lord said. They took me to their chambers in another part of the palace. Ma'am, this building is enormous! Anyways, as you know I had lunch with them and we became fast friends. I felt I'd known 'em for years. But the food—pah! That be another matter.' She paused and wrinkled her snub nose with distaste. 'Mrs Russell told me I'd soon get used to it. I remarked how pretty her dress was and as 'ow I felt ashamed in me old black garment. She says to me, foreign like, ''Now don't you worry none, dear. I have this here

Indian tailor who can run up a dress in the time it takes us to eat our meal!"'

'Really?' Elena marvelled, staring at the printed creation. She remembered it had taken her father and herself a week to sew a man's suit. 'And did you have to give the tailor your measurements?'

'Yes, that I did, ma'am. But first let me tell you what happened.' She sighed happily. 'Well, Mrs Russell sends one of her servants to bring this man and he comes quicker 'an a blink of an eye and with him comes a cloth merchant wheeling a cart loaded with them bolts. So before we sits down to eat, I chose the material and Mrs Russell took me into her bedroom. Here this tailor measures me and says he'd be back before sundown with this 'ere dress all finished. And lordy me, ma'am, I'm blessed if he didn't!'

'Certainly this tailor has wrought a miracle. You've forgotten one thing, though.'

'Yes, ma'am?'

'Who paid for the dress?'

'Now then, ma'am, I've had no cause to spend the wages you paid me. The cloth and making of the dress cost me all of five shillings.'

Elena looked at her aghast. 'Why, that's incredible!'

'Pardon, ma'am?'

'I mean it's hard to believe. I paid several guineas for each of the four gowns I brought with me.'

'The tailor promised to come here tomorrow, ma'am; I told him you was sure to order clothes from him. Now that you are to marry my lord, you'll want some more pretty dresses.'

The colour died on Elena's face. 'Aggie, I hope you did not tell the Russells that I am to marry his lordship!'

'No, certainly not, ma'am. I saw that nothing had been settled between you.'

'Indeed not, Aggie. I have no intention of marrying him.'

It was Aggie's turn to gasp. 'Oh, ma'am, if you don't, whatever will become of us? Will—will we have to make that awful sea voyage home again? I dare swear that I shall die!'

'Now don't despair, Aggie. We will have to wait and see what plans we can make. By the way, did the Russells mention anything about his lordship? I mean did they say what his profession is—that is, what he does for a living?'

'To be sure, ma'am; they said he is the captain of a Dutch ship.'

So Aggie didn't know the truth. Stephan must have warned the Russells not to say anything to her.

Elena patted her on her hand. 'Well, he has invited me to dine with him, so I must get ready now. What will you do?'

'I've invited the Russells to dine with us, ma'am. I wanted you to meet them. But if you are to eat with his lordship, I'll take them to my rooms.'

'Good, so long as you are not on your own.'

Aggie had gone by the time Stephan called for Elena. It was dark but lamps had been lit in the arcades and courtyards, the light attracting spectacular moths. A peculiar sound filled the night.

'What's that noise, my lord?'

'You'd better get used to it, lady, because you will hear that every night; it's made by insects called cicadas.'

As they passed along arcades surrounding courtyards bathed in moon radiance and sunken moonlit pools, Elena became aware that they were not walking in the direction of the dining-room. Apprehension touched her spine. 'My—my lord, where are we going?'

She began to withdraw her hand from his arm, but he abruptly placed his large hand over hers, keeping it in place. 'Now don't be alarmed, *mevrouw*. I'm not going to harm you.'

'Then where are you taking me, my lord?'

'I'm taking you to my apartment. Stop struggling. I've said you'll be safe with me.'

'And why should I believe you, sir? I hardly know you.'

'You'll have to take my word for it, *mevrouw*. I would be wasting time if I didn't intend keeping it. You can be sure that no one would come to your help if I had dark designs on you—which I do not.'

'Then—then why are we not dining with the others?'

He slanted her a cynical glance but did not slow his strides. *'Mevrouw,'* he said on an exasperated expulsion of his breath, 'if you recall, when I took you back to your suite after lunch, you mentioned that you wished to ask me a few questions. And I naturally assumed that you wanted to speak to me in private since you invited me in. Ah, lady, you disappoint me with your short memory.'

'Yes, of course, I remember. But ...' she began
warily. 'It is not proper for a respectable single woman
to dine with a man alone.'

He chuckled. 'But, *mevrouw*, again your memory
fails you. You are not a single woman.'

'I consider myself single, my lord, since I never
knew my husband.'

They had by now arrived at a large wooden door
streaked with bands of iron and dotted with studs.
Stephan pressed down the latch and pushed open the
door, standing aside for Elena to enter.

He caught her arm and propelled her through
beaded curtains suspended from domed archways
through room after sumptuous room till he eventually guided her out on to a terraced garden and into
an exquisite marble pavilion agleam in the moon's
radiance. Fine muslin curtains hung in the archways.

Candelabra sat in the centre of an oval table laid
with white damask and set with fine china and silver
cutlery. Stephan strode to a side table and lifted a silver
bell which he jangled. He returned and pulled back
one of the cane chairs and invited Elena to be seated.
She complied and he settled on the opposite chair.

'My lord——'

'Elena,' he interrupted softly, 'I think it would be
better if you eat first before you unburden your
troubles. You will feel more relaxed, and your
anxieties will seem of less importance.'

'I fear, my lord, I haven't changed my mind.'

Just then a servant brought in some dishes, which
he left on the table, and departed. The food was a
light stew made from lean tender fowl cooked with a
variety of exotic vegetables and served with flat rounds
of bread.

Elena politely refused the wine but accepted a glass of mango juice, deliciously cool and refreshing.

After the dessert of stewed fruit, Stephan leaned back in his chair and sipped a second glass of wine. It was a deep red and he held it up to the candlelight. 'It's the same colour as your hair, Elena. I sometimes wonder if you would taste like wine.'

She smiled, rather enjoying the mild flirtation. 'And how could you possibly find out, my lord?'

'Simple. By kissing you.'

Her eyes widened in consternation. 'My lord...'

He sighed. 'All right, Elena, say what you want.'

'My lord, I have thought over what you have said. In—er—the matter of taking me for your bride, and...and I have come to a conclusion.'

'What conclusion, *mevrouw*?'

'That I should remain here for a month. I promise after I have learned about this island and its way of life I shall give you my answer.' Elena was astonished by what she had said. She had meant to ask him to return her home, except she seemed to be impelled by a strong power within her.

'Excellent, Elena. And to improve your knowledge further, it would be a good idea if you join me on my voyages of—er—mercy. We intend to sail within two days.'

CHAPTER FOUR

ELENA stared at Stephan, unable to believe that he would drag a woman off on his nefarious escapades. But then, she told herself, I must bear in mind that this man is a lawless sea brigand and capable of any unconventional deed. Yet, in a vague summation of his character, she discounted the possibility that he was a downright villain, given to the lower practices of violation and cruelty. Her father once mentioned that people who indulged in brutality, in the majority of cases, lacked a high intellect and were mentally too weak to control their baser urges. She estimated that Stephan was a man of superior intelligence; yet he rejected authority and preferred to trust his own instincts in what he considered good and evil. 'I think you need to do some explaining, my lord,' she said, as composedly as she could. After all, her favourable reading of his character might be erroneous. It would be folly to antagonise him.

His smile was one of open amusement. 'If you accompany me on one of my voyages and experience what occurs, I'm certain you'll be convinced that my brand of piracy does not conform to the common belief in the notorious buccaneer.'

'I insist on taking Aggie, my lord.'

Stephan laughed in pure delight. 'Ah, *mevrouw*, that means you are willing to sail with me?'

She bit her pink lip, regretting her indiscretion. Confusion sent a brighter shade to her apricot-tinted cheeks. Even so, she could not quell an intense curiosity to experience at first hand one of the amazing and dangerous voyages of 'mercy' which Stephan had opted for and find out what it entailed. To give herself time to think before taking the colossal stride of consenting, she swallowed some mango juice, but though it was deliciously cool its effects evoked no inspiration.

Meanwhile, Stephan sipped his wine. Then he glanced at Elena, his brown eyes languid. 'I doubt whether Aggie will be happy to accompany you, *mevrouw*. She is prone to seasickness, is she not?'

Elena nodded but he gave her no chance to speak. 'This is August,' he went on. 'Not quite the start of the south west monsoons.'

She put her head to one side and her shapely brows lowered in perplexity. 'I thought the rains had already arrived, considering the downpour twenty-four hours past when we berthed at the Prince of Wales Island.'

'*Ja*, we do get the occasional torrent, for it is not dry for long in this zone, *mevrouw*. The worst has yet to come. In India, however, the monsoon is at its height, and merchantmen on course from the west will take advantage of the winds to sweep them easily through the straits of Malacca. We intend to lie in wait for these vessels and I cannot promise calm seas for your companion's benefit.'

Elena drew in a sharp breath. She had forgotten Aggie's antipathy to sailing. Her violet eyes, which reminded him of the sky at sundown, looked at him, troubled. 'But a lone woman cannot sail with a crew of men. It is altogether improper, my lord. You should know.'

'Ah, but Aggie is not the only woman on the island. You would do better in the company of Shakira—she is Malayan and will teach you the language. And don't look at me suspiciously; she is not my mistress but a Malayan crewman's wife. Besides, *mevrouw*, you, as a widow, are allowed far more freedom than your single sisters.'

Elena straightened her spine as if to give herself confidence and said in a clear voice, 'Very well, my lord, I'll sail with you.' She realised that she should have refused to accompany him on his outrageous mission, but her curiosity proved too powerful to resist. These exotic surroundings might well be responsible for her touch of madness, she reflected with uneasiness, inhaling unsteadily and catching a whiff of candle smoke and the less pleasant odour from green rings of sulphur coils, which were lit to keep mosquitoes at bay, Stephan had told her when she enquired.

His brown eyes sparkled with admiration. 'Good! I'm delighted to know that you are a woman of spirit. Then that's fixed. Was there anything else you wished to ask?'

She toyed with her empty glass and stared at it, distractedly studying the exquisite workmanship of the cut glass, its facets iridescent in the lamplight. 'Those captains I met at lunch. Are they...are they...?'

'*Ja*, they're buccaneers,' he replied, a mite tetchily.

'And do they...? Are you their commander?'

'*Ja, mevrouw.* Any notion you cherish of asking for their help in getting you off this island, forget about it. If you must know, they mistrust you and believe that if you should succeed in escaping from here you'd betray all of us. I do not need to tell you how busy that would keep the hangman; we all have a price on our heads. Except no one beyond this island knows who those heads belong to.'

'That's preposterous, sir! I would not dream of betraying anyone and staining my hands with blood!'

He shrugged, drawing her attention to the wide expanse of his shoulders. 'Perhaps, but we cannot take risks. In idle gossip you might give us away. That is, if you manage to leave Pulau Mutiara.'

Her violet eyes widened. 'Does that mean I will have to live here for the rest of my life? What about the promise you made that I could think your—your proposal over for a month?'

'And I abide by my promise. You can take one month or a year to think things over, but your decision will make no difference to your leaving here. You would not have been permitted to step off this isle had Anthony been alive.'

'That means I am a prisoner, my lord?'

He drained his glass and idly twisted the stem. 'It depends on what your definition of prisoner is, *mevrouw*. You are free to roam Pulau Mutiara—with an escort, of course. There is plenty to see. But——'

'Yes, yes, I heard you—I cannot leave here,' she chipped in on a weary note.

'I mean it, Elena.' Soft and caressing his voice, yet it held steely determination and the hardening of his jaws confirmed it.

Elena dabbed her mouth with the snowy napkin and pushed away from the table. 'I think, my lord, it is time I returned to my chambers. If I tarry, I fear I may bore you with my repetitious requests to return home,' she said stiffly and stood up.

Hurriedly Stephan left his seat and pulled back her chair. 'You could never bore me, *mevrouw*,' he said, his brown eyes looking deep into hers, his smile so full of charm that her heart began a strange dance. He placed his hand on her back at her waist and guided her out of the pavilion.

Outside, the moon peered from its indigo cushion sprayed with huge stars and threw its silver radiance across the exotic flowers which suffused the air with their exquisite perfume. Somewhere in the distance, a player strummed a stringed instrument and a lone voice sang in an unfamiliar but soul-stirring strain, in keeping with the enchanting setting.

The song with its romantic intonation had an effect on Elena. Her senses were alert with a keen awareness of the handsome man by her side. His hand at her back slid round her waist with a casualness that betrayed a wealth of sensual experience and sent a ripple of faint rapture down her backbone. She glanced up at him surreptitiously from under her lashes and saw his intent gaze on her.

Stephan slowed his pace to a stroll and held her close to his side; Elena perforce did the same. She tried desperately to ignore the pleasure of his hard body pressing alongside hers. Through the thin material of both their garments she felt the lean power of his ribcage, the muscular strength of his thighs brushing hers. She forced herself to concentrate on how she could slip out of his embrace with a casualness that would give no offence. Yet every time she stepped away, supposedly to avoid a crack in the path, he tightened his arm, intensifying the throb of—of—was it desire?—deep within her.

'Elena,' he said, coming to a halt and turning her to face him. Both his hands held her waist lightly, drawing her close so that their bodies touched. As her

eyes gazed entranced up at him, her arms hung helplessly by her sides, powerless to resist as he gathered
her hard against him. 'Has a man ever kissed you—
like this?'

She watched his face, sharply etched and silver in
the moonlight as it slowly approached her own. Her
lips parted to voice her feeble protest, but no sound
emerged. Stephan's mouth came down firmly over
hers, sending an unexpected jolt shaking through her
body. When he forced her mouth wider to facilitate
his probing, another shock raked down her. Her reaction to him frightened her. She now broke out of
the spell and struggled to be free, but soon realised
she was no match for Stephan. One of his hands came
up to cradle the back of her head and the other
clamped round her waist, dragging her harder to him.
Her body rendered powerless, Elena became aware of
her heightened senses: the taste of Madeira on his
mouth, his wine-scented breath, the soap-clean tang
of his skin, the freshness of his laundered clothes and
the pressure of his powerful body. All held her sensually spellbound.

As his kiss grew more demanding, Elena's fear re-
surfaced. If she did not stop him now, she reflected
in alarm, he would assume that she was welcoming
his advances. She was not so naïve that she did not
know where it would lead. Exercising all the strength
she could summon, she tore her mouth away from his
and gave a shuddering sob. It seemed to bring him to
his senses; he abruptly released her and they both
staggered back, breathing erratically, staring at each
other.

Stephan seemed to recover his equilibrium before she did. He straightened his coat and cravat and asked in a low voice, 'Have you?'

In a daze she gaped at him. 'What?'

'You didn't answer my question, Elena. I asked if any man had kissed you like that.'

Gracious! After so mighty an upheaval did he still remember that question? Thank goodness the moon's radiance did not betray the heat in her face. She swallowed. 'No, my lord.'

He laughed quietly. 'Is it still "my lord"?'

She said nothing, feeling quite piqued that he appeared to attach little significance to the kiss which had shattered her. Kissing women must be routine to him, she supposed, feeling chagrined.

'Come, Elena, it's time you retired.'

She nodded as he offered her his arm. Neither of them spoke till he left her at the door of her chambers. Then, lifting her hand, he barely touched it with his mouth. 'Goodnight, Elena.'

'Goodnight, my lord.'

Stephan Van Coen frowned as he strode back to his apartments. He was angry with himself for his lack of control which he had shown when he had given in to the impulse to kiss Elena. Clearly the girl had been disturbed and, more amazingly, so had he. True, he intended to fulfil the terms of Anthony's will and marry her, not out of a sense of duty to his friend or for love—how could he love Elena, since he had met her little more than twenty-four hours ago?—but because as his wife she could not give evidence against him if he were ever caught and charged with piracy. Except neither Anthony nor he had considered the possibility that she might have a mind of her own and not agree to marry anyone else. That untimely kiss would harden her resolution to return to England.

Heaving a weary sigh, Stephan entered his apartment, sending bead curtains clicking as he tossed them aside, and came upon Captain Porrot, who was lounging on a divan in the hall which Stephan used when he received guests. 'Why, Henry, this is a surprise.'

Henry Porrot rose and gave Stephan a courteous nod. Then he straightened and the two men eyed each other levelly. Both were of the same height but Porrot had a lanky build. From the expression in Henry's grey eyes, Stephan deduced that there would be confrontation. The two men were not the best of friends normally, because Porrot preferred to act on his own orders and not through discussion with the other captains in Stephan's flotilla. None the less they were bound by a single bond: to thwart the exploitation of the natives by European traders. Porrot, however, carried this commitment to an extreme that could be described as fanaticism. He believed that the officers and crew of captured ships should be executed and thus they should destroy all evidence of piracy. He and Stephan had argued this point on several occasions. So far, with the backing of his other captains, Stephan had won. He wondered whether Porrot was going to prove awkward again on the subject of their forthcoming mission.

The Englishman looked at the long clock in the far corner of the large chamber and said apologetically, 'I dare say, Stephan, it's time the candles were snuffed.'

'What brings you here at this hour, Henry? Is it some disagreement over the plans for our next—er—expedition?'

Henry's thin, tight lips curved in a semblance of a smile. 'No, sir. It is about Mrs Drew.'

Stephan stiffened inwardly. Outwardly he remained bland. Since his first encounter with Elena, he had taken it for granted that she was his business alone. 'Let us be seated, *mynheer*, and talk in comfort.' He kept his voice carefully controlled. After they had settled on the divan, he carried on, 'What about Mevrouw Drew?'

Porrot raised his beetling grey brows and stared thoughtfully at his stubby fingers, which were out of proportion to the rest of his lanky frame, and examined his clean nails. Then with a sudden jerk of his head he glared defiantly at Stephan. 'I don't trust her.'

Stephan grimaced impatiently. 'Look, *mynheer*, we have been through all this before, if you recall, at our meeting with the others before luncheon. We decided that in no circumstances must she leave Pulau Mutiara except in my company; therefore she cannot do any harm.'

'I believe she is a spy, Stephan.'

Astounded by the accusation, Stephan made no attempt to hide his amazement. 'Spy?' It had never crossed his mind that Elena could be an agent. But it was not impossible. She certainly had the intelligence to act out the part. So he found his urge to defend her illogical. 'Spy for whom?'

The steel-grey eyes of his colleague glittered in triumph. Porrot removed an imaginary speck from his grey coat. Why did this Englishman do nothing to enliven his all-grey image? Stephan thought irrelevantly and irritably.

'Since she is English, my assumption is that she is a spy for my former employers, the British East India Company. We do a lot of damage to their shipping and they no doubt have a suspicion that this island is a hotbed of pirates.'

'So why don't they raid us?'

Porrot lifted his bony shoulders and spread his peculiar hands. 'Lack of proof, no doubt. They know Pulau Mutiara belongs to you and to all intents and purposes you are or were a respected director of the Dutch East India Company. I hear it has gone bankrupt.'

'*Ja*. The British East India Company has claimed monopoly of the spice trade since they can grow all the commodities demanded in Europe, in India. But continue.'

'Even so, if they organise a raid which misfires, they might well be destroying the fragile peace existing between the Dutch and English, in these waters if nowhere else.' Henry leaned forward and tapped his own grey-covered knee. 'So to be in possession of proof the British East India Company could have decided upon the ingenious idea of planting a beautiful woman in our midst, to seduce and extract vital proof from us. Let's face it, Stephan, a woman of Mrs Drew's age and beauty would have been snapped up for marriage in her teens. But she remains single from choice because she values her freedom and can make a lucrative living from spying.'

'Your theory is mere conjecture, *mynheer*. I have proof that she is Anthony's wife.'

Porrot stretched his lips in exasperation, his steel-grey eyes narrowing with anger. 'My dear Stephan, spies are a clever breed and they have been trained by ingenious teachers. She would have been well instructed in her role to overcome likely pitfalls before she set sail for the Far East. I admit she could not have known Anthony would die, but she might have been instructed to annul her marriage on some pretext or another. Fortunately for Mrs Drew, Anthony did die.'

Seeds of doubt began to germinate in Stephan's brain. What Porrot said did make sense. 'Go on.'

'I suggest, Stephan, that we interrogate this woman again more closely. Remember we were witnesses to Anthony's dying words. He insisted that we question her, not because he feared she was a spy but because she might be an impostor.'

Stephan released his breath loudly and slapped his thigh in impatience. 'My dear Henry, I have already done that, as you know. She has convinced me that she is Anthony's wife. I thought I made this clear at the meeting.'

'Then there are but two choices left.'

'And they are?'

Why had he not noticed before how cruel Henry's smile was? And yet Henry was blessed with an amazing sense of justice and kindness to the Malayan peasants whom he loved. 'One is for you to marry her, as Anthony wished. This will prohibit her from giving evidence, if such is needed.'

He knew what the other choice was, yet he asked, 'And the other?'

Henry grinned evilly. 'Why, my friend, what else but for her to dangle from the rope or make her walk the plank!'

This man hates European women, Stephan speculated. He probably has been wounded deeply by one. But that is no excuse for him to take out his grudge on all of them.

A bitter rage which he found difficult to quell boiled up inside Stephan. 'I think you had better leave, *mynheer*,' he said, his voice soft, deep and terrifying in its menace. Ruby sparks flew from the flecks in his eyes.

With satisfaction he watched Porrot's pale face grow grey with apprehension as he hurriedly rose and backed from the room. Even so, the bravado persisted. 'I'm not convinced this woman is Mrs Drew. If she were, she would have immediately donned widow's weeds on learning of Anthony's death. The woman shamelessly shows herself in all that finery.'

Stephan sighed. 'Henry, she did not come here expecting to be widowed, and hence brought no black gowns with her.'

'She could have had one made by one of the palace tailors.'

'She probably doesn't know about them. But we argue over trifles.'

'I think not. As a spy it would not have crossed her scheming mind to dress in mourning. If you don't take any action, Stephan, I shall!' he snarled, turning, and with a loping gait passed through the curtain of beads.

For a while Stephan sat listening to the fading of Porrot's footfalls, the shutting of the entrance door and the continued clicking of beads till they fell silent. The prevailing sounds that remained were the distant chirr of cicadas, the buzz of mosquitoes and other night insects and the thunder of his heart. He rose, crossed the length of the room to a Chippendale drinks cabinet. From it he extracted a bottle of brandy and a tumbler.

When Elena entered her apartment after Stephan said goodnight, she was hoping that Aggie had retired to her suite. So she knew disappointment when she spotted the elderly spinster seated in a cane chair in Elena's bedchamber.

In normal circumstances she would have been pleased to see Aggie looking so smug and anxious to talk. But Elena was suffering from the after-effects of Stephan's disturbing kiss. Her lips still burned and her body throbbed with bewildering sensations. Her immediate inclination was to quickly undress, snuggle into bed, and purge her mind of the kiss which she had wantonly allowed from a man she scarcely knew. She had met him only last evening and... 'What is it you want, Aggie?' she asked brusquely, aware of the beginnings of a headache. The punishment of guilt, she accused herself mutely.

Aggie's happy eyes clouded with hurt. 'It's not all that late, ma'am,' she remarked defensively. 'I thought p'raps you would like to know that Mr Russell be joining my lord's ship soon and when he goes, his wife, Gertha, has offered to take us to a headland to see them pearl divers at work, ma'am.'

'Mm, that's why this is called Island of Pearls,' she murmured vaguely. 'But, Aggie, I fear you will have to go alone with Mrs Russell.'

Aggie's grey eyes were clear, trusting and popped a little. 'Oh? Why so, ma'am?' she cried, her high voice riven with alarm.

Elena had wanted to keep the news till the morning when her headache would, she hoped, have cleared and her tiredness gone. 'I'll explain tomorrow, Aggie. I feel quite worn out.'

'Oh, ma'am!' Aggie wailed. 'I'll ne'er get ter sleep being curious like!'

'You won't be able to sleep at all when you hear what I have to say.'

'Well, if it makes no difference either way, why don't you tell me now, ma'am?'

Elena sighed, silently chiding herself as a fool. Why did she have to open her mouth?

'Tell me, ma'am, and I swear I'll bother you none afterwards. I'll be gone in a trice.'

'All right, Aggie, brace yourself. I am going with Lord Stephan on his voyage.'

Aggie groaned. 'Mercy me! I can't let you go alone with him—though I'll have to go through all that sickness again.'

'No, Aggie, you can stay here with Mrs Russell. His lordship has arranged for another woman to accompany me.'

'That be good, ma'am. If there be another woman with you then I'll feel easy. An' if you want to be with him, ma'am, then 'tis natural, ain't it? I mean you being 'is betrothed an' all.'

Elena felt a little mystified that Aggie had not reacted more forcefully, until she realised that her companion still knew nothing about Stephan's involvement with piracy. 'But I haven't consented to be his bride yet, Aggie.'

'Ah, but you will, ma'am. Everyone thinks so, anyways.'

'Really?'

'Yes, ma'am. The Russells——'

'You told them?'

'No, ma'am, they guessed.'

'They're not "everyone", Aggie. But let it go. Will you be all right on your own? You could ask Mrs Russell to share your suite till her husband and I return.'

Aggie brightened. 'That'll be wonderful! But what about you? Will you be all right, ma'am, these being uncivilised parts? And, begging your pardon, ma'am, my lord himself being one of them foreigners.'

'Why, Aggie, I had not thought you could be a bigot! But I'll be all right.'

Aggie rose. 'Then I'll be getting along, ma'am. Goodnight.'

'Goodnight, Aggie.'

Nightmares bedevilled Elena's sleep. She dreamt she was on the high seas surrounded by masked men who were dressed in black and wore the skull and crossbones on their chests. They stripped their masks off and she screamed; their faces were identical to Stephan's.

Storm clouds gathered just after she and Aggie had breakfasted the next morning. Elena suggested a stroll outdoors to inhale some fresh air. Her mood was lighter since her headache had disappeared.

The garden was enclosed within high walls, but its spaciousness did not give the impression of being hemmed in. In time she would learn that the abundance of floral bushes were jasmine, hibiscus and different varieties of orchids. And the butterflies; she had never seen such beautiful creatures with such enormous wings.

Suddenly lightning streaked across the grey heavens. 'I think we'd best go in, ma'am,' Aggie said, cowering in fright. Shortly after, thunder gave an ominous growl and the two women hurried back to the palace.

A smiling woman servant waited for them at the back door. She made signs that someone wished to see the *mem* in the big chamber.

Elena felt certain that the visitor would be Stephan and she knew an excited anticipation. But the disappointment was deeper than she expected when the man in question turned out to be Captain Porrot. Uneasiness assailed her; she knew instinctively that he disliked her. His steely eyes blatantly conveyed the impression. 'Good morning, ma'am,' he greeted her, bowing stiffly.

'Good morning, Captain,' she returned coolly.

'May I speak to you alone, ma'am?' he asked, sending a haughty glance in Aggie's direction.

'I am sorry, sir. Aggie is my companion and I wish her to stay.'

He shrugged indifferently. She did not offer him a seat nor did she intend to sit herself. It was a subtle indication that she did not wish him to stay for long. 'What is it you have to say, Captain?'

'Madam, I believe Stephan has proposed to you.'

Elena drew herself up indignantly. 'Indeed, Captain, you are intruding on my privacy.'

He continued as if she had not spoken. 'I suggest you marry him as soon as possible; else your life will be in considerable danger.'

A streak of lightning flashed through the chamber, thunder crashed and rolled as if underlining the horror of his words. And then he was gone.

CHAPTER FIVE

'CAPTAIN PORROT!' Elena called, listening to the ring of his boots as they disappeared. No answer. The distant slam of the entrance door proclaimed his eventual departure.

Aggie's eyes popped in astonishment. 'Now why did he have to tell yer that, ma'am?'

Elena felt a daunting bafflement. 'That's what I'm trying to solve. Why are they all so insistent that I marry Stephan Van Coen?'

'That Captain Porrot, he be a nasty gent for an Englishman, ma'am.'

Elena laughed sourly. 'Do you suppose all Englishmen are models of rectitude, Aggie?'

'Models of what, ma'am?'

'I mean—goodness.'

Aggie's wide mouth turned down at the corners as she gave Elena's answer a moment of thought. She scratched the tip of her snub nose, shrugged her left shoulder and said, 'P'raps they ain't all good at home, but 'ere among them foreigners they should be!'

Elena shook her head and smiled in amusement at Aggie's turn of logic. 'That's beside the point. Why is he determined that I should marry Stephan?'

'Well, I thought you was going to. He might be a foreigner but 'e be a good gent, and also a lord! What more can a young lady wish for?'

'What about love? Isn't that important?'

Aggie cackled. 'I am of a mind you already love him, ma'am. Oh, you don't know it yet, but it be so. And don't look at me as if I 'ad turned into a monster! Anyways, did yer not marry Mr Drew without knowing him, leastways loving 'im?'

'Let's go outside,' Elena suggested, not wanting to be reminded of her marriage to Anthony, which had plagued her with uneasiness on the long voyage East. 'It's stifling in here. Perhaps I'll be able to think better in the garden.'

'It's raining, ma'am. Did you not hear the thunder?'

Of course she had; Porrot had departed on the advent of the storm. Elena shook her head; she must be going mad. Glancing out of the window, she saw sheets of water slanting down and could hear the rush of the torrent. 'I suppose I was too absorbed with anxiety listening to Captain Porrot. He threatened my life, Aggie. I wonder if my lord set him up to it?'

To Elena's surprise Aggie said, 'Oh, no, ma'am. My lord ain't the sort to send some other body to do 'is dirty work. Oh, no, he'd come 'isself. Mark me word 'e would!'

Elena flopped on a divan and fanned herself with a handkerchief.

'I'll call a servant to pull the screen fan on the ceiling, ma'am. They call it a punkah. That much I do know!'

Anxiously Elena hoped for Stephan's arrival to apprise him of Captain Porrot's visit and threat, but he failed to turn up.

She did, however, meet the Russells. In an attempt to divert Elena's mind, Aggie persuaded her to invite the couple to lunch. 'As you know, ma'am, I can't read or write. If you send 'em a note they'll be more 'an happy to come.'

So while Aggie clumped away to summon a servant, Elena hunted in the rooms for paper and pen. She came across a chamber with an ornate escritoire, Queen Anne chairs and shelves of books. A woman servant was busily dusting the furniture and looked up as Elena stepped in. She smiled and brought her hand to her forehead in greeting and Elena nodded graciously. 'I'm looking for some paper to write a note to Mrs Russell,' she said, in the hopes that the woman would understand English. To Elena's delight she did and immediately led her to the desk, opened its roll top and pointed to the shelves filled with paper and an inkstand with quills. Elena had barely settled herself on the stool in front of the desk when she heard Aggie calling out and a mumble of voices.

'I'm here, Aggie. I've discovered the writing-room!' She pushed away from the desk and asked the servant to guide her back to the main hall lest she lose her way. The smiling woman beckoned Elena to follow her. She arrived back in the large entrance chamber to encounter not only Aggie but a couple, whom she supposed were the Russells.

The man did not wait to be introduced, but stepped forward and held out his large hand. A tall, rugged-featured individual with a deep tan. 'I'm Midshipman Russell, ma'am, and this is my wife, Gertha.'

Elena smiled in welcome and gave him her hand. He bowed over her wrist, and she noticed his short dark-brown hair.

Gertha bobbed in a quick curtsy and, in awe, eyed Elena's tall, shapely form which was dressed in yellow muslin. Her voice was strangely guttural coming from so tiny a person. 'Pleased to meet you, *mevrouw*,' she said in slow English.

'I'm very happy we've met at last. Aggie has told me a lot about you. I was in the process of writing you a note asking you to join Aggie and me for lunch.'

'What a coincidence, ma'am. We thought we would drop in and introduce ourselves. I'll be sailing at first light on the morrow, ma'am, and would like Gertha to stay with you and Aggie. She'll be a help with the servants.'

'Please sit down,' Elena invited, an uneasiness settling on her. She led them to an area where wicker chairs were arranged in a half-moon round a large divan against the draped wall. If Stephan was sailing tomorrow then she would probably have to go with him. This burly compatriot and his olive-skinned wife with her extraordinary slanted green eyes obviously knew nothing about Elena taking the voyage as well, so she decided not to mention anything. She caught Aggie's eye and frowned a warning, hoping her companion would understand. On the other hand Stephan might not intend to take her on this particular run.

A servant came in then and addressed Gertha, who immediately translated. 'She wants to know whether you want to lunch in the dining-room or here.'

Elena laughed. 'Quite frankly I have not the slightest idea where the dining-room is. I've only seen a few chambers and the bathroom. I think we should eat in the appropriate chamber lest we come in the servant's way in here. Perhaps you could ask the servant to show Aggie where the dining-room is.'

Gertha smiled and spoke rapidly to the servant, then she said to Aggie, 'Go with her, Aggie.'

'You come with me too, Gertha. If she talks to me I won't know what she says.'

'Forgive my appalling manners. You both will stay for lunch, won't you?' Elena asked, and the couple acquiesced with alacrity.

'You have a pretty wife, Mr Russell. She looks enchanting in that lovely floral gown.' After the two women had left, Elena spoke quickly, feeling a little awkward alone in his company. She put it down to the fact that she had rarely found much opportunity to socialise at home and meet members of the opposite sex. Her spare time had been invariably occupied in working for her father. It had always been he who dealt with the customers. As a result she had grown up inclined to reticence.

'Aye. You can have gowns made up like that for a pittance. Gertha will arrange for a tailor to come here if you wish.'

She smiled and nodded. 'Thank you.' She hesitated and then went on, 'Mr Russell, I would be grateful if you would not divulge to Aggie what kind of—of work Stephan, you and perhaps all the people on this island are involved in. She does not know, and as she has a pious nature and observes a strict code of ethics she would be appalled if she ever learned the truth. It is best that she remains ignorant and happy.'

'Rest easy, ma'am,' he said gently. Elena was beginning to like this big man in his sober brown coat and pantaloons. 'My lord has already warned us. He probably judged her character correctly. But I can assure you, ma'am, that our business is not what you imagine. We are not engaged in barbarous piracy.'

She gave a half-hearted laugh which conveyed her scepticism. 'That's what I've been given to understand, sir. Still, piracy, whether good or bad, is considered an illegal practice, as you are aware.'

Russell leaned back in the wicker chair and looked at Elena defensively. 'And yet our greatest men in history were pirates. Consider Drake and Raleigh, to name just two.'

'Yes, but they were working against an enemy of England.'

'And we are working against the enemies of vulnerable people. Unlike the Spaniards they have no means to defend themselves or their rights against the might of the European shipping companies of Britain, Holland, Portugal and France. They have only us. And we mean to protect them.'

'And is there any profit to be gained from this enterprise? I cannot believe it is entirely philanthropic.'

'Sure, ma'am. It is purely philanthropic and conceived by my lord—he prefers to be known as Captain Van Coen. But we must also live. We divide the profits fairly between the Malayan growers and ourselves. I'm talking about the sale of the produce cultivated on this island. I can assure you the money is considerable. What we acquire from—er—the sea is an added bonus.'

'The latter is a dangerous occupation, wouldn't you say, Mr Russell?'

'Indeed, ma'am. But the excitement is worth it.'

'Do you ever have any qualms?'

He sighed and smiled ruefully. 'Sometimes. Only in so far as if anything happened to me, Gertha would be on her own. Even so, I have made provisions for her should I die or be taken prisoner.'

'Did you know that I am due to sail with my lord Stephan on one of his voyages? It might not be on the one you'll be leaving on tomorrow.'

Russell jerked, clearly taken aback. 'No, ma'am, I didn't know. As far as I am aware, the captain has never allowed women to board his vessels when he planned a run. Nevertheless, if you do go with him, you'll have nothing to fear. What I did hear is that you are to marry him.'

It was her turn to be taken unawares. 'Erm...erm... Nothing is decided yet. Did Aggie tell you that?'

'No, ma'am, please don't blame her. Sorry, ma'am. I didn't mean to intrude. It's none of my business.'

Elena did not wish to broach so sensitive a subject, and immediately asked, 'What was my husband, Anthony Drew, like?'

'A good man, ma'am. A great friend of Captain Porrot.'

She felt a chill of fear as she recalled the steely eyed captain. At that moment Aggie and Gertha returned, chatting merrily, and Elena knew profound relief. I am a coward, she chided herself, I like to deviate from troublesome issues in the hopes they will fade away.

The conversation became general and when a servant announced that lunch was ready they all withdrew to the dining-chamber, which was decorated like all the others in Elena's suite except that a long, low table had been placed in the centre and cushions heaped around it. This was the Malayan mode of dining, Russell explained, and, much to Elena's amusement, he sat cross-legged on the cushions. The ladies tucked their legs to one side and nibbled daintily at the spicy food, its appetising aroma

filling the room. Elena had quickly acquired a taste
for it.

Two hours later the Russells departed, Gertha
promising to move a few things of hers into Aggie's
suite in the late evening, and vowing to bring the tailor
to measure up Elena for cotton dresses in cool floral
materials.

The rain had stopped and Elena decided to take a
stroll in the freshly washed outdoors rather than
follow Aggie's example and opt for a siesta. She
needed to think, and the quiet seclusion of the scented
garden seemed the correct place for such an exercise.

She was about to push open the long shuttered door
of her bedchamber that led on to the back terrace
when a step behind her made Elena swirl round.

A pleasurable spasm of surprise affected her abdomen as she encountered Stephan, who was strolling
with easy masculine grace towards her. 'Ah, there you
are, *mevrouw*. I thought you were about to take your
siesta.'

'And is it your habit, my lord, to enter a lady's
apartment without knocking first?' Faint indignation
lent a purple spark to her eyes.

'I did knock, and called out as well, but received
no reply. I thought——'

'You thought you could barge in here? You could
have embarrassed me if you had caught me in a state
of undress, my lord.'

'Do you undress when you take a siesta, Elena?'
The soft sensual tones unwittingly tended to titillate
her senses.

'Er—yes. I do not get into bed fully clothed.'

'Do you get in fully *un*clothed?'

'My lord!'

'Is the skin of your body as soft as that of your face? Are your...?' He stopped speaking, allowing his gaze to take over, to continue its silent quest. The flecks in his eyes shimmered as his look caressed her figure, resting on the full curves of her breasts then the flatness of her stomach, and running all the way down to her feet.

She felt her nipples burgeon against the silk lining of her dress. They tingled as if he had physically caressed them. Her cheeks flamed with some shame and a vast amount of arousal, which he had the power to evoke, without touching her, by the mere tone of his voice and the potent gaze of his ruby-flecked eyes. Faith! Was he a handsome warlock who could run rings of enchantment round her whenever the mood took him?

Conscious of just the two of them, the intimate aura permeating the room, Elena sought for calm reason. She swallowed and asked in a slightly tremulous voice, 'Why were you seeking me, my lord? I know it was not to say—er—say what you have just said.'

He sighed, as if unwilling to leave the intimate scene. 'I came to tell you that we shall be sailing at dawn tomorrow and that I shall be coming to collect you, Elena.'

'I'm an early riser, my lord. I'll be waiting for you.'

He raised a brow. 'You will?'

'I will.'

He laughed, brought her hand to his mouth and murmured, 'That sounded as if you were taking your marriage vows.' He kissed the back of her hand, gazing at it, smoothing the soft skin with his thumb. Then, brusquely, he said, 'I'll see you in the early hours, *mevrouw*. Don't change your mind.'

With slow reluctance he released her hand and un-expectedly Elena felt bereft. 'I shan't my lord.'

'Good. I am pleased to know that there are some women who try to keep their word. Tomorrow will tell.'

Dawn broke clear and hot. Elena had been wide awake since the long clock, two rooms away, had chimed the half-hour after three o'clock. She had risen and taken a refreshing cool bath, and slipped into the new floral dress of crisp cotton which Gertha Russell's tailor had sewn last evening. Gertha had explained that every adult of the tailor's family—and he had a horde of them, ranging from grandparents, parents, wife, sib-lings, cousins and in-laws—had worked on the dress so that it would be ready in a couple of hours. Elena had been delighted. She now stood outside her bedroom and inhaled the air of the perfumed garden just beginning to lighten in the pale dawn.

The long clock chimed the half-hour after four, and Elena stepped back into the bedchamber, closed and bolted the shutters, picked up a leather travelling-bag packed with a few changes of clothing, and made her way to the large front chamber which was the re-ception hall. She perched stiffly on the edge of a wicker chair. Twisting the handles of her reticule in a fever of suspense, she awaited Stephan's arrival.

She checked in her mind that Aggie would be all right and that she would be in good hands. Last night she had said goodbye to her companion so as not to wake her early this morning. Aggie had wept a little but Elena had assured her that all would be well. However, now that the time was nearing for her to leave, Elena was filled with misgivings.

Horrendous thoughts rose to haunt her. Supposing Stephan's ship were captured, she conjectured, along with her? If the victorious vessel happened to belong to the British East India Company then she'd be able to return home unscathed. What of Stephan, though? Would he be handed over to the Dutch authorities and hanged? Or forced to walk the plank? On the other hand supposing they were taken by another pirate ship with a ruthless captain. Would Stephan cleverly wriggle his way to freedom? Or, if the pirate captain demanded, would he offer her up for slavery as the price of such freedom? A blind panic assailed her. 'No!' she cried out loud.

Stephan suddenly appeared and doffed his tricorn. 'Good morning, Elena. "No" what?'

Elena had been staring blankly at the long clock while she gave rein to her morbid imagination. On hearing Stephan's voice she abruptly stood up, tipping her reticule from her lap, and half stumbled over the travelling-bag. 'Good morning, my lord,' she mumbled, bending to retrieve her belongings. 'What did you say?'

'You called out "No" when I walked in. "No" what, *mevrouw*?'

She could feel a flush staining her cheeks. 'It was nothing, my lord. Just a train of thought.'

'For a moment I assumed you had changed your mind about accompanying me,' he remarked mildly, relieving her of the large bag.

'No, of course not,' she said, admiring his uniform of navy broadcloth with gold fringed epaulettes and gold frogging down the front and edging his sleeves. She and her father had worked on uniforms not unlike this and she had often wondered whose broad shoulders they were designed for, and, though she had conjured up images of handsome young men, none in her imagination had turned out as good-looking as Stephan.

He caught her elbow with his free hand and guided her along. 'And may I ask what your train of thought was, *mevrouw*?'

'I wondered what would be the consequences if the tables were turned and the ship you attacked defeated and captured yours. We would all be prisoners.'

'Why, lady, I did not know you were a pessimist,' he reproved placidly.

'I prefer to consider the result of one's actions, and it is best to do so from all angles.'

'Do not worry your lovely head, Elena. We have taken everything into consideration. I have played this game long enough to take care of all eventualities. The bugbear in this game is if any of us falls ill. Or if a natural catastrophe occurs. But these are risks that are unavoidable.'

The sun had already risen, a scarlet orb in a shroud of mist, when they reached the entrance doorway to the palace. Sentries saluted smartly as Stephan and Elena appeared and opened the vast doors for them. They descended one side of the curving double flights of steps leading down to the front courtyard.

Elena could see no waiting cart or carriage and looked questioningly at Stephan. He smiled. 'We're using horses to take us to the dock.' He guided her to a couple of the animals tethered to posts with a groom standing between them.

'But I fear I cannot ride, my lord,' she confessed in dismay.

'No trouble. You'll share my saddle.'

'I see,' she said, not seeing at all. 'But what is the other horse for?'

'Oh, the groom will ride him and accompany us so that he can bring Bliksem back again. By the way, Bliksem means lightning in Dutch.'

While Stephan handed Elena's luggage to the groom and spoke to him, she eyed Bliksem warily. The stallion was as silver as a streak of lightning and probably just as dangerous, she thought as she watched the magnificent animal pawing restlessly at the ground, impatient for his exercise.

Elena backed away and then felt Stephan's hands firmly clasp her waist from behind. 'He won't harm you, *mevrouw*. Not while I'm here. Now come. Let me lift you into the saddle.'

Her stomach heaved as he hefted her on to the front of the saddle and then swung up behind. 'Just rest back against me, lady, and you'll have nothing to fear.'

Elena relaxed as he suggested, and knew a contented security. The swift gallop of the horse whipped up the still air into a cooling breeze that exhilarated her. Closing her eyes, she wished that this exercise could go on forever instead of taking her to join a vessel bent upon a dangerous mission.

So immersed was Elena in enjoying this man's nearness—the hardness of his chest as it rubbed against her back, the strength of his arm as he held her close, the muscularity of his tightly encased thighs as they moved against hers in rhythm with the galloping horse—that she had not taken particular note of the route. She roused herself sufficiently to see that they were not using the same road to the jetty along which she and Aggie had travelled by cart. Besides, they appeared to be taking a long time reaching their destination considering they were galloping at full speed.

She twisted a bit to stare up at him, and saw that he looked ahead. His eyes were narrowed but not against the glare, since much of the strong sunlight filtered through the thick foliage of the forest they galloped through. He, therefore, must be deep in thought. She decided to draw his attention to the fact that she was aware of the unfamiliar route.

'My lord, I do not remember passing through this forest on our arrival on the island. Nor have we come across cultivated fields and villages. And I don't see any other people riding to join the ship.' She attempted to curb the alarm in her voice, and knew she was not succeeding. 'Wh-where are we going?'

He shook his tricorn-covered head as if bringing himself out of a reverie. Stephan transferred his stare to her exquisite violet eyes that could spell danger for a fool. Perhaps he was one. '*Mevrouw*, not only have you the most beautiful eyes I have encountered but they are as sharp as I have been given to believe.'

'Given to believe, my lord? I don't understand. Have I been a subject for discussion?'

'Naturally, all newcomers are. We have to be wary of whom we allow on to this island. Time enough to discuss that. You wanted to know where we are going.'

'Yes, I want to know where you are taking me.'

'I thought you already knew. We are heading for my ship, of course. It is in the Bay of Porpoises on the southern seaboard, a sheltered marina which cannot be seen from the open sea; thus our ships escape detection. Our vessels ride at anchor here when they are idle. Today, however, two will be in use.

One will be commanded by myself and the other by Captain——'

'Captain Porrot?'

Stephan pulled on the reins to slow Bliksem down. He spoke to him gently in Dutch and the animal subsided to a trot. 'No, it's Mynheer Vans Paul.' A pause. 'What do you know about Captain Porrot, *mevrouw*?'

She shifted uncomfortably and leaned forward in the saddle. He tightened his arm and forced her back again. 'He came to see me yesterday.'

'And?'

She drew in an anxious breath, wondering if she should have kept quiet. Stephan might brand her the typical harridan with a wagging tongue. It was too late now. 'He warned me, my lord.'

'Indeed? Warned you against what?'

'Against *not* marrying you. A strange threat, I own. Usually a threat on this subject of marriage is one of forbidding to do so.'

'What else did he say, *mevrouw*?'

'Nothing. His words were to the effect that if I did not marry you, my life would be in danger.'

Though he spoke softly, Elena detected a controlled anger in his voice, as he replied, 'And what did you say, Elena?'

'I didn't get the opportunity to say anything, my lord. He turned on his heel and vanished from the apartment. I did call him back. Naturally I felt furious that he should have the temerity to barge in and then deliver a threat!'

'I'm afraid he thinks you were after Anthony's money and rejects your statement that you married him to save your father from prison. Henry Porrot, I fear, is a misogynist. I can't think why. He believes all women are evil. Besides, he was very fond of Anthony—naturally...'

'Why naturally, my lord?'

'Porrot is Anthony's illegitimate brother.'

CHAPTER SIX

THE surprising revelation temporarily set Elena to musing. In the interim Stephan persuaded Bliksem into a trot and, for a while, they continued the ride in silence.

She stirred herself into asking, 'If Mr Porrot is Anthony's half-brother why wasn't he a beneficiary of the will also?'

'He is a beneficiary of the will. I did not mention it to you because it concerned only Henry. Porrot receives half of Anthony's land holdings in Britain, his parents the other half. He owns shots of land on the common of Shotgate in Essex. Do you know it?'

'Yes, I stayed at the King's Head Inn there when I broke journey on the route to Deptford,' she replied. Elena felt stunned that in the event of her returning home she would be in no position to claim an inch of Anthony's land there. Unless she decided to contest the will, prepare herself for a legal battle. That meant considerable expenditure in appointing competent lawyers to fight her case. And she did not have the immediate cash to make it possible. Moreover, if she lost, she and her father would be back to facing a debtors' prison. Her dream of returning home and claiming her rights as Anthony's wife tumbled like an avalanche, and her hopes were smothered.

Stephan continued, 'And Henry also inherits a large slice of his half-brother's fortune. But Anthony knew Henry would refuse to have anything to do with your

welfare, let alone marry you. So the responsibility fell
to me.'

His last sentence sounded as if he considered her a
tiresome burden which had to be endured in view of
the fact that no one else was prepared to have her. A
deep mortification affected Elena. She was here on
sufferance and the tragedy was that neither of them
could do anything about it. If it had been left to
Stephan, she felt sure, he might have tried to return
her home with enough money to sustain her father
and herself, and would probably have felt relieved to
be rid of her. Alas, he was bound not to let her off
this island except in his company, and now Henry
Porrot by his threats made matters worse by forcing
Stephan and her to wed. To further her humiliation,
Stephan had already stated that he wished to marry
her out of convenience so that she could not give evidence against him should the occasion arise. Of love,
the main ingredient necessary for a successful marriage, there was none. Oh, he had kissed her with
much fervour last night. Perhaps to delude her that
he cared for her? she wondered. But what did a single
kiss matter to a handsome buccaneer, who probably
indulged in affairs with beautiful women, like tasting
several brands of wine but settling for none? It should
make no difference to her—unfortunately, she re-
gretfully owned, it did. What manner of woman am
I, she asked herself in silent reproval, that I can be
drawn so easily to a man of questionable reputation
and in so short a time? Faith! It is but two days since
I met him!

Stephan urged his horse into a gallop and said in
explanation, 'We must sail with the tide.'

Soon after, the trees fell away and the ground sloped sharply to a sandy shore. Before Stephan steered his horse down the slope, Elena caught sight of the Bay of Porpoises which he pointed out. Its beauty snatched away her breath for a moment of marvel. It curved like a pincer, creating a natural harbour, and ended in two high promontories. Even at this early hour the water looked blue, and in its marina ships like vast birds heaved slightly at anchor.

They reached the quayside where two large merchantmen were berthed, one behind the other, cannons bristling from their hulls. 'These are the ones scheduled for our expedition,' he said in an offhand tone as if the imminent voyage would be routine and harmless. Perhaps he considered it as such, she pondered, having accustomed himself to this hazardous way of life.

There appeared to be no stevedores, only people fiddling with coils of ropes and crews on the decks dashing about busily and climbing the rigging. Stephan dismounted and helped her down. He spoke to the groom who had ridden behind them, helped him unload the two pieces of luggage, and watched as the youth remounted his own horse and led Bliksem by the reins.

'Come, *mevrouw*, let us embark,' Stephan said cheerfully, lifting the bags and leading the way up the gangway.

Now that the hour had arrived for her to actually board ship, Elena experienced overwhelming qualms that for a moment drowned out her curiosity and excitement for adventure. Smells of timber, tar, rope and sailcloth affected Elena with familiar sensations; this was how she had felt when she had embarked on the *Eastern Command* at the docks at Deptford. The consolations then were that she had had Aggie and the merchantman had been assigned to an honourable task.

Elena knew a temptation to look back and gauge whether she had a chance to escape. Except such a reckless move would climax in a hopeless bid, considering her lack of knowledge of this island and the language of its people. So, saying a silent prayer for all their safety, she followed Stephan aboard.

She glanced up at the masts, fearful that she might spot the dreaded skull and crossbones of the Jolly Roger, banner of the buccaneers; instead she saw several flags with three broad red, white and blue horizontal bands, fluttering lazily in the gentle breeze, and assumed they were the ensigns of Holland.

Stephan led her along the deck, where tars and lascars were busy scrubbing the timbers, to a cabin beneath the poop. Accommodation in this area comprised the living quarters of the captain and his officers, she knew from her voyage on the *Eastern Command*.

In the spacious cabin with large windows waited a local woman elegantly dressed in her national costume. 'This is Shakira,' Stephan said, smiling at the woman and placing Elena's bag on the wide bed.

'*Selamat pagi Besar Tuan,*' Shakira said, bringing her tiny hand to her forehead.

'*Selamat pagi*, Shakira,' Stephan repeated and Elena guessed they had exchanged greetings.

'Shakira has a fair command of English and she'll look after you during our voyage to the Malacca Straits. I'll leave you in her care.' Ever the gallant, he took Elena's hand in his and bowed over it. '*Au revoir* for now.'

When he had gone, she swept off her hat and fanned herself.

'You feel hot, *mem*?' Shakira asked, smiling, her slanting eyes mere slits above high cheekbones, her teeth gleaming.

Shakira's voice had a nasal twang which rose and fell and Elena half expected her to break into song. 'In this climate I always feel hot. Don't you?'

'I get used to it, *mem*, no? I will open window and you go on small deck. Cool breeze blow there. Come, I will show.'

Elena had thought the windows opened directly on to the sea and was pleasantly surprised when she stepped out on to a tiny balcony with a rail. 'It's lovely,' she remarked, closing her eyes and drawing in deep gulps of salt-tanged sea air. The cool breeze teased the curls at her temples and stray wisps near her ears.

She heard the voices from the quayside and the sound of the sails being unfurled. Commands, shouts, chanting, rent the air and caused her blood to tingle with excitement. The ship began moving in a slow half-circle, then ploughed towards the Indian Ocean. 'What is this ship named, Shakira?'

'*Uitdaging, mem*. It means *Defiance*, in Dutch. But the name is not put on outside.'

She nodded, knowing exactly why Stephan needed to keep the name hidden. Fascinatedly she watched the vessel's progress between the two promontories that completed the bay. Elena narrowed her eyes against the glare and spotted men in loincloths diving off the cliffs. 'What are they doing?' she asked, pointing to the headland.

'Those are the pearl divers, *mem*. It is hard work finding oysters with pearls. But when they do, they make good money. Our *tuan*, he sees no one cheats them. He is good man, our *tuan*.'

Elena made no remark, her mind now hovering on what the outcome of this trip would be; yet an exhilaration impregnated with fear took hold of her.

'Would you like a cup of tea, *mem*?' Shakira asked, leaning on the rail beside Elena.

'Oh, yes, please, Shakira.'

Shakira nodded. 'I go make.'

She had barely left when Elena heard someone softly calling her name. Spinning round she peered into the darkened cabin, her eyes adjusting from the brightness outside to the sudden gloom. Iridescent shapes danced in front of her for a moment. Then she espied the bundle crouching beside the bed.

'Who are you?' she called apprehensively.

The figure straightened, quickly crossed to the door and shot the bolt. Elena's eyes adapted to the dimness of the cabin, and she gasped as she recognised Lucy Vans Paul. 'Lucy, what are you doing here? Why are you not on your husband's vessel? He is on the same run as Stephan, isn't he?'

'I've escaped and I need your help. I know you are anxious to be free as well. We could go together.'

Elena's knees seemed to have lost their strength and she staggered to the bed, slumping down on it. 'But— but how did you get away? You don't have any disguise,' she pointed out, her breath coming in gasps. Swiftly she observed that Lucy wore a white muslin dress sprigged with green leaves and a wide green taffeta sash round her waist.

'Jan, my husband, brought me on board. I told him I wanted to have a chat with you and that Stephan would escort me back to his vessel. I asked an officer where your cabin is and slipped inside here and saw your servant lead you to the window balcony, so I hid under the bed. I waited for her to leave, as I knew she would in due course make you a drink or bring in refreshments.'

Elena's violet eyes stared in dismay. 'But what if your husband realises you haven't returned to his ship?'

Lucy shrugged indifferently. 'He will think I persuaded Stephan to let me stay with you till we dock.'

'I—I don't understand, Lucy. Why do you want to run away?'

'I hate it on Pulau Mutiara,' the girl blurted out, 'I want to return to my Netherlands. All my people are there. If I had a child perhaps it could have been different but I lost the baby not three months past.' Tears appeared in Lucy's eyes and she hastily brushed them away with the back of her hand.

'What of your husband? Does he not mean something to you?'

Lucy sighed heavily and shook her head. 'No. I married him because I wanted to live on Pulau Mutiara then. I wanted to be near Anthony. It was he whom I loved.'

A fierce anger shook Elena. 'You dare admit you were in love with Anthony, knowing that he was my husband!'

'Oh, if it is any consolation to you, Elena, he did not love me. He just wanted an affair till he acquired a wife——'

A knock sounded on the door and Shakira's irritable voice asked, 'Why do you lock door, *mem*?'

Lucy put her fingers to her lips and dived under the deep damask frill overhanging the bed.

The rapping grew sharper. '*Mem*, are you all right?'

'I'm coming, Shakira,' Elena said, moving to the door and unbolting it.

Shakira came in with a silver tray holding a delicate china teapot and cup and saucer. She looked enquiringly at Elena.

'I forgot you were returning with some tea, Shakira, so I—I decided to take a nap. The rolling of the ship made me feel rather sick. But I'm better now. The short rest must have done me good.'

Though Elena flushed with guilt, owing to her lies, and spoke in short nervous jerks, she seemed to have convinced the servant. Shakira clicked her tongue compassionately. 'You drink tea. It will make you well. Then I will leave you to rest. *Tuan* left message to say he will come and take you to lunch at one of the clock.'

Elena tried to compose herself, but dared not speak lest her troubled voice give away her extreme agitation. She sipped the refreshing, scalding tea and wondered what she could do about smuggling food in for Lucy. For the moment she shelved that thought.

'There will be storm at sea tonight. Officers all in *tuan*'s cabin,' Shakira imparted cheerfully.

Finding her tongue after a spell of silence, Elena said, 'You don't sound worried.'

'We have faith in *tuan*. He is very good captain.'

'Do you know what port we are headed for?' Elena asked casually.

'No one knows—only *tuan*.'

The effort to remain placid effected an almost intolerable strain on Elena. 'Thank you, Shakira, for the tea. You may go now, but leave the tray. I might have another cup later on. I think I'll take a rest.'

'As the *mem* wishes,' the servant said and departed.

'All right, Lucy, come out and finish what you were saying. Would you like some tea?'

'That's thoughtful of you, Elena.'

Elena carefully wiped the empty cup with the white napkin on the tray and poured the drink for Lucy.

'What was I saying?' the girl asked, sitting beside Elena on the bed and sipping the brew gratefully.

'You had an affair with Anthony,' Elena reminded her drily.

Lucy appeared oblivious of the sarcasm. '*Ja*. It was his baby I lost.'

Elena jumped and stared at the girl. 'What?'

'*Ja*. I lost it when I became ill after Anthony died. I think I contracted the fever from him. I wish I had died along with the baby. But as you see I got over the illness. If the baby were alive I would have had something to remain on Pulau Mutiara for. But now I wish to return home.'

'With what? You need money and much help to get you to the Netherlands, to say nothing of the danger involved.' Then, narrowing her eyes on Lucy, Elena asked, 'Where do I come in?'

'Oh, I have money. Much guilders and also jewels. They are stitched in pouches which I carry round my hips, where they won't show under the full petticoats. As for you, Elena, I hear you are opposed to marrying Stephan as decreed in Anthony's will. You too wish to go home to your people.'

'I have only my father. And, yes, I do want to go home to him, but it will sound our death-knell; unlike you I have no money and will not inherit any from Anthony's will unless I marry Stephan.'

'Ah! But I have enough guilders for both of us. My father is a banker in Rotterdam. He has banks not only in the Netherlands, but also in England and France.'

'But what help can I give you, Lucy? I am but a woman and, worse, a stranger to this part of the world. I do not know the language even if I do resort to disguise. Why have you chosen me?'

'On this run, Stephan and Jan are going to attack a Dutch merchant ship. You and I must try to board it.'

Elena could not believe she heard aright. The Dutch girl looked so frail and helpless, unsuited to intrepid ventures. 'How, Lucy? This sounds harebrained.'

'Not at all! While they are occupied fighting we can jump ship.'

'Listen, Lucy. Just supposing we do manage to climb aboard the Dutch ship, what if Stephan and your husband capture it and discover us there?'

'This is a chance we must take.'

Elena shook her head. 'It won't work. Your plan is full of holes. I suggest you own up to being here and Stephan will have you conveyed to your husband.'

'Your reward for helping me will be two thousand guilders in gold.' Lucy tried to bribe her desperately. 'Do you not wish to be with your father?'

'You haven't listened to what I have said. It won't work!'

Lucy's face crumpled, she covered it with her hands and cried. 'Don't let Stephan return me to Jan and that hateful Captain Porrot whom my husband invited aboard.'

Elena felt disturbed on hearing of Porrot's presence on Jan's vessel and wondered what his involvement was on this run. Nevertheless her heart swelled with pity for Lucy. She placed her arm round the girl's frail shoulders. 'My dear, your place is with your husband. He does not ill-treat you, does he?' Lucy shook her head. 'Then perhaps you can persuade him to take you to Holland.'

'None of us is permitted to leave Pulau Mutiara. Did you not know that, Elena? We are prisoners there for the rest of our lives.'

'Yes, I know, but there are exceptions to every rule. If you and Jan discuss it sensibly with Stephan he might agree to let you go.'

'I think not, *mevrouw*.' A familiar male voice intruded.

Both women jumped and stared at Stephan, who was framed in the doorway. He came in, unhurriedly shut the door and leaned against it. His cold gaze rested on Lucy. 'You have no right to be on my vessel, Mevrouw Vans Paul. Jan has just sent a flag signal that I was supposed to have escorted you back to his ship, and that you were probably in Mevrouw Drew's cabin. And here I discover the pair of you hatching a plan to escape.' Shifting his gaze to Elena he remarked, in a voice dripping with cynicism, 'I agree with you, Mevrouw Drew, it is indeed a harebrained scheme.'

Elena stood up, the light of war in her violet eyes. 'How much of this conversation have you heard, my lord? I had no notion that you made it a habit to eavesdrop?'

'It is immaterial what you think, *mevrouw*. What matters this instant is for Mevrouw Vans Paul to join her husband immediately. Both vessels have dropped anchor and you, Mevrouw Vans Paul, will be conveyed by boat to the *Onoverwinnelijk*. Do not delay. Your husband awaits you.'

Lucy turned a tear-stained face to Elena. 'I want you to see me off, Elena.'

Elena lifted her chin and looked defiantly at Stephan. 'Do I have your permission, my lord?' she questioned in a tone as arid as a desert.

He bowed, a faint cynical smile touching his mouth, and with suitable mockery replied, 'But certainly, *mevrouw*.'

Lucy hung tightly to Elena's arm and both girls followed Stephan.

The heavens were overcast when they stepped on the main deck and the sky meeting the horizon was black. Yet the sea appeared relatively calm with the occasional swell. Lucy hugged Elena before she stepped into the dinghy, which was then lowered. Tars scrambled down ropes to land in the boat and row it to the ship anchored a short distance away. Elena remained on deck till she saw Lucy safely boarded and standing between her husband and the hard Captain Porrot; then she waved and turned away. Her heart ached for Lucy; she felt distressed she could not assist the unhappy girl.

'May I, *mevrouw*?' Stephan offered her his arm. 'I'll remind you that we are to lunch together.'

She slanted him a cool look. 'Yes, my lord, Shakira informed me.'

His quarters were just a couple of doors away from hers—as spacious and elegantly furnished. He ushered her into an antechamber where a round table covered with a snowy cloth was laid with silver cutlery, and a cut glass wine decanter plus tumblers.

As always he exercised courtesy but Elena knew he was furious. His smiles did not reach his eyes, where the ruby flecks were smouldering.

'A squall is building up on the horizon. We will be in the midst of a storm tonight. Does that frighten you, *mevrouw*?'

She knew he was filling in time while the servants placed food and drinks before them.

'No, my lord, not yet. I wasn't unduly afraid when the *Eastern Command* ran into a storm while rounding the Cape of Good Hope and again at Cape Comorin.'

'Ah, a natural sailor.'

'Perhaps because Britain is a seafaring nation. It must be in my blood.'

'But that cannot be said for your companion, the good Aggie.'

Elena could feel the blood warm in her cheeks. 'I was generalising about my race, my lord. There are always exceptions.'

'*Ja.*' He turned to the servants and spoke in their language. They salaamed and left the room.

'You can help yourself from the dishes in the centre of the table, *mevrouw*.' He lifted the carafe, and raised an eyebrow in query. 'This white wine will go well with the fish. Try some?'

'Thank you, I'll try a little.' She thought it might give her a dash of courage to brave the severe reprimand she expected at any time now.

For a while they relished the food in silence.

'Why did you invite Mevrouw Vans Paul to meet you in so furtive a manner? I would not have objected to her accompanying you on this voyage.'

Elena placed her knife and fork down. 'I did not invite her, my lord. Since you heard part of the conversation you should have known she stowed away. I was astonished to discover her in my cabin.'

He frowned, his eyes seeming to pierce her brain. 'However, the bribe she offered is tempting. If I had not arrived she might have persuaded you to collaborate with her to escape. Oh! I admit you gave her some very sound advice. But later perhaps you might have thought differently.'

'Look, my lord. Lucy is extremely unhappy and is not strong enough to adapt to the life of a pirate's wife. She wishes to go home to Holland to be with her people. I have an idea that her marriage to Jan was forced on her.'

'You're wrong there, lady. No one forced her to marry Jan. She professed to be in love with him—till she met Anthony. Did she tell you that?'

Elena put a piece of fish in her mouth and thoughtfully chewed it. She took a sip of wine which tasted pleasantly dry, and did complement the fish. 'Yes. She told me a lot more—in confidence.'

She watched the slow smile on Stephan's face and wondered why Lucy hadn't fallen for him. But, then, she had felt the strong dislike he carried for the girl.

'That she was pregnant by Anthony? That she contracted his illness and, despite looking delicate, survived but lost the baby. That her husband knew it all and idolises her in spite of her misdemeanour?'

Fires of rage sparked from his eyes and automatically Elena leaned away from him. 'She didn't tell me about her husband.'

'Nor would she. The woman is like a spoilt child. Several men have committed suicide on her account.'

'No!'

'Most certainly, *mevrouw*!'

'You sound bitter enough to have been attracted to her once yourself.'

'*Ja*, I was.'

His bald acknowledgement caused a ripple of fierce resentment to slice through her abdomen. She was appalled to admit that the sensation could well be jealousy. 'Oh? What happened?' She wondered unhappily whether Lucy ranked as one of the 'wines' he had tasted but rejected.

'I soon discovered her type.' A smile of amusement touched his mouth. 'Why? Does that disturb you?'

'N—no, of course not. It is none of my business whom you had affairs with.' She drained her wine glass and held it out to be refilled. 'Did you arrange for Lucy to marry Jan?'

He laughed and watched her nervously sip from her freshly filled glass. 'No, *mevrouw*, he met and married her long after I ceased to find her fascinating. Incidentally, for your peace of mind, she and I never indulged in an affair.'

She decided to put an end to the discussion of Lucy. In truth she did find it disturbing, but preferred not to ponder over it. She said, 'What is Captain Porrot doing on Captain Vans Paul's ship?'

'They are friends. We all are. Sometimes we accompany each other.' His eyes suddenly narrowed.

Very softly, as if speaking to himself, he said, 'Now, I wonder?'

Elena was in no mood to pay much attention to him as her head began reeling. The cabin seemed to heave and roll. At first she thought it was the effects of the two glasses of wine she had impulsively imbibed. But now, as she saw Stephan grab the decanter before it could slide off the table, she recognised that the ship was pitching. He staggered to a row of built-in cabinets where he deposited the bottle. Then servants stumbled in and helped him gather up the dishes and crockery and put them into the cupboards.

Stephan lunged over to where Elena sat clinging to the arms of her chair and lifted her out. He hugged her to him as he rolled with the ship, out on to the corridor between the cabins. Elena did not ask what was happening. She knew. A sudden squall had blown up, forerunner of the storm. She could hear a distant roar.

Stephan carried Elena into her cabin and kicked the door shut. She could see the angry scowl on his face. As he laid her carefully on the four-poster riveted to the floorboards, she said, 'Why are you cross, my lord? Faith, it is nobody's fault that a storm is brewing.'

'It is the fault of those dolts on watch. They should have known what was about and informed me at once. They know where to find me!'

But then over the roar came keening voices and feet padding up and down the corridor. She thought she heard the words, 'Man overboard!'

'What the devil——?' Stephan yelled and flung out of the chamber, leaving Elena's door slamming in the wind.

She glanced at the window and saw it was still open and, beyond it, she perceived in alarm, the waves rising grey and high. Elena swung out of bed and, weaving with the motion of the ship, managed to reach the window. Already the water swelled over the balcony. With all her strength, she tugged on the catches and, even as the wind tore her breath away, she hauled with all her might, slammed the window shut and with a sob secured the catch.

As she lurched to the door, Stephan appeared. He stood swaying in the aperture, his clothes sodden, his face the colour of the waves.

'What is it, Stephan?' she cried, trying to reach him.

He stepped into the cabin, shut the door and, forging towards her, caught her by the waist. Bracing himself against the tossing of the ship, he made it to her bed, sat her and himself down.

'Stephan, I heard it: "Man overboard!" '

'It wasn't a man.'

'Then it was a wrong call?'

'No, it was no mistake, *mevrouw*.'

'I don't understand.'

'It was a woman—Lucy Vans Paul.'

CHAPTER SEVEN

Lucy dead! She had been here but a short while ago. Elena tried to speak the words but all she could emit were a series of choking noises. Then to her own surprise she burst into tears and buried her face in Stephan's shoulder.

Immediately he gathered her close, saying nothing, his sympathy conveyed by rocking her slightly, much as a parent would soothe a child. She was not the first woman to cry on his shoulder, he reflected wryly; others had used this ruse to snare him. Except Stephan knew that Elena's tears were in genuine grief for the woman she had known briefly. He amazed himself by how disturbed and protective he felt towards her.

She eased away from him and dried her tears with a handkerchief she kept tucked under the wide violet sash she wore to match the violet flowers in the print of her dress. 'I—I am sorry, my lord. I didn't mean to make a spectacle of myself. I—I have grown singularly fond of Lucy though I had met her but twice. Do you think she will be rescued?'

'I understand, *mevrouw*,' he said in a soft voice. 'Of her being rescued alive, there is a remote chance in these heavy seas. However everything is being done to recover her body. I fear her husband is distraught. It is as well he has Mynheer Porrot to console him.'

Stephan experienced a bout of anxiety as he watched the colour disappear from Elena's face. Even in her pallor, he marvelled, she looked as beautiful as a marble madonna.

His arm still held her waist lightly. She did not feel like cold marble; on the contrary, like the warm flesh and blood of an extremely desirable woman. With little effort he pressed her back on the bed. Oblivious of all else, he became absorbed in the enchantment her violet eyes wielded over him. The paradox was that they sought not to bewitch, their expression one of shock and sorrow at Lucy's mishap.

She smelled of lavender, her breath sweet and clean. He traced a long finger along the side of her face to her parted lips. Staring down at them he became alive to the incipient arousal igniting his body. To his delight she did not try to push him off. He ran his hand up her arm feeling its smoothness, softness. Then, gently tilting her chin, he looked his fill at her unlined forehead, the dark natural brows with their delicate arches. Colour had returned to her face: a sun-kissed apricot tint. His eyes were drawn to the mesmeric violet eyes and their thick fringes of lashes. Finally he could no longer resist her mouth. He lowered his to brush hers with feathery touches, testing her reaction to him, and felt her shiver, but knew it was not from revulsion. Pleasure? Perhaps he expected too much. 'Elena,' he murmured and brought his mouth down decisively on hers. She did not resist as his kiss started a gentle but thorough exploration of her sweet depths. His passion mounted as he felt her first stirrings of response.

Stephan lay partly across her on the bed, enjoying the soft fullness of her breasts as they rose and fell with her breathing, and rubbed against his chest. Without releasing his mouth from hers, he shrugged out of his coat. Tossing it out of the way, he stroked her bare neck, brought his hand in caressing movements to the frill covering her shoulder and tried to push it down. The material did not budge; it had been secured by a ribbon running round the wide neckline. Stephan shifted his body till he found the bow in the centre of her chest and pulled it loose. Then he eased the frill off her shoulder to beneath her breast.

'Mm,' he groaned softly in pure ecstasy as his large hand covered her fullness and fondled the up-thrusting peak. He became conscious of her thigh stiffening, but she made no attempt to push his hand away. Moreover, to his joy she widened her mouth beneath his. And he knew beyond doubt that he had succeeded in arousing her, that she was enjoying his lovemaking.

Stephan raised his head just for a moment, studying the languid desire in her eyes, the parted lips now blatantly inviting. His enraptured gaze slipped to her perfect breast and the rosy, jutting nipple, begging for his caress. With a quick indrawn breath, he lowered his mouth to drink his fill, and at the same time he pressed himself against her thigh, making her aware of his arousal. The ache for fulfilment she would not know—unless she felt the same way.

Then, to his frustration, he sensed her withdrawal. Despite his disappointment he was forced to admit that this woman had her wits about her; not for her the complete abandonment which could result in pregnancy. She knew the importance of restraint and he admired her for it. He too was capable of controlling himself, had done so with other women, else he would have a brood of illegitimate children, he recalled cynically. However, he had to admit that his desire for Elena went beyond the norm and tested him to the limit.

He rolled on to his side and watched her arrange her dress to its original style of decorum.

Elena silently reproved herself for her wanton behaviour. As she sat up and retied the ribbon that Stephan had unfastened and the one holding up her thick wine-red tresses, her face burned with shame. What must he think of her, she wondered, and would she be able to face him again after this? She must force herself to do so, or he would think her a nincompoop. Of course he had kissed her before, but it had not advanced to the extent that she had allowed him access to her breast. In this moment of tragedy, how could they have made such passionate love? So carried away had she been by the pleasure of Stephan's lovemaking that she had not heeded the tempest raging outside, rocking this great ship as if it were a toy.

She could not find a thing to say. To tell him she resented him for what had occurred would be a downright lie; never in her life had she enjoyed an activity as much as his lovemaking, she reflected guiltily.

He broke the silence by taking her chin and looking deep into her eyes, saying quietly, 'You have no reason to blush or feel ashamed, Elena. What we did is perfectly natural between man and woman.'

She smiled hesitantly. 'I know, Stephan. But going beyond kisses is allowed only in the marriage bed.'

His eyes smouldered. 'Does that mean you have decided to marry me?'

'I—I . . . It's far too early. I have known you but a couple of days.'

She saw his jaws harden and the light die in his eyes. 'Ah, I see, a grand lady finds it lowering to marry a degrading buccaneer,' he sneered. 'Is that it?'

Elena stiffened. 'I am no grand lady, as you are aware, my lord. It is you who are the aristocrat and I a maid of a humbler class. But my principles——'

Stephan brought the side of his right hand in a cutting motion on his left palm. 'Damn your principles, woman! Right is what matters——'

A knock on the door curtailed what threatened to develop into an argument, and she felt thankful for the interruption.

He shrugged into his coat and asked who was there. A male voice answered in Dutch. Stephan translated. 'An ensign, with more news of Mevrouw Vans Paul,' he said, quickly moving to the door. 'I'll come and fetch you for dinner, Elena. Don't move out of the cabin, or you may fall and hurt yourself.' The side of his mouth lifted in a slow smile that seemed to rock her heart as the sea rocked this ship. 'I can't have that, my love.' He rolled with the motion of the vessel as he made his exit, and she marvelled at how easily he could keep his balance.

For the rest of the afternoon Elena stayed on the bed and worried about what was going on: whether poor Lucy had been rescued and was alive. She prayed that it would be so. In spite of her troubled mind, which included mixed feelings for Stephan, she dozed fitfully, vaguely conscious of a change in the motion of the ship.

'*Mem*, I have brought tea and some sweetmeats, for dinner is long time away.'

Shakira's melodious voice startled Elena awake. At once she noticed the stability of the vessel compared to the previous storm-tossed movement. The cabin too had changed from gloom to brightness. 'Thank you, Shakira,' she said, swinging her legs off the bed, but remaining seated. From here she could see clearly out of the window. The sea looked comparatively calm and refraction from the sunlit water dazzled her.

'Has the storm passed over, Shakira?'

'No, *mem*. We moved away from it. *Tuan* gave orders for ship to return to Pulau Mutiara.'

'Oh, is it because of Mem Vans Paul? Is she alive?'

Shakira shook her head woefully, and poured tea. 'Alas, *mem*, no, but they found her body.' She passed the cup in its saucer to Elena. 'Tuan Vans Paul is much grieved and cannot put his mind to work, so *Besar Tuan* thought it best to return home because the wind has changed.'

For a second or two Elena stared at the bit of tea-leaf floating in the cup. She felt sorrow that Lucy had died so young and for the pain her loss caused her husband. She also knew relief that Stephan would not be endangering all their lives in a risky venture.

The fragrant tea had an enlivening effect on Elena. She decided to take a bath in the quaint large cask which did duty as a tub and stood filled with sea water in a corner of the cabin.

Elena considered her pale mauve muslin dress sober and simple enough to honour Lucy's death. Stephan and she dined in his suite as before but in calmer circumstances, without fear of plates and dishes sliding off the table. However, another, not quite calm atmosphere prevailed between them.

A keen awareness of Stephan affected her, the like of which she had not experienced before with another human being. Every movement of his sent faint, pleasant vibrations of sensation through her body.

She stole surreptitious glances at him whenever the opportunity arose and his eyes were diverted elsewhere. He looked fresh and relaxed in a clean uniform, the white cravat enhancing the copper tan of his skin, which was glowing with good health in the light of the swaying lanterns. His wavy fair hair had been neatly brushed back and secured with a wide navy ribbon on his nape. He glanced up from eating the main course of shrimps in a curry sauce with fried wholemeal pancakes and caught her gaze. His eyes locked with hers, causing ripples of feeling to go coursing down her spine. He smiled, and she decided he was the most devastating man she had had the misfortune to meet. Yes, misfortune, because of the deplorable career he had deliberately chosen. If he were honourably employed she might—she might consent to marry him immediately. But marry him or not she could not deny the power of his charm.

'I suppose Shakira informed you about Lucy,' he said, but the glow of his eyes spoke of other topics—the seduction of her, Elena Drew.

'Yes. I thought those who died at sea were interred there,' she said, dragging her eyes away from him and concentrating on her meal.

'Jan wanted her to be buried at Pulau Mutiara, beneath a tombstone by which she could be remembered.'

'Yes, that makes sense, my lord.'

'My lord!' he jeered to the bulkhead. 'Must she keep addressing me thus?' He dropped his voice, the soft tones low and seductive, and directed his gaze on her. 'You called me Stephan, when we made love. Why can you not do so at other times?' He watched the colour rise in her cheeks and was smitten with the urge to snatch her up in his arms and make passionate love to her in his bed, to get rid of this ache which happened every time he thought of her or looked at her and increased a hundredfold when he was with her. Perhaps then he would be purged of Elena as he had been of those other beauties who had travelled from Rotterdam to Bantam, either to find husbands or pleasure their compatriots in a professional capacity. He had forgotten about them the moment he had left their beds. But he knew it would not be like that with Elena. He had experienced sensations with her that he had not undergone with any other woman. Damn! Why did she not marry him and solve both their problems? She would have all the money she wanted and he would have her. She and her confounded principles!

'Very well, Stephan,' she said and smiled, conveying her amusement. For a while he stared at her, wondering what the devil had gone wrong with his heart, which was leaping about in his breast.

'Good.'

'When do we arrive back at Pulau Mutiara?'

He studied the long clock which had been fixed into place at one end of the cabin, and screwed up his eyes in attractive contemplation. 'In an hour or so. Just after nine o'clock.'

'Will you—er—will you try again?'

His eyebrow lifted. 'Try what again?'

She detected the innuendo and wished she could control her annoying flush. 'I mean . . .'

'I know what you mean, Elena,' he said, laughter rippling in his voice. 'You're wondering whether I intend to carry out another piracy engagement.'

'And do you?'

'Indeed I do, darling. Perhaps in a few days' time.'

'Can I not dissuade you from your odious career, Stephan? I would not like to see you...' She spread her hands in despair.

'See me hang? Others seem to think that is exactly what you do wish to see.'

Her smooth brow creased in a puzzled frown; yet it did not detract from her beauty, Stephan noticed.

'What others? I don't believe I have confessed such a barbarous desire to anyone, my lord. Nor have I even thought that.'

He picked up his wine glass of claret and lifted it to the lantern, admiring the deep colour with lazy nonchalance. 'Some even say that you are a spy.' And, while she gaped at him speechlessly, he went on, 'It is believed that you have been planted on Pulau Mutiara by the British East India Company to find out for certain whether it harbours the pirates that have been crippling their shipping. Your mission is to seduce me, the main suspect. And I have to own that you are succeeding immensely.' He let his head drop back a little and scrutinised her through the thick mesh of his lashes. 'Who are you, Elena?'

She rose abruptly but fell back at once when the ship rocked. 'You know full well who I am, my lord.'

Stephan sighed and pressed his lids shut for a moment. When he opened them she perceived the irritation in his eyes. 'It's back to "my lord", is it?'

'Surely you do not expect me to address you familiarly, when you have the gall to accuse me of spying without the slightest proof!'

He slammed his fist down on the table, making the wine splash, plates rattle and Elena jump. 'Then we must find proof, *mevrouw*!'

She refused to be intimidated. 'How do you propose to do that, my lord? Wring a confession from me by applying thumbscrews?'

'Barbaric methods do not produce the truth. Victims will confess to anything to avoid excessive pain. Besides, I am averse to torture. We use a subtler and more effective system, *mevrouw*.'

'Such as?'

'Such as detailed interrogation and observation.'

She shook her head in exasperation. 'You have already subjected me to interrogation. I proved beyond doubt that I am Elena Drew.' She let out an incredulous laugh. 'Spy? Me? Surely that is a male occupation. Women are not physically strong enough to indulge in such a task. We do not possess the stamina to endure the hazards entailed in spying. If we were caught the consequences would be horrendous.'

'You're wrong, *mevrouw*. Women are physically endowed to ensnare a man. You have tried to do so with me.'

She looked at him aghast. 'What?'

'You heard me, *mevrouw*.'

'You're being singularly absurd, my lord.'

'No. You are a clever woman, therefore you would use effective methods.'

'Why do you not interrogate me? I have nothing to hide. Proceed, sir!'

His brown eyes sparkled with humour. 'Ah, I admire a woman of spirit. All right, let us proceed. First, how old are you?'

'I thought you knew from my baptism certificate.'

'I have not seen it. How old are you?'

'I will be twenty-three in November.'

'How is it that a woman of exceptional beauty like you are was not married at an earlier age?'

'Mainly because, as I have earlier explained, I had to help my father; therefore neither of us could find time to socialise. Our main concern was to keep ourselves out of debt and alive.' Bitterly she went on, 'What do you know of survival? From your cradle you have never suffered hardship or experienced what it feels like to go hungry. Whereas I have.'

'Precisely. Which means you, a well-educated young woman, decided there were more lucrative ways of making money than sewing men's garments, and picked upon the highest source.'

'That is mere conjecture on your part, my lord.'

'Then it is up to you to convince me that it isn't, *mevrouw*.'

'Since you are not prepared to take my word for it, you will have to write to Mr Drew, Anthony's father, but I fear you will have to wait three years for a reply.'

He laughed contemptuously. 'By then I might well be rotting in an unconsecrated grave after public execution.'

Her face turned white. 'No! I would rather die than be responsible for anybody's death.'

'Would you, now, *mevrouw*?'

'Oh, how can I make you believe that I am not a spy?'

'A very easy way, *mevrouw*.'

'Tell me, sir!'

'Why, marry me, of course. That will prove beyond doubt that you do not have ulterior motives.'

'I asked you to give me a month to make up my mind and you agreed, my lord.'

'At that time nobody suspected that you might be an undercover agent. And anything can happen in a month. You may find a way of escaping from Pulau Mutiara and betraying us. We, of course, do have limited resources of weapons for an invasion, but if a fleet attacks the island then we may well be massacred.'

'All right, my lord. I give you full permission to keep me under armed guard or house arrest, if you do not trust me. But I insist on waiting a month before I give my answer to your proposal.'

A pain stabbed her heart when he said in a cold withdrawn voice, 'As you wish, *mevrouw*. Allow me to escort you back to your cabin.'

It was late when they arrived at the palace. At the Bay of Porpoises, Stephan had hired a horse and cart to take them back via a coastal road, instead of through the interior jungle. He pointed out the jetty where she had disembarked on her arrival at Pulau Mutiara. She made out a ship lit up with lanterns and guessed the vessel was the *Stephan*. Though he treated her with faultless courtesy, his coolly polite attitude hurt Elena and made her feel as if she were no more than a mere acquaintance. She knew his reason for adopting this behaviour: he desired her body, was impatient to possess her and to do so was prepared to marry her in haste. Except she was determined to abide by her decision to wait for the expiration of a month in which they could become better acquainted with each other, not sensually but intellectually.

In the next twenty-four hours the palace was unusually hushed as a sign of mourning for Lucy's death. Elena sent a written condolence to Jan Vans Paul and wore a black ribbon on her upper arm.

The following morning Stephan, along with his captains, conducted Elena and Aggie to Lucy's funeral service in an exquisite Dutch church just outside the boundary of the palace—Elena was surprised that these buccaneers had had the audacity to build a church—and followed the procession to the graveyard in the church grounds. After the burial the mourners soon dispersed, except Jan Vans Paul, who stood at the graveside, his cocked hat in hand and head bowed. Elena's heart swelled with pity for him.

As she turned to follow the others a hand touched her arm. Moving her head, she saw Stephan, looking smart in his uniform but sombre. 'Would you care to see where Anthony is buried, *mevrouw*?'

'I would appreciate that very much, my lord.' She lightly tapped her companion and said, 'If you do not wish to accompany me, Aggie...'

'I'll come, ma'am.'

'Good. We'll not tarry, then.' Stephan offered his arm to Elena and the three of them walked along the paths dividing the graves.

'There seem to be a lot of graves here,' Elena remarked. 'It is quite a large necropolis.'

'*Ja*, during an epidemic a goodly number of people died. But this is the Christian graveyard. There is a Muslim one near the mosque; and burning-grounds near the Buddhist and Hindu temples.'

'I don't know much about the Eastern religions,' Elena said, relaying a curiosity in her voice.

'I'll show you their places of worship one day. For the present, here is Anthony's grave.'

He brought her to a halt at a rectangular stone slab with Anthony's date of birth and the year of his death written across it. She made a swift calculation and said out loud, 'He would have been thirty years old.'

'*Ja*, the same age as I am.'

'Not much of a tombstone, ma'am. Look at them ones with marble statues of angels,' Aggie criticised bluntly. 'Don't seem proper for Mr Drew to 'ave only a stone slab with nothin' much writ on it.'

'Mejuffrouw Davis,' Stephan said, frowning heavily at Aggie, 'the marble has to come from Makrana in the Indian desert and then be carved here. I might tell you all this takes considerable time. But be sure that a headstone will be erected with a suitable epitaph on it. And it will be approved of by Mevrouw Drew herself!'

Aggie sniffed; she had no idea what an epitaph was, yet she needed to have one last dig at Stephan. 'Why are there no pretty flowers on Mr Drew's grave like them speckled ones on the one next to 'is?'

'They're of a valuable species of bloom called orchids. There would have been an abundance of them on Mynheer Anthony's grave except that he hated flowers.'

Elena looked at him, startled. 'Really? It is a rare person who does not like flowers.'

He shrugged and squinted at the sky. 'He complained they made him sneeze. We all have our likes and dislikes. If you've finished here, *mevrouw*, let us get out of this hot sun.'

Elena bowed her head and silently recited a few prayers. She wondered briefly what her life with Anthony would have been. 'I've finished, my lord.'

'Good.' He caught her elbow and steered her to an avenue flanked by tall trees, their branches of lush foliage meeting in an arch overhead.

'Ah, this shade be better, ma'am,' Aggie puffed, face red, as she hooked her arm through Elena's and tried to keep up with her and Stephan.

Elena heard a man walking behind them clearing his throat, but did not turn around, assuming he was one of the mourners. They all came to a sudden halt when they heard Porrot's harsh voice.

He came abreast of them and stood near Stephan. Leaning forward slightly, he ignored Aggie and gave Elena a hard smile. 'Good day, ma'am.' He doffed his grey cocked hat.

This man's name should have been 'Grey', she thought, wishing he would leave them and go ahead. 'Good morning, Captain Porrot,' she returned, coolly.

An awkward pause ensued as they all walked along together. Stephan broke the silence. 'I thought you were with Jan, Henry.'

'Yes, I was, but he told me not to wait for him. He is much distressed and wished to linger by his wife's grave. I fear he has taken her death badly. He slept little last night and refused breakfast this morning. I told him if he continued as he is we'll have another funeral soon.'

Elena gasped. 'Not a very pleasant thing to say to someone who is grief-stricken, Mr Porrot!'

'Jan was fond of his wife, Henry,' Stephan rebuked. 'Give him time to get over her death. Meanwhile we must give him all the distraction he needs.'

'Oh, I agree, Stephan. You could give him that distraction if anyone could.'

Henry looked past Stephan to Elena. She could not read the message in his cold grey eyes except that they made her shudder.

'Certainly not for the moment, Henry. Only time can heal grief . . .'

'Or diversion.'

'Pray explain what you mean, Henry.'

'I'm sure Mrs Drew knows what I mean, Stephan.'

'I regret, sir, that I haven't the foggiest notion,' Elena said stiffly.

'Very well, I'll do my best, ma'am.' Porrot suddenly seemed to realise Aggie was walking abreast of them and to his disgust had her arm through Elena's. Such familiarity bred contempt in Henry Porrot. 'Do you always permit your servant to be free with you, Mrs Drew?'

Elena could hear Aggie making indignant and spluttering noises, but obviously she was so furious she could not speak. 'Aggie is my companion, sir,' Elena said coldly. 'I treat her as a friend, not a servant. I think I have informed you of this before, Mr Porrot.'

'Indeed you have, ma'am. May I point out that a servant's place is *behind* her mistress——'

'Enough, Henry! I thought we had done with arrogance! Now speak of this diversion you mentioned, to help Jan.'

To Elena's surprise she saw a tinge of colour rise in Porrot's face; moreover, he did not pursue the persecution of Aggie.

'Why, Stephan,' Porrot said with a hint of contempt, 'you and Mrs Drew seem much in accord walking arm in arm along this avenue. It would create marvellous diversion and cause for celebration for all of us if you and Mrs Drew adopted this same manner but—down an aisle.'

CHAPTER EIGHT

IN THE next fortnight Stephan offered to show Elena parts of the island and she was delighted to accept. He took her in a gig over the flat surfaces. 'The interior is too hilly, with rampant jungle and only footpaths,' he explained, admiring her new muslin dress of small flowers printed on a pale green background, which went well with the locally crafted wide-brimmed straw hat, made to her design and sporting a band of the same material as her gown.

He drove her to a couple of *kampongs*, villages, where she met the smiling residents, but Elena felt frustrated that she could not speak directly to them. Stephan, however, proved an able interpreter. She watched him talk to the people and their children, his face alight with affection. For a fleeting moment she thought how wonderful it would feel to be loved by him. Every day he drove her to a different locality. Once they enjoyed a picnic lunch in idyllic surroundings on the outskirts of the jungle near a sapphire-blue pool fed by a waterfall. It was here that she saw the largest reticulated snake she could ever have imagined, wrapped around the branch of a tree.

Through sheer terror Elena screamed and threw herself into Stephan's arms. He held her close but made no attempt to kiss her. 'It's a python and at present harmless, considering the bulge in its body. Don't be afraid, Elena. I won't let anything hurt you,' he soothed. 'Even so, be wary of snakes as they are common on this lush island and there are poisonous species among them.' Her heart slipped in misery as he gently, firmly put her from him. Finally Stephan drove her to one of the promontories that formed a pincer round the Bay of Porpoises. From here she watched with great interest the pearl divers at work. Knives in mouths, their small wiry bodies poised gracefully for a moment, the divers cut cleanly through the blue-green waters of the bay and stayed down for an inordinately long time.

'Isn't that dangerous?' she asked Stephan. 'It is a miracle they do not damage their lungs holding their breaths for so long.'

'It is indeed dangerous. Perhaps that's why they enjoy diving. It's a challenge. They more often than not come up with plenty of oysters but a meagre supply of pearls.'

A few nights later after a spell of scorching heat and dry weather the monsoons broke in earnest. Hardly a day or night passed when lightning did not strike and thunder did not roll. At first the rain on dry earth smelled pleasant, but, as one wet and humid day followed the next, mildew formed on every conceivable surface. When Elena enquired how the washerman dried the clothes, Shakira explained, 'He lights a charcoal brazier in his hut and hangs garments on washing ropes above it.' Consequently they smelled of smoke.

Shakira had now been appointed as Elena's language tutor, courtesy of Stephan. Since Aggie could not read and write she tried to pick up what she could by sound.

Elena was glad of the occupation; learning required full concentration. Moreover, it left her mentally too weary to brood over whether or not she should marry Stephan and try to wean him off piracy, and at the same time inherit the fortune left to her in Anthony's will. It would enable her to buy her father the cottage she had in mind, with ample funds left over for him to retire from his work and live his remaining days at ease.

Ever since Lucy's death Stephan had not taken a ship out and Elena began to hope that perhaps he had recognised the risks involved in the lawless trade, and decided it was not worth the efforts, considering the harsh penalty of death should he fail.

Her hope was squashed one night at dinner. Stephan had called for her as usual and as always she looked forward to seeing him. During the past fortnight he had made no amorous overtures. Elena told herself she should be thankful that he did not undermine her will; except a new worry rose to haunt her. Was he still attracted to her? Perhaps he had found a more willing female to share his bed. The image of such an act sent a shaft of pain through her heart. She consoled herself with the faint belief that if he had found someone else he would not have put himself out to escort her round the island and to dinner every night. Elena admitted silently that her thinking had become a muddle of absurd contradiction in that she should fight her attraction for Stephan instead of needling herself with jealousy.

Tonight they dined indoors because of the lashing rain. Once they were served and the servants departed, Stephan came straight to the point. 'The *Uitdaging* sails with the evening tide the day after tomorrow.'

Elena closed her eyes and said despondently, 'No, not another mission!'

'Open your eyes, Elena. That's better. You should have known that sooner or later I would have to sail and that you would be on board the same ship as myself.'

'I hoped you had undergone a change of heart and decided to dispense with piracy. My lord,' she pleaded, her violet eyes wide and earnest, 'do not risk your life. Whether you are acting in a good cause or not it will not prevent the powerful companies from exploiting the people of the East. You are merely a minor annoyance, soon forgotten.'

She saw the determined set of his well-honed jaw. 'You're right, Elena. Except that tiny annoyance, as you call it, does benefit the people of this island. It cannot go on forever, I am aware. Even so, I do have my own plans for the future.'

'What are they, sir?'

He shook his head. 'It does not matter. Meanwhile be ready to sail on the appointed day.'

'I suppose Shakira will be accompanying me.'

'*Ja*. She tells me you are progressing very well with Malayan. I'm not surprised; a clever lady like you would have no difficulty. You need to be proficient in the local tongue since you are destined to spend the rest of your life on this island.'

'As a prisoner, coerced by you and Captain Porrot,' Elena pinpointed bitterly.

Stephan sighed and squeezed his nose as was his habit when he grew bored. He dropped his hand heavily on the table. 'Let's not go into that futile argument again, lady. Accept your lot and make the most of it.'

The rest of the dinner period continued in faintly hostile silence punctuated by flashes of lightning, resonant thunder and a gushing downpour.

Later that night, when Elena told Aggie about the forthcoming voyage, the older woman objected vociferously. 'Why does my lord wish to take you, ma'am? Seeing as 'ow poor Mrs Vans Paul drowned. I be thinking my lord be uncommon hard! Them ships is no place for ladies! I beg you not to go, ma'am!' Aggie's voice rose to the pitch of panic. 'An' what about me, staying behind and worrying no end?'

'You're welcome to accompany me, Aggie.'

Aggie let out a loud squawk. 'Mercy, ma'am! What with me being bedevilled by the sickness?' She shrugged and displayed a martyred air. 'Anyways, if it be your wish, I'll come.'

Elena's soft lips twitched in amusement. 'That's thoughtful of you Aggie, but I have no desire to see you suffer as you did on the *Eastern Command*. However, it's different for me; my lord insists I accompany him.'

'You have a mind to refuse 'im, ma'am!'

'I dare say you do not understand the circumstances, Aggie.'

'I understand 'em well enough, ma'am. It don't be right to take women off on trading jaunts. They should be left where it is safe.'

Elena saw the futility in continuing the discussion which was getting them nowhere. Wearily she said, 'The hour is late, Aggie, so I'll wish you goodnight.'

'Goodnight, ma'am,' Aggie said, a little peeved. Lifting her head in comical outrage, she sailed out of the chamber.

*　　*　　*

On the evening of Elena's departure, Aggie became tearful. 'Now you be careful, ma'am—don't you go wandering about topside. Stay in your cabin. See that Shakira looks after yer. I'll be prayin' to the good Lord to see you safely back. Oh, ma'am!' she sobbed and threw her arms round Elena.

Elena hugged her companion affectionately, disturbed at how near to crying she herself was, and wondered if it portended ill. No, I must not be superstitious, she remonstrated with herself. I am overcome by Aggie's solicitude, and naturally Lucy's death has unnerved both of us. 'Now, now, Aggie,' she said aloud. 'I'm not going away forever. I'll be back in a sennight, if not sooner. So cheer up. You have your friends the Russells with you.'

Aggie brushed away her tears with a handkerchief she kept tucked up her short sleeve. 'Aye, I'll have Gertha, but Mr Russell will be sailing with you and m'lord. She is like to be troubled too, for look at the weather.' As if on cue lightning streaked through the palace and thunder growled all over the sky, causing both women to shudder. 'See what I mean, ma'am?'

Shortly after, Elena and Stephan set out for the Bay of Porpoises by horse-drawn carriage via the coast road. Uneasiness assailed her; they appeared to have become reticent in each others' company since dining together two nights past. The flashing sky and rolling thunder were reminiscent of the inner tension and clash of personalities prevailing within the tight confines of the box-like carriage.

Even so, Elena's curiosity outweighed her taciturnity. For a few seconds she gazed up at the swaying lantern which had attracted a number of winged insects, among them huge moths, while collecting her thoughts.

'My lord,' she said, raising her voice so that he could hear above the tempest raging outside. 'Tell me, why have you chosen to sail in weather like this?'

He turned to look her full in the face. Tonight he had chosen a cocked hat to go with his navy and gold uniform and to Elena he appeared more devastating than ever. In fact, in her eyes his male beauty enhanced day by day.

'I think I have explained before, *mevrouw*,' he said, his voice deep and faintly dry, 'that our expeditions are carried out during the monsoons when Indiamen take advantage of the winds that sweep them with little effort through the Malacca Straits.'

'Yes, but I cannot imagine how a ship can remain on its beam in this storm.'

The hint of a smile touched his lips and it had the power to send her heart dancing. 'It is not as bad as it seems, *mevrouw*. We have sailed in worse weather than this. It depends on the skill of the sailors and the navigation of the captain. I can assure you, my crew are highly experienced in manoeuvring this vessel.'

'They must be, my lord. Else only raving lunatics would venture out on so tempestuous a night.' She stared out through wooden slats in the window. 'I feel sorry for the driver of this carriage. He must be soaked on his perch.'

'He's boxed in and the horses love the rain more than they do the sun.'

On arrival at the docks, Elena had little time to observe the surroundings. Stephan held a large umbrella over her head, and hustled her on board the

Uitdaging and into the cabin she had previously occupied. 'Don't attempt to open the windows,
mevrouw,' he ordered sternly.

'Credit me with some common sense, my lord. I
have no wish to allow half the sea into my cabin, nor
do I cherish the wild idea of swimming!'

He laughed. '*Ja*, that's right. Now, if you will
excuse me. I must go on the quarter deck. Shakira
will be in shortly to give you some refreshment.
Goodnight, *mevrouw*.'

Quite without volition she suffered a jab of anguish;
he had no intention of dining with her tonight.
'Goodnight, my lord.'

Once the ship ploughed out to sea, it seemed to
have stabilised enough for Elena to leave her seat on
the bed and sway unsteadily to the windows. All she
could see were droplets streaming down the diamond-
shaped panes, and all she could hear was the in-
cessant roar of the sea.

A short while later she answered the knock on the
door, hoping it would be Stephan; instead she let in
Shakira bearing a tray of food. '*Selamat petang,
mem.*' She wished Elena good evening.

'*Selamat petang*, Shakira.' Elena returned her
greeting. They now spoke partly in English and partly
in Malayan, and could understand each other very
well. 'What a night!'

'We are out of the worst of the storm, *mem*,' she
said, smiling. 'Now the winds will take us to the straits.
Nothing to worry about.' She put the tray on the table
and urged Elena to eat. 'Nice fish I make. Good for
you.'

Elena wished she could share the Malayan's optimistic outlook. 'Are you never afraid when you sail on these—er—missions, Shakira?'

'No, why? *Tuan* great captain. He has always succeeded.'

'And how many times is that?'

Shakira spread her arms out to their widest extent and brought them round in a circle. 'Lots and lots of times, *mem*.'

Elena had to laugh. 'And you have been on all those voyages?'

'Not me, *mem*, but my man has. He brings me fine presents and good China tea.'

'From captured ships?'

'Yes. But *tuan* insists on throwing away the opium.'

Elena stopped eating and stared at Shakira. 'Did you say opium, Shakira?'

The servant nodded gravely and grimaced. 'Very bad, *mem*. It is the devil's drug. Very expensive. It makes you sleep and have false dreams of paradise. The more the victim smokes or eats opium the more he craves for it, until he dies. Before that he will have committed several felonies, perhaps even murder, to steal the money to pay for the drug. Sometimes if the slaves of opium cannot get the money they kill themselves.'

In her extensive reading, Elena had learned something about opium. In its positive form it was useful in medicines; the negative form effected by the abuse of the drug resulted in horrendous consequences. 'Go on, Shakira.'

'The big trading ships take opium from Hindustan, where the poppy is grown, to China and exchange it for tea. Our *tuan*, he does not like.' Shakira wrinkled her small flat nose in distaste. 'He says it is wrong. So he robs the Indiamen and throws the opium in the sea.'

Later, after Shakira had taken the tray away, Elena locked herself in the cabin and made ready for bed. She shed her clothes and slipped into a sleeveless nightdress made of fine cotton, part of her trousseau which she and her mother-in-law had purchased at an exclusive shop in London.

So that was Stephan's chief aim: to cripple the opium trade and save a few people from the ultimate destruction of drug addiction, she reflected in admiration. Why had he not told her? Why did she have to learn it from Shakira? As she lay in bed, rocked by the gentle waves and listening to the rush of the sea, Elena drifted towards sleep, but before oblivion overtook her the answers to her questions emerged from the mists of semi-consciousness. Stephan had not confided in her because he believed she was a spy.

Elena shot up in bed. She must warn Shakira not to mention to anyone what she had conveyed to Elena regarding the opium. Stephan would be furious and perhaps both Shakira's and her husband's jobs would be in jeopardy.

The jarring of the ship, as if on impact with something heavy, had Elena wide awake and swinging out of bed. She lurched to the window but could see only blackness; no rain trickled down the panes. The storm must have passed on, she supposed vaguely. What was happening? Then she heard men yelling and gunshots. Elena knew they were gunshots because the gunners on the *Eastern Command* regularly practised, in case of an attack by pirates or hostile vessels.

Faith! Was the *Uitdaging* under fire? she wondered, her scalp crawling with terror.

A pounding on the door caused her to spin towards it. She released the bolt and Shakira fell in.

'What's going on, Shakira?'

'*Tuan* sent me to you, *mem*!' she shrilled, more in excitement than fear.

Panic built up in Elena. 'Where is he? What is he doing? Have we been attacked?'

'No, *mem*. It is *tuan* who has attacked a merchantman.'

Elena put her head to one side and strained to listen. The shots and shouts appeared to be distant, not coming from the deck overhead.

As if reading Elena's thoughts, Shakira enlarged, 'The fighting is not on our ship, *mem*. *Tuan* boarded the other merchantman.'

Elena disliked the idea of Stephan's wilful provocation. How many people would die as a result?

The door suddenly crashed down and a man wearing the mask of a skull and a black cloak stepped into the cabin. Elena shrank back, a silent scream locked in her throat.

She noticed out of the corner of her eye that Shakira was not in the least perturbed.

'Come,' the masked man said and to Elena's relief she recognised the deep timbre of Stephan's voice. He held out a black cloak and an eye mask to her. 'Put those on, *mevrouw*. You wanted to see what manner of piracy I performed, now is your chance to do so.'

'But . . . but . . .'

'Are you coming or not, *mevrouw*? There is no time to lose.'

His masterful tone of voice pressured her into complying. Still bewildered, she flung on the cloak and placed the mask over her eyes, fastening the tapes round the back of her head.

'Find something to cover her hair. We mustn't take any risks; she might be recognised by its colour,' he told Shakira. The servant darted to Elena's bag and pulled out a fringed shawl. 'That'll do,' he approved. Shakira helped Elena to cover her head and then all three left the cabin.

The deck was deserted. Overhead, clouds had dispersed and stars glimmered in an indigo sky. The fresh tang of the ocean breeze caused her to breathe easily. The sails of the *Uitdaging* had been furled and the ship rode at anchor. To port lay a large merchantman. From its deck came all the shouting and gunfire which Elena had heard, but now that had calmed down. Those dressed similarly to Stephan, she assumed, were his men. They had the terrified crew and officers of the captured ship covered with pistols.

'That is a British East Indiaman,' Stephan said calmly. 'It's carrying cotton and other commodities from India for trade in China. It'll call at Malacca on its return voyage, load up with spices for which the company paid a pittance and take them back to Europe. But we will not allow them to do that. We will dump the dangerous merchandise in the sea, take the cotton and gold and return to Mutiara.'

For 'dangerous merchandise' she read 'opium'. 'How many people have you killed, my lord?'

'None, *mevrouw*.'

'But I heard gunfire.'

'We took them by surprise—in their beds. Fired over their heads. All their guns are captured, cannon out of action. So even if they do come after us they have no weapons to fight with, nor sufficient money to buy them.'

'Was there no one on watch?'

'*Ja.* We hoodwinked them by running up the Union Jack and signalling that we were passing by.'

'Very trusting, I dare say. Don't they exchange secret codes to assure themselves that you are captain of a British Indiaman?'

'Oh, certainly. We have the right code. I too have my spies, *mevrouw.*'

'You still believe I am one?'

'You apparently know a great deal about codes.'

'Captain Copeland of the *Eastern Command*——'

'The captain is to be commended. He's an able instructor.'

'If I were a spy, sir, I'd hardly impart so much knowledge to you.'

Elena's attention was diverted as she heard the masked men on the other ship ordering the captive bunch of officers, but could not distinguish what was being said. 'What are they doing with those prisoners?'

'The captain and his officers are being ordered to his cabin where they will be locked in. The crew goes down the hatches, secured with locks,' Stephan said in a hard voice. 'Then we start loading all the cargo on to the *Uitdaging.*'

Elena's pity went out to the men of the British Indiaman named *Courage.* Indeed they would need it. Stephan had allowed the officers to be released at gunpoint after completion of the transfer of goods.

Once his men were back on the *Uitdaging*, Stephan gave the order to weigh anchor.

He said to Elena, 'You had best get back to your cabin, *mevrouw*. There is nothing else to see.'

But she felt disturbed and angry that her compatriots on the East Indiaman had been left defenceless and perhaps without food.

She allowed herself to be steered back to her cabin where she shrugged off his hand and untied her mask. And watched him do the same with his frightful one. Then she drew herself up and glared at him. 'You are heartless, my lord!' she said candidly, heedless of the consequences.

His eyes narrowed. 'What the devil are you talking about, woman?'

His anger, she confessed, was daunting but she persisted, her voice rising. 'You have left those men defenceless and without food. To all intents and purposes you might have shot them. Hence you are guilty of their deaths!'

A single dark brow rose and now she could see the unnerving red sparks of anger in his eyes. 'Indeed?'

'Yes, indeed, sir! If you tried to convince me of the humane mode of your operation, you failed. I am not in the least impressed!'

His face turned white. 'So be it, *mevrouw*. I would, however, wish to justify myself on one point: we have left the entire store of food for your compatriots' voyage. They will probably sail to the Prince of Wales Island, which is closest. Rest assured that no one will die. Goodnight, *mevrouw*.' He sketched her a deep and ironical bow and departed.

The *Uitdaging* docked at the Bay of Porpoises the following day at dawn. To her disappointment it was not Stephan who saw her safely back to the palace but his French captain, Monsieur Fourier.

For an unspecified reason, the Frenchman had abandoned the hostility he had displayed towards Elena when she had first encountered him at lunch on the day of her arrival at Mutiara. He mentioned that he had taken part in the operation, as he referred to the piracy which Elena had witnessed. She did not encourage him to speak about the incident; instead asked him about himself, if only to keep her mind off Stephan. 'What made you leave France, *monsieur*?'

'I joined the Compagnie des Indes Orientales, *madame*, but, like Lord Stephan and our other captains, I was dissatisfied with the injustice meted out to the natives who toiled to produce the spices that have enriched the European companies.'

Unbelievable, all this philanthropy, she thought. 'Do you profit from your way of life here, sir?'

'*Mais oui, madame!* We must live, no? Everyone on this island benefits. We have a bank where reserve funds are stored for emergencies, such as outbreak of diseases. Medicines cost a great deal of money.'

Elena admitted that Monsieur Fourier was charming, agreeable and courteous. He kept her amused till they reached the palace, and escorted her to her apartment. Before his departure, after he had observed conventional etiquette, he said quietly, '*Madame*, it would be in your interest and everybody else's for you to marry Lord Stephan.'

She had no time to brood over his words, as Aggie opened the apartment door and gave her a suffocating hug. 'Ma'am! I be that glad to see you!'

'But you looked alarmed, Aggie. What is it?' Elena held her companion away and examined her features. The woman's eyes protruded and darted about in fear.

'Ma'am,' she whispered.

Elena could not hear the remainder of her words. 'Speak up, Aggie. What are you afraid of?'

Aggie cleared her throat and tried again. 'Ma'am, this island be a nest of pirates!'

Elena picked up her bag and brushed past to her bedchamber. She heard Aggie scuttling behind.

'Did yer hear me, ma'am?'

'Yes, I heard you, Aggie. Who told you?'

'Gertha, ma'am. She did not mean to. It came out accident- like. But 'tis true, ma'am. I am much afeared.'

'I've known all along, Aggie. Don't be frightened, dear. No one will harm us. You like it here, don't you?'

'But, ma'am, they're pirates and my lord he be chief of 'em! I always says them foreigners is no good.'

'It's a pleasant island, Aggie,' Elena continued with feigned enthusiasm as if her companion had not spoken. She must not allow Aggie to panic or cause a disturbance which might change these courteous buccaneers into barbarians. 'It might be a trifle hot but we'll soon get used to it.'

'Ma'am, are you feeling all right? I fear the voyage might have——'

'Do not distress yourself, Aggie. Now listen carefully to me. I am to marry Stephan Van Coen. He is ruler of this island and cares for its people. Today I witnessed his kindheartedness. So, please, no more talk of pirates.' Elena played on Aggie's loyalties, for that was one of her companion's greatest virtues. She would never betray Stephan if her mistress married him. Hence it was imperative that she wed Stephan as soon as possible.

Aggie looked confused but answered dutifully, 'Yes, ma'am.'

Elena smiled indulgently and patted Aggie's shoulder. 'Good. Now please call a servant.'

When the woman arrived, Elena asked for a message to be delivered to Lord Stephan. Half an hour later she returned with a male colleague, telling Elena that *tuan* would see her in the library and that his servant would escort her there.

On being ushered into the library, Elena saw there was no sign of Stephan. '*Tuan* will be here soon, *mem*, please take a seat,' the servant said.

She thanked him and he departed. For a while she sat in the chair opposite the desk in which Anthony's will was kept. A glow entered her heart because soon she would tell Stephan that she would marry him. The simple truth was that she had developed a—a fondness for him. Was that right?

A sudden compulsion drew her to the desk. Casually she lifted the lid and right on top lay an open letter. She recognised the writing as that of Anthony's father and her eyes rapidly scanned the missive.

A hundred gongs seemed to ring in her head as, with trembling fingers, she lifted out the letter, letting the lid of the desk slam back.

The next instant Stephan entered the library and she stared at him with stricken eyes.

Her voice came in choking gasps. 'Why, why did you not t-tell me, my lord, th-that my father was—was dead?'

CHAPTER NINE

'WHEN did this come?' Elena demanded, staring from the sheet trembling in her hand to Stephan. 'And is it a despicable habit of yours to read letters addressed to another? You indeed need lessons in manners, sir. How dare you?' Her words lacked the volume normally associated with outrage. The shock of grief for her father, the one person whom she believed cared about her and whom she loved deeply, had robbed her voice of its natural strength. In her struggle to restrain the tears shimmering on the brink of her lids, Elena emitted her words in laboured breaths.

A sharp pain, like a knife twisting in his abdomen, afflicted Stephan as he held out his arms and moved towards her. 'Elena——'

'Don't touch me, my lord!' She backed away, staring at him with huge heart-wrenching eyes. 'I—I demand to know why you did not hand the letter to me.' She glanced down at the date. 'My father-in-law wrote it a week after I sailed.'

'It arrived the day following Lucy Vans Paul's death,' he apprised her, his sympathy turning cool at her relentless accusations, which gave him no chance to justify himself. 'I read it because I did not want you to be distressed. There is nothing you could do about your father's death, Elena, even if you did return.'

'How did you know the contents of the letter before you even opened it? Clearly you are no mystic!' Her outrage mounted at what she considered scandalous bahaviour.

'I wondered why you were receiving a letter sent through the East India Company's London office. Why would they write to you and not Anthony?' he defended coldly. 'They cannot as yet have received the information about his death. That should arrive at London, at the earliest, a year from now.'

'I do not believe that was the main reason, as plausible as you deem it. I feel sure I know why you kept it from me.' She tossed her head back and glared up at him in challenge. 'You think I am a spy and assumed the letter asked me to forward information.'

His eyes glittered with the chilling sharpness of icicles, his face wooden; he wanted to hurt her as much as she was hurting him. *'Ja.'*

'Faith!' Elena choked, aching to warm up his coldly harsh face with a resounding slap. Except her temperament abhorred any form of violence. 'You have the gall to admit it. And do not delude yourself, my lord, I have no intention of marrying you. I demand to be taken to the British governor on the Prince of Wales Island, and I demand it today!'

'Your demands be damned! You cannot leave Pulau Mutiara, *mevrouw*—you are aware of that.'

She disregarded the steely warning in his voice. 'Ha! To save your skin?'

'No, it is my responsibility to save every skin on this island. In your present state you will promptly betray us to the governor. When you have calmed down, ask me again. For now I'll take you back to your suite. Incidentally, what did you wish to see me about before you spotted the letter, *mevrouw*?'

If he but knew! 'It is of no importance, my lord.' She felt relieved that he did not press her.

Elena hesitated as he held out his arm, marvelling at his display of courtesy despite his ill temper. Indeed she was in no mood for civility; she wanted to brush past and run to her chambers, but her knees felt uncommonly weak. She might make a goose of herself by falling in an ungainly heap right here under his eyes. With all the dignity she could muster she placed her hand in the crook of his arm. Before long she found herself leaning heavily against him. Her legs quaked, her mind revolved in a trauma of agony chanting a dirge of, Papa, oh, Papa! why did you go so soon? Her throat hurt with the control she exercised to hold back the tears.

Eventually her legs sagged and with a sweeping motion Stephan lifted her into his arms. Feebly she tried to resist him. 'I—I . . .'

'Don't speak, *mevrouw*,' he said, his voice softening. 'And do not feel ashamed to cry. It's the best way of relieving your grief at the moment.'

But, with a stoicism she did not know she possessed, she refused to 'humiliate herself' as she labelled it, certainly in his presence.

When Aggie opened the door to Stephan, he strode past the bewildered woman, straight to Elena's bedchamber and laid her gently on the four-poster. Then without saying a word he left the apartment.

As soon as she heard the outer door close, the tears poured forth from Elena like the intermittent spells of monsoon torrents.

Aggie sat on the side of the bed and wrung her hands. 'Ma'am, oh, ma'am, what ails you?'

Elena sat up and flung her arms round her companion's thick red neck. 'Oh, Aggie! It's my father. He—he's gone.'

Aggie's protruding eyes bulged to their utmost extent. She uttered a loud 'No!' of shock, brought Elena's head down on her generous bosom and rocked the girl's slender body, which was heaving with sobs. 'Mercy me! Are ye saying Mr Worth 'e be dead, ma'am?'

Elena nodded vigorously, her storm of tears showing no signs of abating. 'Why did he have to d-die before I c-could give him the comfort h-he sorely needed? I had so much p-planned for him. Here, read this.' She shoved the crumpled letter she still clutched at her companion.

Aggie released her mistress and smoothed the sheet of paper out, admiring the copperplate writing, then looked at Elena helplessly. 'You be so upset, ma'am, you've forgot I ain't able ter read. You tell me what's it about.'

Feeling a little foolish, Elena sat up straighter, dried her tears with the handkerchief she drew out from under her sash and laughed shakily. 'Oh, I'm sorry, Aggie. Give me the letter. Thanks.' For a while she read quietly. 'It's from Mr Drew. He writes that my father was taken ill one afternoon and by the evening he was dead. Heart failure, the doctor said.' Elena paused to gulp back the threatening tears. 'Mr Drew goes on to write that since I am now family and unlikely to return home he has taken over Papa's shop. He believes Anthony will take care of me. Indeed he is sure I am leading a life of indolence with servants at my beck and call and rich enough to buy the best in gowns. Then he mentions he'll be writing to

Anthony. That's the lot. Before you ask, let me mention that Mr Drew doesn't know of his son's death yet. Lord Stephan has informed him, I think, but the letter will take many months to arrive in Maldon.'

'Be comforted, ma'am, that dear Mr Worth was ever a good man and now in the arms of 'is Maker.' Aggie sniffed, attempting to prevent herself from breaking down. 'I am of a mind yer'll be wantin' to go 'ome, ma'am.'

'Yes, Aggie, I fear both you and I must go back. There is nothing for us here. My lord is against us leaving because he thinks I'll betray him and for this reason he wishes to marry me.' She sighed and wearily drew the back of her hand across her forehead. 'I'm tired of arranged marriages—one example is enough.'

'But what will we do for money, ma'am?' Desperation laced Aggie's voice.

Elena lifted her shoulders in hopelessness and sighed. 'I don't know, Aggie. I will only inherit money from Anthony's will if I marry his lordship. And that is not possible now.'

'Aye, ma'am, I understand. 'Tis ungodly to wed them as is a pirate!'

In her present mood of acute depression, Elena felt disinclined to convince Aggie that Stephan had proved his brand of piracy was indeed philanthropic to the people of the island. At the moment, however, her opinion of him had dropped low, considering his audacity in reading her letter. She could not imagine why his lack of trust in her tended to wound so deeply. 'Pray leave me now, Aggie—I need some time alone to plan for our future.'

'I feel troubled to think of you fretting all by yerself, ma'am. Can I order something for you? A drink, maybe?'

'No, thank you, Aggie.'

Elena watched her companion clump reluctantly from the room. She lay back on the bed and stared up at the ornate ceiling without seeing anything and let her mind wander back to Maldon where she had known much happiness and unhappiness. Right through it all she had had her father's unstinting love, and now he'd gone before she could give him the joy and comfort he deserved. There is nothing left for me to live for, she told herself. Tears gathered in her eyes and rolled down her cheeks and she made no attempt to stem them.

In the next couple of days Elena's grief reached abnormal heights. She refused all refreshment except the occasional glass of water. Stephan had not called to take her to dinner, not that she cared. An apathetic listlessness affected her; she existed in a void.

'Ye can't live like this, ma'am! Yer be starvin' yerself, you be! I'll tell m'lord if you refuse yer food again! I dare say them servants will do that anyways. Come, now, I thought you to be a brave lady.'

Elena rarely exerted herself to quell her companion's chiding. Her senses appeared to have atrophied. She no longer possessed awareness or concern about what went on around her; she existed in a twilight world. Only one person kept focusing in her mind. All she became capable of uttering was, 'Papa!'

On the third day of her self-imposed fast, a servant announced that my lord wished to speak with her and that he waited in the front hall.

She did not take the trouble to reply, nor make the slightest effort to rise from the bed. However, in spite of her physical lethargy, she did observe personal cleanliness. Through force of habit, Elena had woken each morning, taken a bath, dressed in fresh clothes then lain back in bed again. A numbness had claimed her mind and body, obliterating all feelings of discomfort from the damp heat and, mercifully, mental agony.

'Elena!'

Stephan's voice startled her. She turned a wan face to him. 'Please leave me alone, my lord,' she said in a croaking voice through dry lips.

The look of horror on his face did not daunt her in the least. 'Elena! What are you doing to yourself? You have become a mere shadow. I've come to have lunch with you here. Let me help you up.'

She shook her head. 'I'm not hungry.'

'You haven't eaten for three days, I hear. And you are upsetting Aggie and a number of servants who are fond of you.'

'Nobody cares for me nor I for anybody. I'm tired of life, my lord. Please go away.'

He clenched his teeth so that his jaw stuck out. 'No, I shall not. You have everything to live for.' In a swift movement he carried her off the bed and stood her on her feet. Elena swayed, clinging to him.

Despite her debilitation, she had to admit that he possessed an uncanny power to bring her alive to his presence, his proximity. His clean, warm male scent floated around her, his arm supporting her caused a delicious tingle along the length of her backbone. Whatever demise she wished for herself, her nubile body spoke another glorious language; it enjoyed the thrills this compelling male evoked. I am becoming increasingly crazy, she reflected in dismay.

'Put me back on the bed, my lord. I fear I feel dizzy.'

'I'm not surprised, if you have deprived your body to this extent,' he said drily. 'Now, come on. Put one foot in front of the other while I support you.'

She did as he ordered only because she felt too weak to offer any opposition, or so she convinced herself. Slowly he helped her to the eating-chamber where, to her surprise, the smell from the dishes of food already laid on the long table rose to stimulate her appetite.

Stephan lifted Elena and settled her in the dining chair. Then he sat beside her and helped her to some food.

'Why do you not leave me to die, sir? I thought you would welcome that.'

'Do not be so melodramatic, Elena. Why should I wish you dead? A beautiful young woman like you should not dwell on the macabre.'

'Hear him,' she told the screen fan suspended by ropes from the ceiling, wafting to and fro. Turning her weary eyes on Stephan, she said weakly, 'If I should die you will have no fear of my betraying you and your people, my lord.' She paused to take a breath. 'I envy Lucy. She's out of this wretched life, enjoying the peace of eternal sleep.'

'I'll not listen to such morbid talk. I'm more concerned with the living than the dead and that means you. Now try and eat a little, Elena.'

Though she had felt hungry when she first began eating, her appetite dwindled after a few mouthfuls of the carefully and tastefully prepared Malayan dinner. Even so, she did manage to quaff a great deal of thick, cool mango juice.

Stephan surreptitiously noticed what Elena consumed, yet he understood that her body had adjusted itself to the lack of food. He felt thankful that at least she drank plenty of nourishing liquid which would prevent dehydration, which was a real danger though the island heat was humid. It could, however, become dry should a couple of days' harsh sunshine suddenly invade. He decided not to show too much concern at her rejecting the meal lest she chose to be contrary and prolong her fast.

'I'm sorry, Elena, that I did not pass Mr Drew's letter on to you. You're right, it was indeed ill-mannered of me.'

She smiled woefully and shrugged. 'It matters not, my lord. I can understand your suspicions since you and your people are living in constant threat of danger. I fear in my grief I sought to blame someone else for Papa's death. I realise that whatever I said gave me no satisfaction. Moreover, nothing will bring Papa back.'

He covered her slender hand with his large brown one. 'I appreciate your magnanimity, Elena. To reward it I have decided to give you the inheritance Anthony willed to you.'

Her violet eyes widened. He marvelled at the unwitting magic they wrought over him. 'You mean you will give it to me regardless of whether I marry you, my lord?'

He nodded. 'Precisely.'

He waited in anticipation to see her face and gorgeous eyes light up but he was disappointed.

'That's considerate of you, my lord. I thank you.'

'What is more, Elena, you are free to leave Pulau Mutiara. I will personally take you and Aggie to the Prince of Wales Island and hand you over to the governor.'

'In spite of the fact that I am liable to betray you, your captains and your islanders?'

He lifted his eyebrows and shoulders in resignation. 'That's a chance I must take. It isn't the first time I've taken a chance and it certainly won't be the last, *mevrouw*.'

She tried to stifle the unexpected hurt she experienced. What manner of idiot am I? she asked herself. He is giving me all I could want and yet I feel this misery which has nothing to do with Papa's death. 'When can Aggie and I leave?'

He drained his glass of wine. 'I advise you to recoup some of your strength; else you'll not survive the long voyage to your country.'

'Yes—yes, of course, sir.' Considering the circumstances, she should be heartened by the thought of returning home; not feeling as if her heart had suddenly acquired the heaviness of iron and plummeted to her dainty slippers.

'You do not appear to be overly happy, *mevrouw*.'

'One does not leap for joy when one is mourning a loved one, my lord.'

'Quite. My apologies,' he said coolly. 'If you've finished dinner, I'll help you to your bedchamber.'

'Thank you, my lord.'

In the next couple of days Elena's strength returned, though she fretted when Stephan made no appearance. He sent word to say he would be away for a few days 'on business' and urged her to recoup her health.

In those few days the rain kept off after sundown and she, Aggie and Shakira were able to take leisurely strolls in the large garden courtyard attached to the suite. The scent of night-flowering blooms hung with heady heaviness on the warm air stirred by a balmy breeze. In this tranquil atmosphere her grief lessened and no longer did her mind dwell on death. What she did dwell on was how much she missed Stephan.

One morning in the garden she and Aggie sat on rattan chairs beneath a tall tamarind tree that spread cool shade. Elena watched birds of exquisite colours and listened to their enchanting trills. She was so engrossed in discussing their beauty and their singing with Aggie that she was oblivious of everything.

'Good morning, Elena.'

She started and turned her head to see Stephan standing right beside her. The warmth of pleasure glowed in her face. 'Oh—er—good morning, my lord. You did startle me.'

He appeared dressed for riding in a beige outfit and as always looked stunning. His eyes danced with amusement as he regarded her. 'You look recovered, in fact exceedingly well, Elena.'

She bowed her head graciously and gave him a radiant smile. 'I thank you, my lord.'

'I came to ask if you would care to see the mosques and temples I promised to show you.'

Her eyes sparkled with joy. 'I would be delighted. Are we going now?'

'*Ja*. But first let me advise you to wear a hat and carry a parasol. We'll be making the tour in an open gig.'

'Is Aggie coming with us?'

'I think Aggie will feel happy in Mrs Russell's company. The good lady will be on her way here soon,' he said with a smile. Elena admired his adroitness in keeping Aggie happy and at the same time getting her out of the way, and for once she did not object; she had missed Stephan more than she cared to admit.

'Aye, m'lord,' Aggie said. 'Gertha said she'd be coming. I'll get Mrs Drew's hat.'

Stephan lowered his tall figure into Aggie's vacated chair and gazed deeply into Elena's eyes. 'Do you know, today makes a month since you stepped on this island?'

'Yes, I know.'

'And if the situation were different it would be the day for you to give me your answer.'

'And I might have said yes or no,' she said evasively.

Their gazes locked. As she felt herself drawn into the bottomless grandeur of his eyes, Elena became conscious of her heart swelling as if with glorious music. The sublime sensation stayed with her when Stephan led her out to a light carriage waiting in the drive of the palace.

A slight breeze, effected by the movement of the gig, tempered the steaming heat. Stephan drove her inland through an avenue of trees on either side of which were fields and villages with neat bamboo and straw huts propped on stilts. She held her breath a little as she spotted the mosque at the far end of the avenue, its domes and minarets plated with gold, dazzling in the bright sun. As Stephan helped her out and they neared the gate, he said, 'Infidels are not permitted to enter the mosque, but it's bare inside. The beauty is all on the outside.'

'It's magnificent,' she gasped, her eyes widening in wonder.

Elena had barely spoken when the peace was disturbed by a powerful baritone that seemed to echo across the land. She looked around for the singer, her face bewildered. 'Where is that coming from?'

Stephan chuckled. 'It's coming from the minaret, one of those tall slim towers.'

'Oh? And what is he singing?'

'He's calling the faithful to prayer. He says, "God is great, there is no God but Allah and Mohammed is his prophet". He does that five times a day.'

'It's fascinating,' Elena enthused. 'Tell me about it.' She watched the various expressions of interest flit across his handsome face as he gave her a brief outline of Islam.

From there they branched off to a Buddhist temple. This time they were allowed to enter provided they removed their shoes. Here too Stephan gave her a summary of the religion. 'That gold statue sitting cross-legged is the founder of Buddhism and naturally he is the Lord Buddha. But he is not a god. Mainly Chinese come here to worship.'

Elena observed people lighting joss-sticks and bowing to the image then going down on their knees and touching their foreheads to the floor.

'And now, lastly, we visit the Indian temple. It is the most colourful of all as there is a pantheon of gods in the Hindu religion.' He gave her a self-deprecatory smile. 'It is not a straightforward religion to explain because it is deep and involves a complex caste system. I do not understand a great deal about it myself. Nevertheless I'll tell you what to expect.'

The path he took her led part way into the jungle lush with undergrowth, dense with tall palms, bamboo thickets and trees dripping with moisture. She cried out when she spotted a vast monkey, with sparse reddish hair, swinging in branches just above them.

'That's an orang-utan, which means "wild man" in Malayan. Quite harmless I assure you.'

Elena laughed unsteadily and placed a hand on her chest. 'Are there dangerous animals here?'

'Oh, yes, the large spotted cat known as a leopard. Then there are snakes which live in the trees in the heart of the jungle.'

'Look at those butterflies!' She clapped her hands in pleasure as she watched them flitting about, their iridescent wings a delightful distraction. 'Those orchids, are they not superb, especially the yellow-flecked purple ones?'

'Ah! Here we are, Elena.'

The temple suddenly burst into view. Elena stared up at the façade which rose in a triangle with its point chopped off, and all the way up were a cluster of brightly painted male and female statues, some with blue skins and all with tall gold crowns. It was a work of art. Here too people entered the open-sided, pillared building and did homage to various gods enshrined in niches. 'These people appear to be very devout.'

'*Ja*. Religion to the peoples of the East is a way of life. For them their faith works.'

'Enjoyed it?' he asked after they returned to the palace and he guided her to his private chambers.

She laughed in pure delight. 'Yes, it was wonderful, Stephan. I thank you.' She offered her hand to him.

The smile gradually faded from his face, the red flecks in his eyes blazed. 'You can do better than that, *mevrouw*.' He caught her proffered hand and drew her closer to him till their bodies touched.

The vibrancy of the physical contact killed the laughter in Elena's throat. Her face grew grave, her violet eyes took on an enchanting and pleasurable gaze as she allowed him to manipulate her into his strong embrace. She pushed her head back and looked up at him through her long dark lashes in unconscious allure. Of their own volition her arms crept up his wide chest, her hands cradling the back of his head, revelling in the thickness of his wavy hair. Elena raised herself on tiptoe till her parted lips were a hair's breadth away from his. 'Will that do, my lord?'

'Not yet, my lady,' he murmured and brought his warm and moist mouth down hard on hers. She opened wider to him, responding with a passion that delighted him. Shudders of pleasure racked their bodies. Eyes closed in ecstasy, they strained to lock themselves closer to each other.

Without lifting his mouth from hers, Stephan swept Elena up in his arms and carried her, she did not know where, till she felt the softness of a bed. For a while he released her to throw off his silk coat, waistcoat, cravat and shirt. She gazed languidly at his magnificent body. As his mouth lowered to her throat, she gave a shudder of ecstasy and arched her neck for his easy access.

Meanwhile he undid the three buttons that held the front of her low-cut muslin dress together. He released her mouth to stare in wonder at her full upthrust breasts, the pink nipples jutting and ready for his caresses. He cupped the full swells and buried his head in the deep valley between. 'My God, Elena, you were never lovelier,' he breathed.

As he kissed her breasts, Elena's veins ran with singeing passion, her heart danced to erotic music. 'Oh, Stephan,' she whispered. Her body grew moist with the yearning for his. It was when Elena felt his hand pushing up her skirt and touching her vulnerable centre that she came to her senses. She shoved him away, rolled off the bed and stood quivering with her back to him as she fumbled to fasten her dress.

She felt him behind her, gripping her upper arms. 'Why, Elena? Why this sudden change?' He kissed her neck. Elena swung away from him.

'No! You attempt to seduce me and leave me with child on the eve of my departure. I fear I cannot allow that, my lord.'

She did not turn around as his hands fell away and she heard him shrugging into his clothes.

When next he spoke his voice was like an icy blast. 'I'll see you to your chambers, *mevrouw*.'

Elena nodded, turned and followed him, her eyes staring at the floor.

Only after Stephan had left did she realise with shattering force and too late that—she had fallen in love with him.

CHAPTER TEN

AFTER he had left Elena at her chambers, Stephan Van Coen immediately strode to the stable yards at the side of the palace.

In the veranda in front of the stalls, grooms had placed their *charpoys* in readiness to enjoy the two-hour afternoon recess following the eating of their midday meal. They usually stretched out beneath the shade of the huge jack-fruit tree not far away, but at the moment occasional fat drops of rain splattered down, threatening to develop into a downpour. Since it was the custom for everyone to retire for the siesta during the hottest part of the day, rarely were the grooms disturbed.

Therefore it came as a surprise to them when the ruler himself, the big master, Besar Tuan Van Coen, strode into their midst.

He apologised for disturbing them. 'I'll saddle Bliksem myself. Go back to your rest,' he told the stallion's groom. The youth did not argue but the quizzical look on his and his companion's faces revealed that they wondered what had come over the *tuan*, attempting as he was to ride in what threatened to become a deluge.

Elena was what had come over him, Stephan reflected dourly, drawing the bridle over Bliksem's head. In no way did he intend to spend the afternoon lazing around dreaming about that teasing wench. The woman threatened to become an obsession and so far he had not allowed himself to suffer this mental malady for any female. He swore to banish the frustration and anger that plagued him because of Elena's recent rejection, and what better way than riding in the rain?

He positioned the expensive saddle, tightened the girth, then, placing his booted foot in the stirrup, swung up on Bliksem. In a matter of seconds he was cantering along the sweeping drive leading out of the palace.

Stephan headed for the coast road and from there rode on to the wet sand. By now the deluge had started. He gave Bliksem his head and the horse, snorting in exhilaration, streaked along the sodden shore.

The rain stinging his face, the hard riding and the smell and roar of the sea failed to distract his thoughts from Elena.

How the hell had he become emotionally embroiled with the woman? He swore long and hard. Although he had reconciled himself to marrying her, as he had promised Anthony on his deathbed, Stephan had vowed to remain heart free. But fate had chosen to play pranks on him—although there was no hope of his marrying Elena now, his heart was in danger of being ensnared. He should be happy she would be leaving the island soon and thus would allow him to continue his life as before. Instead this black mood had cloaked his soul and this punishing ride, which he had assumed would be an effective antidote, did nothing to shrug it off. He finally settled on another means to ostracise Elena from his mind and that was to visit Malacca where he could be sure of a welcome in the bed of the beautiful Portuguese widow, Maria

Fernandez. His visit to her was long overdue. Stephan smiled grimly; he'd set sail with the morning tide on the morrow.

Elena now had fully recovered her health after her period of depression following the news of her father's death. And now she waited for the summons from Stephan informing her of the date she could set sail for the Prince of Wales Island. But nearly a week had elapsed and no news from him. She had tried to persuade herself that she was merely infatuated with Stephan after he had made love to her and that she would soon forget him. Alas, as the days progressed, she found her thoughts lingering on him. He was a compellingly handsome man, she ruefully admitted, and it would be some time before she could eliminate him from her mind, but get him out she must!

Monsieur Fourier called one bright and steaming morning in a gleaming carriage and offered to take Elena and Aggie to the villages and bazaars. 'Stephan regrets that he is unable to do it and has asked me to act as substitute.'

Fourier turned out to be excellent company, and Elena felt pleased that he did not treat Aggie with disdainful condescension as Henry Porrot had done. 'I am happy you do not look down on my companion, *monsieur*.'

His black brows rose, wrinkling up his high forehead. 'How can I look down on any human being, *madame*? After all I am a revolutionary Frenchman and abide by my country's rousing slogan: *Liberté, Egalité, Fraternité*. Alas!' He spread his hands and turned down his lips, affecting a sombre expression which suited his black frock-coat and high-crowned hat. 'I am disillusioned by the outcome of our revolution. All we did was eliminate some aristos and a great many innocent people in a reign of terror. Our colonies should be set free but slavery and oppression continues. Worse, French colonising is expanding in the Far East. How then can our slogan be justified? For this reason I rebelled and joined Lord Stephan.'

'I thought you detested aristocrats, *monsieur*,' Elena pointed out a trifle drily.

'*Mais oui, madame*, but he is an aristo with a difference. True, he has the wealth of an aristo, but he uses it to create prosperity for the people of this island. Most pleasing of all he has the brain of a revolutionary. *Voilà!* He is my ideal. If there were more men like him...' Fourier sighed morosely and finished with a Gallic shrug.

The bazaar was in the marketplace of a large village and sold everything worth selling. Strong aromas of ripe fruit, spices and flowers were rife in the sultry air.

Monsieur Fourier behaved with meticulous gallantry; the first thing he did after handing the ladies down from the carriage was to buy them several sprays of orchids in a variety of colours. He smiled indulgently as they thanked him effusively and watched their faces light up with pleasure. 'This man,' the Frenchman said as he paid the seller, 'possesses an orchid farm and ships rare species to the Prince of Wales Island to grace the governor's table. Lord Stephan has arranged with him to export the bulbs through his company to the Netherlands where they have produced ideal conditions in houses of glass to grow the plants. In fact all these vendors you see here have export markets for their goods, thanks to

Stephan. He sees to it that no poverty exists on this island.' Elena noticed that Aggie was quite bewitched by Fourier. Indeed, Elena herself found him charming. However, she was more impressed by Stephan's benevolence to the island people.

The trio wended their way through the colourful crowd and stopped near a stall selling rich materials. 'Ooh, ma'am! Look at them bolts of silk,' Aggie gushed, running her fingers along the fabrics.

'They'll be no use to you at home, Aggie. We have enough light clothes. What I think are worth buying are rugs to take back for the cold floors during the harsh winters. Look at them!' Elena quickened her step to the carpet stall and gazed in wonder at the display of rugs woven from cotton, silk and wool in jewel colours. 'What do you think of this one?' she turned to ask Fourier and was astonished to see the stunned expression on his face. 'Why, Monsieur Fourier, what is wrong? I dare swear you have seen an apparition!'

The pallor of his skin was almost as white as his immaculate cravat. *'Madame,'* he half whispered, half croaked. *'Madame*, did you say you would be going back to *Angleterre*?'

'Yes. I recently received news that my father has died and I—I feel I must return home.'

'But, *madame*, you cannot do that. Stephan will not allow it!'

'It was my lord who agreed that I should go. Aggie and I have done most of our packing and are now waiting for him to name the date on which we will be sailing for the Prince of Wales Island. From there we hope to embark on an Indiaman en route to Britain.'

'*Mon Dieu!* Is that so?' At Elena's decisive nod, his eyes widened in sudden understanding. 'Ah! Now I comprehend why it is that Stephan has gone to Malacca.'

Elena's wide brow pleated in a frown. 'Why has he gone there? I thought he was making arrangements for Aggie and myself to be shipped to the Prince of Wales Island. Surely he's not involved with—with—er—business?'

Monsieur Fourier did not appear to pay attention to Elena. He stroked his smooth chin. 'So the wedding is off, yes?'

'Of course. Now please tell me why my lord has gone to Malacca, *monsieur*. Does that mean he has reneged on his pledge to send Aggie and me home?'

'No, *madame*, he would not do that.' Fourier hesitated for a moment then gave his unique Gallic shrug and continued, 'Since you will not be marrying him, there seems no point in keeping secrets. He has a paramour in Malacca, the beautiful Maria Fernandez.' And added, as he saw the shock in her eyes, '*Madame*, we are no monks.' As if that explained it all.

Elena could not speak.

'Ma'am!' Aggie shouted in consternation. 'Ye look ill. There be no colour in yer face. Yer not goin' ter faint, are ye?'

Monsieur Fourier caught Elena's elbow. 'I think we had better return to the palace, *madame*.'

She made no demur and throughout the drive back sat taut and white, the corroding acid of jealousy eating into her soul.

'How long will it be before my lord returns from Malacca, *monsieur*?' she asked as he bowed over her hand before taking his leave.

'It depends, *madame*. If the lovely Maria gives him the pleasure he desires, then it may be some time before we see him again. A word of advice if I may. Marry my lord and you will have no further cause to worry. Adieu, *madame et mademoiselle*.' He sketched them a charming bow and left.

The moment the two women entered the apartment, a servant announced that lunch was ready. Aggie, however, insisted that Elena drink some water. ''Tis the heat, ma'am, that brings on them vapours. The sun be fair fit to fry one in that bazaar. There! Now yer look near to normal after that drink.'

While they ate, Aggie chattered on about how wonderful it would be when they stepped on to home soil. 'Mind you, I'll miss Gertha. Though she be foreign she be a good lady.'

Elena barely listened to her companion; her heart seemed to have crashed into a hundred fragments. Mingling with the anguish and jealousy was an outrage she could not suppress. None of these emotions made sense since it was she who had spurned Stephan; it had been her decision to return home. He had every right to indulge in an affair if he chose; he certainly was not beholden to her or anyone else. Except she could not bear the thought of him kissing and caressing another woman and in a more intimate manner than he had done with her. And, as if that were not torment enough, she wondered if she could live without ever setting eyes on him again once he said his goodbyes at the Prince of Wales Island docks.

Meanwhile, when Stephan arrived at Maria Fernandez's sumptuous house in Malacca, he found the woman a disappointment and blamed it on Elena.

At one time he had considered Maria ravishing, but now the delicate blonde looks of the woman seemed faded, despite the fact that she used liberal quantities of rouge on cheeks and lips. And now he noticed the deepening lines of dissipation and age round her eyes. Her mannerisms had not changed; she still affected the chicanery of the coquette which formerly he had found amusing. Now he felt bored by what he termed her transparent antics. She led him into her boudoir where they had enjoyed many an exciting sexual romp. Maria's body, he owned, was still magnificent, and that night, when he shared her bed to rid himself of the frustration in his loins, it was not she he made love to in his mind but Elena Drew.

On his return to Pulau Mutiara, Stephan set about doubling his work schedule. He visited all the *kampongs* on the island to see to the welfare of his people. To his horror he spotted a white flag on a pole outside one of the villages. As he approached, a villager with a white cloth tied over his nose and mouth rushed up to him and gestured for Stephan to keep his distance. '*Besar Tuan*, do not come closer. Five people have fallen ill with a pestilence.'

Stephan looked beyond the man to the neat arrangements of huts on poles but could see no one about. 'What sort of pestilence?'

'They shiver as if from cold yet their skins are like the heat of hell.'

'Has anyone died yet?'

'No, *Besar Tuan*.'

'I'll send a doctor with some assistants. He might have to take the sick to the hospital. Try and keep your people confined here or they might spread the disease. Have you enough food?'

'For now we have, but I do not know how long this illness will last.'

'I'll have some sacks of grain brought and left here where my horse is standing. I cannot permit the porters to go any closer. In the meantime see that all the water and milk you drink is boiled.'

Stephan felt as if icy fingers had clutched his heart; disease was the one thing he feared, and not a year had gone by since the last epidemic in which Anthony had died. He turned Bliksem round and headed back to the palace. Elena and Aggie would have to leave the island as soon as possible, before the sickness spread, he pondered with concern.

Elena knew a secret delight when at mid-morning she answered the door and saw Stephan on the threshold. He looked haggard and much troubled.

'Good morning, my lord,' she greeted, unable to curb the subtle coldness underscoring her voice, considering the havoc her mind had suffered when she learned of his 'liaison' with another woman. Nor did her imagination spare her with its vivid portrayal of what had probably occurred between Stephan and Maria Fernandez.

But Stephan appeared to be oblivious to Elena's mood. He did not return her greeting; instead he caught her by the elbows and propelled her backwards to a divan where he pressed her down and seated himself beside her. 'I want you and Aggie to leave this island with the evening tide.'

Although she was expecting to do so shortly, a shaft of pain racked her heart. 'We are packed and ready, my lord,' she began steadily, but lost control as she blurted out, 'We have been so for some days while you were at Malacca with your paramour. I expect you wish us out of the palace so that she can occupy this suite!'

He slowly released her elbows and took her chin in his hand, forcing her to look into his eyes. She saw the flames of amusement dancing in them. 'And that disturbs you, *mevrouw*?'

'N—no of course not!' she denied, too hotly for her words to sound convincing. 'It is none of my business, my lord.'

'*Ja*, that's true, you should not have mentioned it because we are not even betrothed to each other. Nevertheless, let me assure you, *mevrouw*, that I don't intend bringing Maria or anyone else here. I want you and Aggie off this island for your own sakes.'

She bent her neck to one side and stared at him curiously. 'I don't understand.'

'A pestilence has broken out in one of the villages—I found out by chance on one of my rounds this morning—and I fear it might grow into an epidemic. In which case there will be fatalities. I do not want you to be one.'

Elena realised how petty her show of jealousy appeared compared to this threat to many lives. 'What about you, my lord? Are you not afraid of contracting the illness?'

'I think I must have built up a resistance to disease; I spent a great deal of time with Anthony and his illness was highly contagious. So do not worry for me, *mevrouw*. I assure you I'll survive. It is you who has not been exposed to virulent diseases who is most likely to contract them.'

Suddenly Elena saw a chance to make herself useful and to repay Stephan for his hospitality to her and Aggie. 'Perhaps you should know, my lord, that I am not the fragile individual you suppose me to be. I too have a strong constitution. My mother died of a highly contagious illness. It was consumption and I nursed her till the end. I could not help feeling nauseated at first, but I soon hardened myself to the necessary chores involved in caring for the sick.'

'Are you telling me that you will stay on and accept the consequences?'

'No, my lord, not accept the consequences but to do something to help those who are ill. I assure you I am a capable nurse.'

Stephan whistled in disbelief. 'There is a difference in nursing your kin and strangers, moreover people of a different race.'

She ignored him. 'Where are the patients, my lord?'

'They should soon be in the hospital; it's situated on the north coast. But wait! You go too fast, *mevrouw*. What about your companion? Will she be willing to stay here?'

Elena bit her lip; she had not given Aggie a thought. 'I cannot speak for Aggie, my lord. I'll call her.'

There was no need as Aggie suddenly plodded into the room and Elena received the strong suspicion that she had been eavesdropping; the paleness of her face and the jutting of her eyes betrayed the shock she had undergone.

'Ah, *mejuffrouw*, you are just the one we wanted to see. Did you hear what we said? Your expression and your sudden appearance at the right time tells me you have.'

Aggie's face took on the colour of a russet apple. 'Beggin' yer pardon, sir. I was not listening.'

Elena sighed. 'Aggie, your face gives you away. Tell my lord what you wish to do.'

Aggie shuffled her feet and twisted her hands. 'I dunno, ma'am. I'll say this much, ma'am, my brother, 'e died of the smallpox an' me ma an' me, we looked after 'im, we did, till the good Lord took 'im away.'

'And no one in your household caught the illness?' Stephan asked.

'Aye, me da did an' many a villager. When Papa died me ma and me moved to Maldon and Mr Worth, the good Lord rest his soul, took me on as a seamstress. Then a few years later me ma died, natural like.'

Stephan leaned forward, elbows on knees, and stared ahead. 'You ladies might be immune to smallpox and consumption, but will you be able to resist this contagion? It is known as malaria, which means "evil air", and is prevalent mostly in hot, moist climates. The actual cause is not yet known. And you, Elena, do you think you can cope with stomach-churning chores?'

He studied the reaction on the women's faces. Elena lifted her resolute chin and looked determined to keep her word to help. Aggie, however, turned white and her protruding eyes conveyed terror.

Elena too noticed her companion's fear. 'I think, my lord, Aggie would be relieved to return home. She will have to put up with seasickness, but it will be tolerable compared to the ravages of disease.'

But Aggie surprised the other two by saying with unexpected resolve, 'I'll stay here with you, ma'am. Mayhap I can help in the palace?'

Stephan smiled in admiration. 'You are brave, *mejuffrouw*. You certainly can be of help. You can oversee your mistress's food and drink. Make sure all water and milk used for cooking and drinking is boiled and do not administer any fruit juice. Above all, if I may be personal, wash your hands before you touch any food and drink. There is plenty of soap available.'

Aggie bobbed. 'Yes, m'lord.'

He rose and caught Elena's hand, drawing her to her feet. 'I will call for you at six of the clock, *mevrouw*, to take you to the hospital. But if you change your——'

'I will not change my mind, my lord.'

He smiled. 'Good.' Then, addressing Aggie, he said, 'It is near lunchtime. Take care to see that the water is boiled and cooled before either of you drink any of it.' He bowed over Elena's hand and she felt a strong compulsion to touch his gleaming hair. 'I will see you later, *mevrouw*.'

The moment Stephan had left, Aggie burst into a storm of tears. Much concerned, Elena pulled the distraught woman into her arms. 'Aggie! My dear, what is it?'

Between sobs and hiccups Aggie managed to get out, ''Tis the sickness, ma'am. A shame that it should be on this island—so like paradise. And the people, ma'am, they be so nice. It don't seem right, it don't. If this be like cholera, then I seen what the sickness can do to one!'

Elena stiffened. 'Where did you see cholera, Aggie?'

'You was a wee one when it broke out in Maldon, ma'am. One of your papa's tailors got it, right there in the workshop. Proper terrible it were. We, your papa, I and some of them other tailors helped to carry 'im out to your papa's cart. 'E were ever so sick, 'e were, the tailor I mean. An' your good pa, God bless his soul, 'e cleaned up the mess, 'e did.'

Elena held Aggie at arm's length, her face aglow with joy. 'Why did you not mention this when my lord was here?'

Aggie gave a rueful shrug of her plump shoulders. 'I had forgot about it at that time, ma'am. Now it be coming back.'

'Do you see what this means, Aggie?'

Aggie blinked. 'Don't see as I do, ma'am. All I sees is that there cholera be a nasty disease. That it do!'

'Aggie,' Elena said with studied patience. 'Aggie, do you not realise that both you and I have built up some sort of resistance to disease if it was there in our midst? Papa would have conveyed the pestilence to Mama and me, but we did not become ill. And *you* actually touched the victim?'

'Aye, but that be a long time past, ma'am. There's no knowing with them bad diseases.'

'True, but even if we do contract this malaria I believe it will not be fatal.'

Aggie dried her eyes and composed herself. Just then the servant came to announce lunch. 'Now don't ye drink no water, ma'am. I'll be seeing to the boiling of it this very moment, I will!'

The siesta proved agony for Elena. She tried to focus her mind on the best form of nursing she could employ to relieve the distress and pain of the sick people she would be meeting this evening. Alas, her thoughts kept roving back to Stephan and Maria Fernandez. I should have agreed to marry him. There is nothing for me and Aggie to return to in Maldon except to live out our lives in comparative comfort thanks to Stephan's generosity. It would be scandalous and brazen of me to inform him that I have changed my mind and now wish to be his wife. It is too late. Stephan has no doubt turned to Maria Fernandez and will in due course marry her.

Elena sighed unhappily. God gives us the odd chance and if we do not take it we lose it forever. I have lost Stephan.

Stephan arrived before the appointed time to take Elena to the hospital. Once they were in the carriage waiting on the palace drive, he handed her a muslin mask to place over her nose and mouth. 'Put that on before we enter the hospital.' Then he handed her a long apron to don. She slipped it on straight away, noticing that it covered her from her neck right down to her ankles.

'My lord,' Elena said. 'Aggie told me, after you left us this afternoon, that she had been in contact with a cholera victim who contracted the disease while working for my father.' She gave him the details. 'It appears that all of us have come in contact with cholera. Would this make Aggie and myself resistant to the disease the people have contracted here?'

He looked up at the ceiling of the carriage and narrowed his eyes in contemplation. And Elena took the opportunity to study his strong profile. In her eyes, his good looks and personal attractions had increased a thousandfold since she knew of his affair with Maria Fernandez, thus intimating that she was definitely in love with Stephan. Those strong brown hands had fondled another woman, she tortured herself further. A short while later he sighed and flicked a speck from his brown silk coat. 'It was a long time ago and I am not sure whether immunity to cholera will safeguard you against this particular disease. Are you afraid, *mevrouw*?'

'Not overly, my lord. I think I am more concerned about the people who are suffering from the ghastly illness.'

Stephan said nothing but he caught her hand and squeezed it. It was enough. She curled her hand into his, her heart singing with simple joy.

The huge red orb of the sun sank into a golden sea as they arrived at the hospital. Elena was surprised to see how solid and large the structure was. It was built with red bricks, European in design, and was a double-storey rectangular building. On the south side, beyond a large field, she spotted three large grassy hillocks. Because they were exactly alike, she assumed they were man-made, and wondered fleetingly whether they were burial mounds.

The strong smell of carbolic greeted her as she and Stephan stepped into the receiving hall where an island woman sat at a desk and questioned all who arrived. She stood up when she saw Stephan, salaamed, and addressed him in Malay, '*Besar Tuan*, we have admitted Tuan Vans Paul. I sent a servant to fetch you. But now that you are here, please come this way.'

Stephan did not waste words with questions but, taking Elena's arm, followed the tiny young woman.

Captain Vans Paul was in an isolated room. He looked deathly pale, but his mouth had turned blue and his eyes were sunken and huge as if he were forcing himself to remain alive.

Stephan released Elena and in a couple of strides reached the bed. He dropped to his knees and lifted one of his friend's limp hands. 'Jan! What ails you?'

'He cannot speak, *tuan*,' the Malayan girl said. 'It is not the sickness, so the doctor said.'

'Where is he? He should be here.'

'I am here, *sahib*, I did not go far,' a dark man answered.

'Ah, Hakim Asaf, please tell me what is the matter with him. Why can he not speak? It is not malaria, is it?'

'No, *sahib*, I gave him full examination and I am thinking he has been—poisoned.'

Elena gasped and Stephan swore. 'My God! Did he inflict it upon himself?'

'I do not know, *sahib*. His servant found him lying on the floor and an empty wine glass was beside him.'

Stephan turned his attention back to his friend. 'Jan! Tell me, did you do this to yourself? Just move your hand if you did and leave it still if you did not.'

Jan Vans Paul did not move his hand. 'Do you think someone did this to you? Move your hand if you believe this, Jan.'

Elena saw Jan's fingers move.

Then his eyes glazed over, his hand went limp.

CHAPTER ELEVEN

STEPHAN stretched out an unsteady hand and drew his friend's eyelids down. He lifted himself somewhat heavily from his kneeling position, the only clumsy movement Elena had known him to perform. He had his back to her, but as always she observed him keenly. Stephan straightened to his imposing height, his back and shoulders rigid, and from his stance Elena presumed that he was deeply moved by Jan Vans Paul's death. As he turned away from the bedside, Elena saw his face, pale and drawn under his copper tan, and the perspiration gathered in drops on his wide forehead, some trickling down his temples.

'When is it advisable to have the funeral, Hakim?' he enquired in English of the Indian doctor, who looked with doleful eyes at the corpse.

'No later than sundown tomorrow, *sahib*. I am thinking it is too hot to keep the body longer than that. It will begin to—to . . . how you say?' He pushed up his turban and scratched his head in thought.

'To decompose?'

'Yes, *sahib*, and that will add to more sickness. We have yet to fight this malaria pestilence.'

Acknowledging that Stephan was too shaken by his friend's death to think of introducing her to the physician, Elena ventured, 'Doctor, I am Elena Drew and have volunteered to look after the stricken patients. My lord has agreed.'

The doctor looked visibly relieved. 'That is very good, *memsahib*. We will need much help. I am hoping that this malaria is the mild form.'

'I think, Hakim, you will have to do without the *memsahib*'s help tonight. In any event I brought her here to look around first. We must get back to the palace. I have to make arrangements for the funeral.'

Back in the carriage Stephan was hardly aware of Elena. He became morosely preoccupied and muttered something in a foreign language which she assumed was his native Dutch. She asked, 'What did you say, my lord?' He shook his head and appeared to rouse himself out of his deep reverie.

'I'm sorry, Elena, I was thinking of Jan. He was the best of my captains and suffered the worst. As far as I know he did not have an enemy on this island—so who could have poisoned him?'

Elena placed a comforting hand on Stephan's coat sleeve. She could feel the rippling of his muscles as they tensed under her fingers and sent a shiver of reaction up her arm. She withdrew her hand immediately like one who had touched a flame. 'My lord, the doctor might be mistaken. Captain Vans Paul might have died from natural causes—heart failure for instance.'

His brown eyes narrowed on her, the red flecks agleam with anger. 'Do not attempt to divert blame from a callous killer. You were there, *mevrouw*, when I questioned Jan. Did you not observe his fingers moving?'

'Yes, I did, but it could have been the twitchings of a dying man.' She desperately tried to relieve his anxiety. The grief of a natural death would in time subside, but murder was wholly unacceptable. And she knew enough about Stephan to believe that he would not rest till he had found Jan's killer.

'No, *mevrouw*, I am certain Jan was murdered.'

'My lord, if you remember, he was very upset about his wife's death. You yourself told me he was devoted to her—he could have decided to end his life.'

Stephan remained adamant. 'Jan was murdered, *mevrouw*.' He rested his head back and closed his eyes, indicating that he was not disposed to further argument. Some of his pain communicated itself to her, causing them to suffer in unison.

However, when Stephan escorted Elena to her apartment, he said, 'I would not advise you to attend the funeral, *mevrouw*; you have your own sorrow—your father's death—to contend with. I don't need to tell you, *mevrouw*, that funerals are gloomy affairs.'

His concern about her own grief touched Elena; yet she knew he disapproved of her being with him at his friend's graveside perhaps because he did not wish her to witness his heaviness of heart. If he were my husband, she thought quite irrelevantly, I would have to attend. I would be able to go everywhere with him, but through my folly I have shunned the opportunity. 'That's thoughtful of you, my lord,' she said with a trace of sadness in her voice.

Elena decided against telling Aggie about Jan's death and the suspicion surrounding it. Her companion was already distraught over the pestilence and Elena did not wish to add to her misery.

She received a surprise when Stephan called for her next morning at eleven o'clock. 'The funeral is over, ma'am, and I thought you would like to help out at the hospital.'

'Of course, my lord.' She allowed him to escort her to a light carriage. Dazzling sunlight greeted them when they left the palace and a torrential downpour awaited their arrival at the hospital. The doctor hailed the couple and took them first to the women's dormitory and then the men's where the first few victims of the epidemic were being treated.

'What is the cause of this ailment? Have you any idea, doctor?' she asked, staring in sympathy at a child who was shivering with ague and moaning.

The hakim shrugged. 'So far we are not knowing, *memsahib*. But we have some cinchona bark to treat the sickness. It will not bring permanent cure, but it will make patient more comfortable. Oh, yes!'

Stephan frowned. 'Have you noticed, Hakim, that whenever there is an outbreak of malaria, those villages near the lake are the first to be afflicted? Do you think it has anything to do with the water?'

The doctor shook his head. 'I am thinking, *sahib*, it has something to do with *still* water; the *kampongs* near the waterfalls and streams do not get the pestilence. Not at first. In fact, those near running water get the pestilence last.'

'Then perhaps we will make it a rule that water for human consumption on this island must be boiled at all times.'

'*Ji*, sahib. It will give some protection. We will also be needing more cinchona bark. The saplings in our cinchona grove are not ready for use.'

'I'll see if I can obtain a good supply from the Prince of Wales Island and Malacca.'

At the mention of Malacca, Elena experienced a stab of jealous pain. She wondered if he intended visiting the port as an excuse to call on his paramour.

Why would he trouble to make excuses? she mused dejectedly; he was free to call and have affairs with whomever he wished, and need not use the pretext of collecting medication. Her sudden paleness caused anxiety in Stephan. 'Elena, are you all right?' he asked, scanning her face. 'Does the sight of these sick people make you squeamish?'

'No, no. I'm well enough, my lord,' she told him with feigned nonchalance. 'I suppose it could be the heat.'

'You don't have to come if you don't want to, *mevrouw*. If you do not have the stomach to tend these patients, their kin will help out.'

Faint derision discernible in his voice conveyed his contempt for what he believed constituted her weakness, her withdrawal from her pledge to help at the hospital.

Elena bristled defensively. 'I will not go back on my word, my lord. Provided someone can bring me here every day I shall do whatever chores the doctor delegates to me.'

The doctor's protruding stomach, spoiling the shape of his smart Indian-style cotton surcoat, shook, his jowls quivered with laughter. '*Memsahib*, you will not be having to do the degrading work, that will be done by the patients' kin. You can give out the medicine and talk kindly to them, no? But I am hoping this pestilence is mild and will not spread.'

Elena took an instant liking to this doctor whom everybody referred to as Hakim. She smiled at him. 'I hope it's mild too for the sake of the people and not,' she swept her eyes in a sidelong glance at Stephan, 'and not because I wish to side-step the work.'

He returned her look with a smile of amused mockery. 'I think we had better return to the palace, *mevrouw*. I must make preparations to sail for the Prince of Wales Island. Meanwhile you will be conveyed to and from the hospital in my absence.'

She inclined her head as regally as a queen. 'As you wish, my lord.'

The rain had stopped as they said their adieus to the *hakim* who saw them to their carriage.

Stephan handed her a fan which lay on the opposite seat. Elena thanked him gratefully and vigorously stirred the sultry air around her face. 'What are Indians like the *hakim* doing in this part of the world, my lord?'

'Good question. They were brought as prisoners to the Prince of Wales Island from South India to clear the jungle and, through bribery, reluctantly did so. They then built the fort. Because of the constant threat of disease, doctors were brought along and Hakim was one of them. In fact *"hakim"* means doctor.'

'I see. How did he happen to be on Pulau Mutiara?'

'Same way as your erstwhile husband. We captured the East Indiaman he was on and he opted to stay with us. Not surprising, since we offered him more money than he had seen in his whole life.'

'Yes, I see,' Elena said and changed the subject. 'Not many people stricken with malaria were in the hospital, my lord.'

'No, *mevrouw*. I had expected the dormitories to be crowded by now, which augurs well. I doubt whether the contagion will reach epidemic proportions. That being the case—you will be able to set sail for home soon.'

Elena stiffened, mildly shocked by his last sentence. She received the impression that by broaching the subject he hoped to be rid of her soon. Well, he would, would he not? If his thoughts dwelt on Maria Fernandez! She fought for equilibrium, but ended up saying in a small voice, 'Yes.'

Stephan hooked his long finger under her chin and turned her face to him. He lifted a single brow in enquiry. 'Am I wrong in assuming that you now prefer to live on Pulau Mutiara, Elena?'

She loved it when he spoke her name in his deep seductive voice. Elena yearned to cast off inhibiting convention and blurt out what her heart commanded—that she wanted to marry Stephan and live on here because she loved him. Pride, however, reined her in, prompted her to think along different lines. She had received her chance to become Stephan's wife but had cast it aside and now she must pay the penalty of knowing he had chosen someone else. For her to remain on, witness and accept that Stephan loved another woman, would be like living life treading on nails. 'You are wrong, my lord. Aggie and I will return to Maldon. There will be much to settle up.'

He released her chin and said a quiet, 'I understand, *mevrouw*.'

In the following week, during Stephan's absence, Elena forced herself to cast him from her mind by energetically working at the hospital, tackling every chore she could lay her hands on till she returned to the palace every night too exhausted to think.

As Stephan had predicted, the malaria had not grown into an epidemic and it would be a matter of a few days before those affected would go home to their villages with instructions to ingest cinchona bark whenever the fever threatened, hence keeping the infection under control.

Henry Porrot surprised her by arriving at her apartment one evening. When a servant announced him, Elena had just taken a bath and was in the act of completing her toilet.

Her first thought was to refuse to see him; on the other hand her curiosity to know what he had to say triumphed.

She did not take extra care over her dressing and wore a plain flowered dress which had been sewn locally and made her feel comfortable and cool.

He was sitting in a straight-backed chair when she appeared in the entrance hall which she thought of as a parlour. He rose instantly and bowed slightly as she moved a little warily towards him.

As usual he was dressed in grey and his cold grey eyes regarded her steadily. 'Good evening, Mrs Drew.'

Though he was her compatriot, Elena could not take to him nor dismiss the uneasiness she felt in his company. She smiled uncertainly. 'Good evening, Captain Porrot. What can I do for you, sir?'

His thin mouth quirked in what she supposed passed for a smile. 'I would be greatly flattered if you would care to have dinner with me, ma'am.'

She took an involuntary step backwards, her eyes widening in apprehension. This man, she knew, disliked her; more to the point she felt sure he hated her; moreover she herself mistrusted him. The only conclusion she came to was that he intended to upset her in some way. Or had he come to fulfil his threat to harm her if she rejected Stephan and decided to return home?

A long time had passed since she had last seen Porrot and as a result she had forgotten about him and his threat. 'Why do you wish to dine with me, Captain?'

He shrugged his thin shoulders. 'Is it so extraordinary for a man to desire the company of a beautiful woman, ma'am?'

'But you do not like me, sir. You think I am a spy, do you not?'

Again his brief unconvincing smile. 'Ah, madam, that is all in the past. We cannot find proof that you are engaged in treasonable activities—treasonable to us on this island, that is.'

She narrowed her eyes and looked at him askance. 'What changed your mind, sir?'

'You, madam.'

'Really? And how might that be?'

'Why, madam, your selfless devotion in giving your services free to the hospital. You wouldn't do that if you were engaged in spying. There is little information you could glean from sick people.'

She did not believe him; yet Elena's curiosity proved more powerful than her suspicions of Porrot. 'Where are we to dine, sir?'

Just for a flash of a moment she saw a gleam of triumphant malevolence ignite his cold eyes; it was so fleeting that she persuaded herself she was either prejudiced towards him or had imagined the look.

'Ah, madam, I take it you accept. There is a festival on in one part of the palace grounds. We are all invited and refreshments will be brought round. I think you will find the evening highly entertaining.'

'May I bring Aggie?'

Immediately she saw his face harden with disapproval. 'Aggie? Who, pray, is this Aggie?'

He knew full well; even so, Elena decided to spell it out to him. 'She is my companion, sir.'

'Oh, *that* Aggie. The servant had escaped my mind completely. I—er—wished to speak confidentially with you, madam, not in the company of anyone else.'

Elena thought it best not to argue since she was anxious to know what he had to say to her. If she insisted on taking Aggie he might withdraw his invitation and she would be left wondering what had been in his mind. There was little fear of him harming her while they watched a festival where she would be cushioned by crowds of people. 'If you will excuse me, Captain, I wish to tell my companion I will be dining with you.' That should warn him that he could not start anything underhanded.

He made no demur, inclining his head amicably. 'But of course, madam.'

The man was too polite, she reflected, as she tugged the bell cord to summon a servant. Elena gave her orders to bring Aggie and in a short while the companion arrived.

Her popping grey eyes moved in suspicion from Elena to Porrot. Even so, she gave the man a quick bob and turned to address Elena, 'Yes, ma'am?'

'Aggie, I shall be dining with Captain Porrot. We are to watch a festival in the palace grounds. Perhaps you could persuade the Russells to take you.'

Elena could have laughed. Aggie had never learnt to conceal her emotions. Her eyes popped further in astonishment. 'Yer goin' with 'im, ma'am?' She jerked her thumb rudely at Porrot. Elena suspected that her companion used her broadest cockney to aggravate him.

His grey flesh took on a tinge of colour and he glowered at Aggie in outrage. Elena found she was beginning to enjoy herself. So he thought Aggie could be trifled with, arrogant ass. Who did he think he was?

'Yes, Aggie. I am anxious to see the festival and I thought it best you should know where I am.'

For a second or two Aggie peered at Elena as if trying to gauge her meaning. 'Hm, I understand, ma'am. I'll go and see Gertha.'

Elena did not deem it worth changing into an evening gown for Captain Porrot. Her floral dress, though tailored for afternoon wear, was neatly pressed and presentable.

'I'll just collect my fan, Captain.'

As he escorted her through arcades and courtyards, Porrot proved himself an entertaining companion, telling her that this island had been in Stephan's ownership for the past eight years. 'We have all worked very hard to make a success of Pulau Mutiara, madam.'

'I'm sure you have, Captain. Why are you telling me all this?'

He brushed his hand airily. 'Oh, just a matter of conversation, madam. I thought you might be interested.'

'Captain Porrot, now that we are alone, tell me what is worrying you? You have something to say in private to me. Now is the ideal time.' They were passing through arcades of a courtyard with not a soul in sight.

'I think, madam, you should enjoy the festival first. Then I promise we'll get down to serious talk.'

'Is it so unpleasant that it is necessary to wait till the festival is over?'

He affected not to hear her question. 'Ah! We have arrived.' He guided her on to an arcade where divans had been placed and waved her to be seated on one while he settled next to her. A number of people occupied other divans and Porrot said of them, 'These are the palace officials.' But he did not initiate any introductions.

On the steps leading down from the surrounding arcades into a vast flagstoned courtyard, she noticed, more people were crowding. It was stifling and, to add to the heat, a large rectangle of glowing charcoal occupied the centre of the square.

Elena fanned herself and was about to ask what the banked fire indicated in this suffocating atmosphere, when drums erupted from one corner of the yard and from the opposite corner came a troupe of exotic dancing girls clad in red, yellow, green and magenta. They swooped and turned in perfect rhythm, their shimmering skirts swirling and dipping as they moved. Bells on their ankles and arms jangled along with rows of glittering bangles. Jewelled rings on fingers and toes and gem-encrusted forehead pendants sparkled in the oil lamps illuminating the area. Strong musky perfume emanating from the women hung in the sultry air.

Porrot did not wait for Elena to ask what was going on. In fact she was too fascinated by the spectacle to question him as to its meaning.

'This is a Tamil festival,' he began. 'Tamil prisoners were brought to the Prince of Wales Island from Madras in India to clear the jungle in the interior.'

'Yes, I know, my lord mentioned it.'

'So, madam, I'll enlarge. Since the jungle seemed impenetrable, the prisoners were reluctant to do any clearing. So Francis Light, a British trader, who was responsible for them, feared he would have a riot on his hands. He came up with the bizarre and ingenious plan of loading the ship's cannons with silver rupees and shooting them into the interior. This was a great incentive to the wretched prisoners who had never seen money for many a year, and they dashed out with machetes to clear the jungle to scoop as much silver as they could.'

Elena laughed with incredulity. 'I dare say, Captain, that this is some fairy-tale you are spinning.'

'It's perfectly true, madam. Ask Stephan when he returns from Malacca.' He smiled maliciously as he saw Elena stiffen.

'You were telling me about the festival, I believe, Captain.'

'Ah, yes. Some of the Tamils—er—joined us here at Pulau Mutiara and brought their culture with them, as did the Chinese, the Muslims and the Malayans.'

'None of the other cultures take part in this ceremony?'

'No, madam, it is exclusively Tamil. Now see for yourself what happens.'

The dance had come to an end and men in *dhotis* with strings across their bare chests and white marks chalked on their foreheads slowly moved into the courtyard carrying oil lamps in branched, brass holders. 'Who are those?' she asked.

'They are Brahman priests. The marks of the prong on their foreheads proclaim them as devotees of their god Vishnu. They are here to lead the ceremony.'

She watched in growing fascination as the priests stepped slowly round the long, wide rectangle of smouldering charcoal and chanted to the beat of the drums and wail of flutes. After they had completed their walk, they lined up at one end of the fire. The chanting stopped, the drums became silent and a hush fell over the crowds.

For a while the queue of priests stood as still as the night air. Then the one in the lead chanted something, held aloft his brass holder of lamps and stepped on to the glowing charcoals.

Elena stared in horror. Her mouth opened to cry out, but she felt Porrot's thick, hard fingers grip her arm. 'Ssh!' he hissed. She could not drag her eyes away from the appalling spectacle that made her skin and scalp creep; yet she watched in horrified fascination the priest moving slowly, surely on the burning rectangle. With every step he took, smoke puffed from beneath his bare feet. At last he stepped off the charcoal and continued walking on the flagstones to prove that he remained unhurt. The air stirred like the release of a breath of relief.

The line of priests chanted loudly and followed each other closely on the fire. They too emerged unscathed. As if that were not shock enough for Elena she watched dumbfounded as the dancers, followed by the crowds, queued up to take their turn on the glowing charcoal.

'What is this supposed to be, Captain?'

'A religious festival called the fire-walking ceremony.' He looked at her smugly. 'Fascinating, isn't it?'

'It's—it's miraculous! None of them seems to be burnt. If I stepped on to...'

'I'll wager you would burn yourself, madam.'

She shook her head in wonder. 'But how...?'

'How are they immune? They are put into a trance. I fear I am not sure how it works, nevertheless there are the results for all to see.'

Once the ceremony was over, servants brought round dishes of food to the privileged guests in the arcades, while vast numbers of laden trays were placed round the courtyard for the people to feed themselves.

Elena found it too hot to eat but drank plenty of water, first enquiring whether it had been boiled and being assured that it had.

'Captain Porrot, why did you bring me here? Please don't hedge any more. I'd appreciate a frank reply.'

Porrot finished his curry puff and wiped his hands with fastidious attention in a napkin. 'You rejected Stephan's offer of marriage, I hear, madam.'

Taken by surprise, Elena stared at him. 'That, I declare, Captain Porrot, is none of your business!'

'True, true. However, it is relevant to what I wanted to ask you tonight, madam.' He gave her a slow, crafty smile that made her suddenly feel chilled.

'And that is, sir?'

He leaned towards her, his eyes boring into hers like steel blades. 'Madam—will you marry me?'

CHAPTER TWELVE

Blood rushed to Elena's brain, blocking off all sound except a constant whirring effected by the shock she had just received. 'Marry you?' she squeaked. 'That's impossible, Captain.'

A frown of irritation added to the map of lines scored on his grey forehead. 'Impossible? Why impossible, madam? You are an unattached woman and I a bachelor, which makes it perfectly possible for us to marry.'

Although she believed he could sense her aversion to him, Elena could not bring herself to tell him the truth; it would be the height of rudeness and she had never consciously been rude to anyone in her life. She improvised with, 'I scarcely know you, Captain,' and soon after perceived her mistake.

He laughed shrilly, the discordant sound jarring through her body. She knew what he would say and tried to intervene, but he got in before her. 'My dear madam, perhaps your memory fails you, hmm? You married Anthony without knowing him.'

Elena swallowed to ease her discomfort. 'Yes, I admit that's correct, but at the time I was more or less coerced into doing so because I had no choice, Captain. My marriage to Anthony relieved my father from debt. Circumstances now are different. My father is dead and I have enough for my needs.'

A gleam of malice appeared in his cold eyes filling her with dread. 'Only enough for your needs? Madam, if you marry me you will be an exceedingly rich woman—more so than if you had married Stephan. Does that tempt you?'

His cynicism was not lost on Elena, motivating her into sweeping him a glance of derision. 'Not in the least, sir. I have no wish to be overly rich. Such wealth isolates one, prompts one to live in fear of robbery or abduction for ransom and promotes bitter envy among one's relatives and friends. One is puzzled as to know who are sincere.'

He gave an exaggerated yawn implying that he found the conversation boring. 'It is a long-held hypothesis of those who do not possess wealth to regard it as evil. A simple case of sour grapes. Believe me, madam, in my experience of human beings nearly every one of us yearns to be rich.'

This discussion was swerving into irrelevant channels, she reflected impatiently. 'I'm sorry, Captain Porrot, I cannot accept your proposal. I promised myself if I should marry again it will be to a man I love, be he rich or poor!'

'Love!' he sneered. 'It's gone in a trice.' He snapped his fingers to demonstrate his point. 'A condition imposed by nature to ensure-procreation.' For a fleeting moment she wondered with a touch of humour what Aggie would make of his choice of words. 'That being the case,' he went on, glancing at her briefly, and speaking with barely perceptible condescension, 'I might find it in myself to give you this mythical—er—love.'

Elena shook her head. 'I'm sorry, sir.' Feeling ill at ease debating the sensitive matter of love with so insensitive an individual as she judged Porrot to be, she did not chance looking at him, in the hope that her action would convey she considered the matter closed. Elena let her gaze absently roam the courtyard.

The crowd was thinning and the musicians were gathering their instruments in readiness to depart. She searched for Aggie and the Russells but could not distinguish them in the dim interior of the arcades. 'I think it is time we left, Captain,' she said without glancing at him.

'As you wish, Mrs Drew,' he agreed with cold cordiality, rising from the divan. Even so, he still observed courtesy by crooking his arm and offering it to Elena. Despite his adherence to etiquette she was alive to the malice emanating from him in angry waves, instilling fear in her. Of a sudden it occurred to Elena that she had not asked him why he wished to marry her. Perhaps for the same reason as Stephan did: to stop her from leaving the island and betraying them all. Except she now felt reluctant to broach the subject with Porrot again. She straightened and took his arm, barely touching his sleeve.

They passed through the interior arcades of the palace leading to her apartment, and then, to Elena's relief, she spotted Aggie ahead with the Russells. She intended excusing herself to the captain, however ill-mannered it might seem, and catching up with her friends when a firm step sounded behind her. Both she and Porrot simultaneously stopped and turned.

Porrot looked enraged but Elena took little notice of him. Her heart flamed like a torch in the darkness of fear. 'Stephan,' she breathed. 'When did you come back?'

A slow smile stretched across his mouth. As always he looked devastating and meticulously clean in a dark purple cut-away coat of fine silk, an immaculate cravat, pale breeches and a lilac ribbon which tied back his gold hair. Only one thing spoilt the effect: the smile did not reach his eyes. Hard, opaque, they gazed down at her. 'Good evening, *mevrouw*, Henry.' He bowed slightly, yet with elegance, to Elena, and nodded to Porrot. 'I arrived back in time to deliver the cinchona bark to the hospital, then go on to the palace, dress and attend the festival.'

'Why did you not join us?' she asked, the flame of happiness in her dying out, her large violet eyes scanning his face in bewilderment.

'I was not far off. There was not sufficient room on the divan you and Henry shared. But I assure you, *mevrouw*, I was perfectly comfortable.'

She remembered, then, that each arch in the arcades was divided by curtains. He must have been screened from her by the drapes. How much had he heard of her conversation with Porrot?

The man himself provided Stephan with the information she sought to conceal from him. With relish he said, 'I brought her here, to propose marriage, Stephan. She refused you, so I thought perhaps she might accept me. Some women prefer the grey-haired father figure.'

Not a muscle moved on Stephan's face and Elena received the uncanny feeling that he had heard part, if not the whole, of her conversation with Porrot.

He ignored Porrot and addressed Elena. 'And did you accept, *mevrouw*?'

'No, my lord.'

Porrot gave his nerve-jarring laugh and said with needle-sharp sarcasm, 'She would have me believe that she intends to marry for love.'

Elena felt her face scorch with embarrassment and supposed that she would soon be an object of ridicule in front of these men. She decided upon a hasty escape. 'I am excessively tired, gentlemen. If you will excuse me. Goodnight, my lord. Captain Porrot.' Not waiting for them to reply she lifted her skirt above her shoes and rapidly walked ahead.

To her relief, back in her apartment, an agitated Aggie awaited her in the parlour. 'Ma'am, I looked everywhere in them arcades for you and the cap'n but I didn't see neither of yer. Where did he take you?'

'It's difficult to explain since all the arcades looked the same. But after the festival when Captain Porrot was escorting me back here, I saw you ahead with the Russells.'

Aggie shuddered. 'Terrifying, weren't it, ma'am? How them peoples walked over the fire with narry a blister, I sure can't tell. 'Twould be witchcraft I dare swear, ma'am; or 'twould be a miracle.'

'Yes, it is amazing.' Elena yawned and realised how tired she felt.

'Well, I'll say goodnight, ma'am, seeing how weary you be.'

'Yes, I have to be up early to go to the hospital. Goodnight, Aggie.'

Before Elena dropped off, she wondered whether Stephan would arrive to take her to the hospital in the morning. Also what he and Porrot had to say to each other after she left them in the arcade.

Stephan and Porrot had watched Elena dash away ahead of them. Neither of the two men attempted to go after her nor call her back. They fell into step as they moved forward.

'Why did you propose to Mevrouw Drew, Henry? I did not know you were interested in her.' Stephan spoke with calm curiosity, but in his breast a blaze of jealousy burned. What the devil had come over Porrot? The man was supposed to be a misogynist.

'Nor am I,' Porrot confessed drily. 'Oh, she's a very beautiful woman; even Alain Fourier, that confirmed bachelor, is smitten with her, but I assure you, my lord, I am not in the least attracted to Mrs Drew.' He dusted his coat sleeve where Elena's hand had rested, as if she might have contaminated him with a pestilence. 'I just tested her to see if her dedication to spying exceeded her love of wealth. I fear I cheated in that I professed to own great riches, more than you do.'

'And you found?'

'And I found, Stephan, that her dedication to spying triumphed.'

'Did it not occur to you, Henry, that she simply was not attracted to either of us? Perhaps she told the truth that she did wish to marry for love alone.'

'Bah! Stephan! Your speculation is completely defeated by the fact that she married Anthony by proxy. If she ever did go through that ceremony, which I doubt. My belief is the woman is an impostor and spy.'

'What would you have done, Henry, if Mevrouw Drew had accepted your proposal?'

Porrot looked nonplussed, but recovered in a flash. 'Oh,' he said, turning his thin lips down and waving a hand airily. 'I knew she wouldn't.'

'I have given Elena permission to leave the island with her companion, Henry.'

Porrot sighed. 'Yes, I know, Fourier told me. That was the main reason why I offered for Mrs Drew—to try and keep her here. I took the chance that she might succumb to the temptation of wealth. Alas, I failed. Even so, I'll not give up. This woman is not going to leave Pulau Mutiara if I can help it, Stephan, and ruin all that we have painstakingly worked on.'

Stephan slanted his friend a look of mock amazement. 'Really?'

Porrot's thin grey face hardened. 'Yes, Stephan, really!'

Stephan laughed incredulously. 'But Elena has no substantial proof that we are involved in piracy. We have kept no written records of our exploits, so that she cannot copy them.'

Porrot was adamant. 'Nevertheless, I mean to see that Mrs Drew does not leave this island, Stephan.'

'We'll see, Henry, we'll see,' Stephan said quietly but with a subtle threat in his voice.

Elena had not long finished a cool breakfast of a slice of papaya and two plantains, washed down with China tea, when Stephan called for her the following day. She greeted him with a smile so bright that he looked taken aback. Watching his changing expression she instantly grew serious. 'Why, my lord, is something wrong?'

He took her hand, bowed gallantly over it and smiled at her. It was Elena's turn to be slightly dazed. 'No, of course not, *mevrouw*. If you are ready——' He swept his hand pointing ahead and, taking her elbow, guided her to the front of the palace where, as usual, a carriage waited.

Her spirits lifted; it was like old times being with Stephan. Moreover, it was early enough for a cool breeze to play on them as the carriage wended its way to the hospital. This coolness, she knew, was transient and would soon be replaced by heat as the day wore on. So, like her short time with Stephan, she decided to take advantage of the coolness and enjoy it to the limit while it lasted.

'You look happy, Elena. Delighted to be going home soon?'

She gazed at him, startled. 'It's such a beautiful cool morning, filled with birdsong, enough to raise the most jaded of hearts.'

'Ja,' he said, opening the glass window on his side and inhaling deeply. 'This is the best time of day on Pulau Mutiara.'

'I'll be sorry to leave, my lord.'

He turned slowly to face her. 'Then why go, Elena?'

Why go? She could not possibly stay on here and witness his mistress, Maria Fernandez, take over the palace along with Stephan's heart. It would be like signing her death warrant. Better to leave and not know what went on. 'There's nothing for me here— no ties. I—I'd be in the way, I dare say.'

He seemed to draw down a curtain between them. 'You know best.' This tersely. 'But I hope you will hold fond memories of this island, *mevrouw.'*

'Oh, I shall! I shall, my lord.' She said it too enthusiastically, she reflected a moment later. Toning her voice down, she went on, 'You always treated Aggie and myself well. We shall remember that you allowed me to benefit generously from Anthony's will. Else we would suffer great deprivation at home. We shall always be grateful to you, my lord.' And I shall always love you, Stephan, she added silently.

On their arrival at the hospital, the *hakim* greeted them effusively. Elena understood his ebullience when he spoke. 'Today, I am thinking, *sahib*, we will be discharging most of the malaria patients. The fever will recur from time to time, but if they take cinchona bark at onset it will be controlled. We are pleased that there has not been one death.'

'Well done, Hakim,' Stephan praised him. 'We are indeed fortunate to have you.'

'Not only me, *sahib*, there was the *memsahib* and the relatives of the patients that tended them well.'

'I take it there will not be any need for me to come here again?' Elena questioned.

'No, *memsahib*, but do come in and say goodbye to those who are about to leave.'

Elena and Stephan went round to the few people in the dormitories and said their farewells. She asked if she could help in any way and was politely rejected.

Then Elena wished the *hakim* goodbye and she and Stephan returned to the carriage. Everyone in the hospital turned out to see them off, as if they knew they would not set eyes on Elena again, though she had not mentioned that she would be leaving the island for good. She considered that the fewer people who knew of her final departure from Pulau Mutiara, the better for Aggie and herself.

'As you know, my lord, Captain Porrot is against Aggie and me leaving this island,' she said nervously. 'I believe he is serious in his intent to prevent our departure, therefore I would be grateful, my lord, if you would not apprise him of the date we are due to sail.'

'Of course, not, *mevrouw*. I am aware that you will be in danger if I were to be so indiscreet.'

'Stephan?'

His eyes were grave and tender as he gazed into hers. *'Ja, mevrouw?'*

'Stephan, now that my help is no longer required at the hospital, could you tell me when we will be sailing for the Prince of Wales Island?'

'We will leave tomorrow night an hour after midnight, provided it is overcast and the moon obscured. Then the *Stephan* can slip away from the jetty without being detected.'

'Thank you. I know that Captain Porrot will go to any lengths to stop me.'

'Even to the extent of asking you to be his wife,' Stephan said drily.

A shiver of apprehension raked through her. 'I am aware that Captain Porrot mistrusts me and is obsessed with the ridiculous idea that I am a spy, hence he is capable of ruthless measures to prevent my escape. I think too that it would not be advisable to mention the day of sailing to Aggie, lest she insist on saying her goodbyes to the Russells.'

'Ja, mevrouw, I was about to suggest that to you.'

They lapsed into a silence that brought her alive to other sensations. The close atmosphere in the carriage seemed to vibrate with a power that honed her awareness to his presence, the nearest she could come to describing this feeling was to define it as a kind of life force.

Impelled by an unseen power, she turned her head, and their gazes collided. The impact was almost physical in its force, enough to shake Elena.

Stephan lifted her hand, first examining the slender fingers and then raising the palm to his lips. Ripples of pleasure raked through her blood. Her breathing became laboured as she watched him close his eyes, the long gold-tipped lashes resting on his cheeks, as he kissed her palm.

'Elena,' he murmured. 'Have dinner with me, tonight.'

'Yes, yes, Stephan, I will,' she whispered, knowing that the night would be the last they would share alone with each other.

The carriage came to a halt in the driveway of the palace, and, as was his wont, Stephan escorted Elena back to her apartment. 'Tonight, ma'am,' he reminded her, sweeping her a bow.

'Yes, my lord,' she promised, giving him a radiant smile.

Neither of them had the slightest premonition of the turmoil the night would bring.

Aggie was not around when Elena entered her apartment. She felt pleased in a way; Aggie's absence gave her a chance to compose herself. Elena made her way to her bedchamber and gazed at her reflection in the tall mirror. Her eyes shone with the brilliance of amethysts and her cheeks and mouth glowed with a pink softness. This then is what love does to one, she reflected dreamily, and tonight I intend to savour every moment of Stephan's company. I will carry the memory in my brain for the rest of my life. At least I will have experienced, for the short period of time I have known Stephan, the great joy of love that the poets and troubadours have described and sung of down the ages.

Aggie arrived at lunchtime to find Elena sitting in the garden courtyard beneath a betelnut palm, staring into space.

'Why, ma'am, have yer been here long?'

Elena jumped, breathing out a startled, 'Oh, you did give me a fright, Aggie!'

Her companion chuckled. 'I did, ma'am? Mercy me, I never knew me step were as light as a fairy! You looked like you were a-dreamin' of a lover, that I swear!'

Elena had difficulty controlling a flush, but laughed lightly. 'Don't be absurd, Aggie, who could I dream about?'

'Why, 'tis plain to see, it be about m'lord.'

Elena's flush deepened. Not giving Aggie a chance to tease her, she hastily asked, 'Is lunch ready? I declare I am famished.'

'So am I, ma'am, I'll go ring for a servant.'

Stephan had not stated what time he would collect Elena for dinner. Nevertheless she assumed it would be at the usual hour of eight o'clock. Tonight she determined to look her best and had set about giving herself a clear two hours to get ready. She enjoyed a cool leisurely bath then donned silk underwear which would lie smoothly beneath her best leaf-green taffeta gown. It had been made by the London modiste and cut on neo-classical lines in the Grecian style: it was high-waisted, falling straight in front and gathered in a high yoke at the back to drape in rich folds to end in a short train. Lace edged the low neckline and cap sleeves and a double row ran round the hem of her dress. The only jewellery she possessed was the gold locket enclosing Anthony's miniature portrait, and she felt disinclined to wear the piece. However, ribbons round the throat had been fashionable at home, and since she owned a number of them, she picked out a thin green velvet one to tie round her neck. Her hair she brushed till it shone and left it loose to hang in heavy curls down her back. She wondered whether to wear it up, secured with a ribbon, or leave it as it was. Eventually she settled on the latter. She decided against wearing elbow-length lace mittens, as it was much too hot. During her shopping spree in London, she had treated herself to a small bottle of French perfume. She used it now in preference to the lavender water she usually applied. She dabbed the scent on her wrists, neck and behind her ears. Closing her eyes, she inhaled the exotic fragrance and hoped Stephan would like it too.

Aggie had been in attendance while Elena dressed and gave help where it was required. She oohed and aahed every so often to show her approval, and sighed for the loss of her own waistline.

'Do you think my hair looks untidy hanging loose, Aggie?'

'Ooh, no, ma'am. I'd say you look proper angel like! I dare swear m'lord will like as not be swept off 'is feet, 'e will! Mark me words. Pity...' she sighed.

'Pity what, Aggie?'

The companion shook her head. 'It's not for me to say, ma'am—— Ah, there's the knock on the door. Sure to be m'lord.'

'What will you do, Aggie?'

'I'll go an' see Gertha, ma'am.'

'Good. I'll see you later. Don't worry to come to the door. Goodnight, Aggie.'

'Goodnight, ma'am. An' you be careful.'

'And you too, Aggie,' she said, dropping a peck on the older woman's ruddy cheek. Then, lifting her train, she swept out to meet Stephan.

To say that Stephan looked stunned when Elena opened the door to him was an understatement. He stepped back as if something had hit him across the head. For a while he stared speechlessly at her and then, to her astonishment, he let out a low whistle.

'Elena.' Her name came out in a breathless huskiness. 'God! You look ravishing. I've never seen a woman look as beautiful as you do.' He held out his arm. 'Allow me.'

She gave him a radiant smile, took his arm, and said, 'Thank you, my lord. I thought I'd wear my best dress, since there will be no occasion for me to wear it on the return voyage or at home. Aggie and I shall not be mixing with the *ton*, that is certain.'

With his innate charm, he said, 'I consider myself flattered that you have chosen the gown to dine with me.'

Stephan guided her to the pavilion draped with mosquito muslin where they had dined tête-à-tête on that unforgettable night when he had first kissed her. Her face taking on a tinge of pink, Elena wondered if there would be a repeat performance.

No servants in the pavilion this time, and Stephan himself poured out Madeira and served Elena with the various exotic dishes which she had acquired a taste for and her body had adapted to so well.

A faint breeze stirred the starlit night, wafting heady perfume from night-flowering shrubs, and abounding with the sound of crickets and mosquitoes. 'What are those?' Elena asked, pointing at what looked like tiny pulsing stars.

'Those are insects known as fireflies, *mevrouw*.'

Elena was fascinated by the sight of the creatures, which were blinking in and out of shrubs and trees in the garden like a swarm of eyes spying on Stephan and herself. 'They're like fairy lights,' she remarked.

He smiled indulgently. 'When we've had our meal, I'll take you up on the roof of the palace and you can see them over a wide area. I promise you won't be disappointed, Elena.'

However fascinating the display of fireflies might be, Elena was more interested in the sight of Stephan. She purposely lingered over the meal to prolong her stay with him. Meanwhile, she drank in his male beauty. The streaks highlighting his gold hair shimmered in the lamplight. She ran an imaginary finger down his broad forehead, over his thick brows above his magnificent brown eyes that gazed softly at her now, along his straight nose and wide mouth curved in a slight smile. She observed his sharply angled jaw and strong chin. If she were an artist . . . But there was no need to paint him; he would be engraved forever on her mind.

'What's the matter, Elena?' Stephan invaded her thoughts. He stretched out his hand and caught her fingers, his touch sending shivers of excitement up her arm.

'Why, nothing, my lord,' she responded.

'Then why the sighs? Having second thoughts about returning home?'

She looked up at him, her violet eyes large and filled with distress. 'I—I don't want to leave.'

He lifted his wide shoulders and asked in bewilderment. 'Then why go? You are welcome to stay here as long as you wish. I have told you this before.'

She vied with her pride and finally arrived at the conclusion that his invitation was like a morsel to her hungry and love-ridden soul. Perhaps if she stayed on he could learn to love her; she was not so stupid that she could not sense Stephan was attracted to her, whatever his relationship with Maria Fernandez was. And here was the crux of the matter. Maria! The splinter beneath Elena's skin that refused to be extracted. 'Yes, I think I will. There is nothing for me at home, now that Papa has died. Anthony's father is a good Christian and will see that my father is given a good burial. And I'm sure Aggie will be happy to stay on. She has taken to the island and its people as I have.'

He smiled slowly and this time the smile reached his eyes, the red flecks gleaming with joy, his strong hand tightening on her fingers. Elena's breath caught, her heart barely moved; she dared to believe that he cared enough to rejoice at her decision.

Yet he did not speak the words she longed to hear; instead he said, 'Let us go on the palace roof.'

He caught her hand and guided her along a narrow path that led from the pavilion to the back of the side of the palace. Steep winding steps spiralled up. It was a long climb and when Stephan helped her up on to the flat roof she put a hand on her bosom and gave a breathless laugh. He laughed with her and casually slipped his arm round her waist, then manoeuvred her to the protective parapet of the flat roof. The rest of the area was taken up with bulbous domes that marched around the vast structure.

'This is where I sleep when the rainy season has ended.'

She caught the edge of the waist-high parapet and looked down at the garden alive with fireflies, throbbing with tiny lights. A balmy breeze blew a tress of her hair across her cheek, and Stephan lifted it away but let his hand linger on her soft skin.

'It must be cool, sleeping up here,' she remarked, gazing up at him, seeing his face distinctly in the starlit night, his eyes dark and grave.

'It would be a hundred times more pleasant if you married me and shared my bed.'

'Oh, Stephan,' she sighed, her heart pumping with joy. She turned slightly in the circle of his arm and rested her head against his lapel. 'If you are proposing to me again...'

'I am, Elena, and I suppose you'll say no.'

'You're wrong there, my lord.'

She could hear the strong beat of his heart and the quickening of his breath. Then his long finger curled under her chin and lifted her face.

'Why? Why have you changed your mind, Elena?'

Elena saw the tautness of his face, could feel his whole body tensing as he waited for her reply.

'I love you, Stephan.'

CHAPTER THIRTEEN

STEPHAN'S reaction to Elena's avowal was neither sweet and tender nor rough and painful. It was strong, confident, born of a sureness mastered by experience to give a woman maximum pleasure.

He swept his hand through the thick silkiness of her wine-red hair, cradling the back of her head, firmly drawing it back to arch her neck, exposing the long slender column. His other hand holding her securely round the waist, he bent her pliant, willing body back a little, slowly lowering his mouth to the hollow of her throat.

At the touch of his warm mouth and the gentle probing of his tongue, Elena held her breath on a silent gasp as if afraid that this blissful desire he evoked in her might end all too soon. Her senses proved oblivious to the outside world, yet heightened in their concentration on Stephan.

She inhaled his clean male smell of unscented soap and fresh perspiration, which was effected by the constant heat, but only enhanced his allure. His mouth moved in tiny kisses from the hollow of her throat, along her jawline. Straightening her body he held her close against him. For a moment his lips hovered over hers and then came down hard but painlessly on her mouth. Insistently he prised her lips open, his tongue invading, playing, curling against hers. She closed her eyes, relishing the taste of his mouth, its flavour of

wine, and inhaled the heady, healthy scent of his
breath.

Elena's blood bubbled with erotic heat; her heart
drummed out sensuous music and her body pulsed
with the moisture of need created by her love for him.
And the restless titillation of his hands intensified her
desire. They swept through the thick curtain of her
hair, then under it to caress her slim back, sending
burning tingles needling the length of her spine. One
arm settled over her hips, the other round her waist.
He lifted her on to her toes and pressed himself against
her, making her aware of his rigid passion.

Suddenly, wrenching his mouth from hers, Stephan
said, his breathing ragged, '*Lieveling*, we cannot do
much up here, there's no bed and too much clothing
between us. Come.' He swept her up in his arms and
raced down the long winding steps.

'Where are you taking me, Stephan?'

He did not answer and she repeated the question
when he stood her on her feet once he reached the
garden. 'You'll see, Elena,' was all he was prepared
to say. He grasped her hand and towed her alongside
the high garden wall to a side gate of carved metal.
Unfastening the bolts, he silently took Elena through
the gateway, out on to a narrow path on the opposite
side of the wall. Five minutes later she recognised that
they had arrived at the graveyard in the church compound. It looked peaceful, but Stephan did not stop
there, he led her to a small house at the back of the
church. He rapped on the door at the side of which
a small lantern hung. Elena grew more bewildered and
tried to read his expression for some illumination of
why he had brought her here. She opened her mouth

to question him. Obviously anticipating her query, he put his finger on his lip.

The soft slap of slippers in the interior heralded the approach of the chaplain. She heard bolts being dragged back and next instant the door creaked ajar. She recognised the elderly clergyman who had presided over Lucy's funeral. When he spotted Stephan he pulled the door wide and spoke in Dutch. Stephan's staccato reply in the same language apparently took the good reverend by surprise; his pale eyes, in a long pink face, stared at Stephan in disbelief and he staggered back a pace. A lively discourse followed that Elena found incomprehensible.

At last the reverend shrugged and beckoned the couple inside. Except for his slippers, he was fully dressed in sombre garb of black coat, breeches, white stockings. He led the couple to a stark whitewashed room, its only furniture a small table holding a black cross and, further down the chamber, a single pew and bench.

With a wave of his hand towards the bench, he invited Stephan and Elena to be seated and departed from the room.

'Stephan,' Elena asked in a hushed tone, 'why have you brought me here?'

'To marry you.'

The jolt of shock made her jump. 'What?' Now she understood why the clergyman had been astonished.

Stephan's straight brows reached for his hairline. 'That surprises you, does it?'

'But—but you gave me no warning.'

'You've had months of warning from the day you landed on the Prince of Wales Island.'

'Yes, I know. But why now, so late at night?'

'It's not late, Elena. You ask why now? You confessed to loving me, and that's reason enough for marriage. I am not giving you a chance to change your mind, or your heart, my love. Tomorrow might be too late.'

Now that the shock had subsided a little, she felt a new excitement mixed with joy running in her veins. Licking her lips, she asked in a choking voice, 'W-where has the good priest gone?'

'To collect a couple of witnesses and to bring the necessary prayer book with the wedding service.' He caught her hand, squeezed it, gave her a lop-sided smile as if pleading her forgiveness for pouncing this event suddenly on her. 'I have asked him to keep this marriage a secret for a couple of days. Else we'll be besieged by well-wishers and not be left in peace. In a sennight I'll order celebrations.'

She was saved from voicing her thoughts by the return of the reverend and a young island couple. Stephan knew them. He greeted them cordially and spoke quietly to them in Malayan, which she understood. He thanked them for coming and requested that they keep the marriage to themselves for the next week. They willingly agreed and the service went ahead. It was short and simple but held all the gravity of a lifelong commitment. After husband and wife signed the register, Stephan pressed coins into the clergyman's and the witnesses' hands. Then the married couple returned to the palace garden. Stephan led her through a series of arcades surrounding garden courtyards.

'Where are we going now, Stephan?'

'To my, or I should say, our bedchamber, my love, where else?'

Once he had entered his apartment, he set her down and secured the door, then, sweeping her up in his arms, he strode through to the bedchamber and, parting the mosquito drapes, gently laid her on his huge four-poster. A couple of lamps in niches on either side of the headboard cast gentle light in the room. Stephan gazed down at Elena, his eyes brilliant with raw desire. Her face was flushed, her lips bright rose, her eyes shedding a soft lilac light of passion.

'Take your clothes off, *lieveling*,' he said quietly, turning away to undress himself.

His voice, though lovingly casual, filled her with alarm. No one had ever told her to remove her clothes and it disconcerted her. She sat up, gaping at him. 'What?'

Stephan had discarded his coat and flung it on a chair. He was in the act of unravelling his intricate neckcloth when she spoke. His hands stilled and he swung round. 'I said, remove your dress, darling. We cannot make love with our clothes on.'

Elena slid off the high bed and backed towards the door. She licked her dry lips and said, 'I'm sorry, my lord, I—I—cannot behave like a common strumpet.'

In a single stride he reached her, gripped her shoulders and hauled her hard against him so that her head jerked back. The desire in his eyes had now turned to rage, the red flecks ablaze, his nostrils flaring. But when he saw the terror in her eyes his attitude softened. 'You are my wife, Elena. There is no way your behaviour can be lowered to that of a strumpet. For this reason I had to marry you; I know that your rigid adherence to moral principles would not allow you to express your love fully. And, God help me, I cannot wait. Don't be afraid, *lieveling*; that ceremony we went through was perfectly legal, recognised anywhere in the world.'

'*Lieveling?*' Her voice took on a husky, dreamy quality, because he was working his enchantment on her again. His hands caressed her shoulders and back, undoing the laces that held her dress up.

'It means "darling" in Dutch.'

He had loosened her dress and smoothed it down her arms to her elbows. Drawing in a breath of admiration he remarked, 'By God, you have beautiful breasts, Elena, made for a man's caress.' He held her tip-tilted fullness, gently rubbing them with his thumbs, then bent and covered one rosy peak with his mouth, arousing the nipple with his tongue till it burgeoned hard and swollen.

Letting out a loud gasp, Elena clasped his golden head to her breast, raking her fingers through the thickness of his hair. Stephan reluctantly straightened, and removed her clothes. When she showed signs of protest, he kissed her long and ardently till her resistance melted away.

He carried her back to lay her naked on the bed and as rapidly as possible shed his garments, lest she revert to a bout of her earlier inhibitions. He could not wait to make her his. No longer did he delude himself; he had fallen irrevocably in love with Elena—else why would he marry her at the first opportunity?

To his delight, she opened her arms to him as he lowered himself on the bed. She caught him to her and opened her mouth wide for his probing kiss, all the while caressing his muscular chest, feeling the crisp golden hairs. He felt so firm and hard, thrilling her with his strength. Heat vibrated in Elena's veins as his hands worked their magic over her, massaging the soft flesh of her breasts and jutting nipples. He slid his hands over her buttocks, kneading their roundness, then his fingers trailed over her stomach and lower to the downy triangle. As he gently pushed her thighs apart and rhythmically fondled her pulsing, moist centre, she groaned deep in her throat and with wanton delight moved against him.

Stephan lifted his mouth from hers and gazed deep into her passion-drugged eyes. 'What do you want, *lieveling*?'

'Oh, Stephan, don't tease me. I want you. Take me, darling.'

'If you're a virgin, it might hurt, Elena.'

'I know. And I am a virgin.'

His eyes blazed with joy at her words. 'I'll be gentle, *lieveling*. Just relax.'

It hurt more than she thought, enough for her to cry out. Stephan waited, kissing her gently, whispering endearments. Then slowly he moved within her and instantly the pain vanished; only a rocking pleasure existed as he took her to unknown heights. Elena wrapped her legs round him and dug her nails into his back as he rode her to the edge of paradise; their breaths harsh, bodies streaming with perspiration, they climaxed together.

They lay enclosed in each others' arms till they drifted off to sleep.

Elena woke to a sound she could not quite define. She removed her arms from round Stephan and raised herself on one elbow, straining to listen. It came again, like a clap of thunder, and it brought Stephan bolt upright.

She kissed his back and chuckled. 'I didn't think you were afraid of thunder, darling!'

Another blast sounded; this time the palace vibrated and Elena frowned.

'It's not thunder, my love. If you remember, the night was clear. That sound is cannonade.' He flung himself off the bed and reached for his breeches. 'If I'm not mistaken, we're being attacked. Come on, my love, get your dress on and I'll see you to your apartment.'

'Attacked?' she asked in dismay, yet did as he ordered. She dressed quickly and caught the hand Stephan held out to her.

'*Ja.* Now let's run.'

Elena trembled so much with fright that she could scarcely keep up with him. Stephan swung her up in his arms and ran till he came to her apartment. He pushed at the door but it held. 'Why is this locked?'

'Aggie said she would stay here tonight.'

Before he knocked he turned Elena to him. 'Please don't say a word about our marriage to Aggie, *lieveling*.'

'I promise,' she pledged, looking solemnly at him, and he gave her a quick hard kiss, as if to comfort her.

Stephan's sharp rapping had a dishevelled Aggie coming to the door and peering out. She yelped when she saw Elena. 'Mercy me! Where 'ave yer bin, ma'am, I's——?'

'Never mind all that, *mejuffrouw*. I want both you ladies to be ready lest we have to take refuge in the jungles. Do not move from here till I return.'

'Stephan, be careful!' Elena called into the darkness, but received no reply. She sighed worriedly and slowly shut and bolted the door.

'Why are yer so late, ma'am? I bin that troubled 'bout yer!'

Elena glanced at the long clock and saw it was only eleven o'clock. However, she agreed it was a late hour for her to be out. 'We had a leisurely dinner. Please don't be worried if I am overly late in the next sennight, Aggie. I shall be dining every night with my lord.'

Her companion looked suspiciously at Elena and she chided herself for not controlling the heat affecting her cheeks.

'Now, ma'am, you be careful. My lord, he be a 'andsome gent, and like as not a maid can lose 'er head an' 'er maidenhead over 'im, I dare swear!'

'Oh, nonsense!' Elena pooh-poohed the idea by waving her hand, but secretly she smiled. How astute Aggie was. 'And don't be so crude!'

'No, ma'am.' Aggie bobbed and they both laughed.

The laughter was soon wiped off their faces when a boom sounded and the floor vibrated. Both women stared at each other. 'Mercy me!' Aggie yelled, slapping both her hands to her cheeks. 'What be that?'

Blood went out of Elena's face. 'That's the blast of cannon. My lord and I heard it before. He said the island was being invaded; but I thought perhaps he had been mistaken when he brought me back here. It seems as if he is right.'

Aggie became panic-stricken. 'Ooh! Mercy me, ma'am!' she cried, wringing her hands in distress. 'What if it be them uncivilised pirates? They care naught for women's sens-sens . . .'

'Sensibilities?'

'Aye, ma'am. What's to become of us?'

'Calm down, Aggie. My lord said if it were anything serious, he would come for us.' As if to refute her words the boom of cannonade rang out again.

'Ma'am, ma'am! Let's get out of here. We could climb over the garden wall!'

Aggie was half sobbing now, transferring her panic to Elena. 'Don't be absurd, Aggie!' She tried to sound unruffled, but a tremor appeared in her voice. 'W-we cannot scale an eight-foot wall.'

Aggie grabbed hold of Elena's arm and began tugging her towards the back door leading on to the garden courtyard. 'We can, ma'am, we surely can! Yer can stand on my shoulders and 'eave yerself over.'

'And how will *you* get over?'

A sharp knocking had both women staring at the door in terror. 'Who—who is it?' Elena's throat was so parched that she could barely whisper the words, and consequently, the rapping came again more insistently, but to her relief Stephan shouted.

'Open up for God's sake, Elena!'

She did not hesitate. With a cry of relief, she rushed to the door and rapidly unlocked it. She threw herself into Stephan's arms. 'Oh, thank God it's you, Stephan!'

He held her close. 'Come, we must leave at once. A Dutch ship is firing cannon. It's at the jetty.'

Elena gently eased herself from his embrace and enquired, 'But do you not have cannon and arms to defend the island?'

'We do, but not in the palace. They're in an arsenal on a hill in the centre of the island and deep in the jungle.'

'Why so far away?'

'For just such an attack as this. If the palace is captured and all the weapons are here there will be no hope of fighting off invaders. But if we have arsenals on various parts of the island then there is a chance that we can repulse an offensive. There are two cannons on the palace forecourt, but they are too far from the jetty. As soon as the attackers move to the palace they will be fired on. Meantime, I have to bring weapons from our arsenal tonight.' He grimaced impatiently. 'But we tarry with too much talk. Elena, you ride with me. Aggie will ride with Luc.' He jerked his head to a burly Dutchman standing behind him with a group of other men. 'He's a good horseman.'

After they collected their mounts and rode out of the palace through a back exit, Elena noticed from her perch on the rear end of Stephan's saddle that they were galloping along an unfamiliar route. She peered round and spotted in the starlit night the rest of the group thundering behind.

A hundred questions launched themselves in her brain, but she did not voice them for fear of deflecting Stephan's concentration from the ride. Uppermost in her mind was that there seemed to be no army, no form of armed defence to protect the people of the island. She wondered who Stephan had placed in command of the palace. These musings on her misgivings would have to wait to be satisfied until they arrived at the arsenal.

The blast of cannonade grew fainter as they penetrated into the depths of the jungle. The vast canopy of trees blotted out the starlight and now the horses had slowed their gait to a walk; the path grew narrower, the night sounds sharper, and soon the jungle

enclosed them. On a couple of occasions, Stephan and
the other men of the group were forced to dismount
and use machetes to clear the undergrowth en-
croaching on the path and hack at long creepers and
aerial roots hanging like immobile snakes from
branches. Moisture dripped from leaves, and the
humid air smelled of damp foliage, earth and rotting
vegetation. The disturbance caused by their passage
through the jungle caused irate and alarmed monkeys
and birds to whoop and squawk in protest.

And then they were climbing a gradient via a path
that spiralled upwards.

'Here is the arsenal,' Stephan said as they reached
a plateau open to the sky and visible in the clear starlit
night. On the flat surface sprawled several low
buildings. Elena also spotted a large number of people
bustling about and realised that not one of them held
lanterns or any form of illumination. 'Why don't they
carry lights?' she asked.

'Because they'd be seen from the coast.' He pointed
down. And there, a long way below, she beheld the
shimmer of the surf and beyond a couple of ships,
which looked tiny at this distance but were brightly
lit with lanterns. 'If we can see them distinctly, they'd
be sure to see us.' Even as he spoke a plume of fire
belched from one of the hulls but could not be heard
from here.

Aggie came abreast of them and gave Stephan a
quick bob. 'M'lord, where do we go from 'ere?'

He gave terse instructions to the group of men who
had ridden up with them, then said to the two women,
'Come. You will remain in underground chambers
specially hewn out to safeguard the people of the
island in the event of an invasion. You could call them

catacombs. But the arsenal is not underground; it's too damp and we have to keep the weapons dry.'

'Who's looking after the palace, Stephan?'

'Captain Fourier is, and Captain Porrot should by now be over at the Bay of Porpoises, to apprise our other captains of the attack and tell them to prepare for all eventualities.'

He led the women into a long low building lit with lamps which were not visible from outside. Filled sacks were piled high, ranged against the rough, strong walls. The place smelled of the mill where Elena used to buy her flour at home. She assumed the sacks held grain to feed the island in the event of a siege. Several people were moving hither and thither, and Aggie suddenly called out, 'Gertha! Am I glad to see yer!'

Gertha rushed to her friend and, on seeing Stephan, gave him a low curtsy. 'Evening, m'lord.'

'Evening, Gertha. Your husband sorting out the weapons? I fear I must part him from you.'

'I understand, m'lord. Do you want me to take care of Mrs Drew and Aggie?'

'If you would, please. But stop here a moment, I wish to speak with Elena.'

He put his hand at the back of Elena's waist and guided her outside. 'Mrs Drew indeed! Soon they'll know you as Lady Van Coen. If—all goes well.'

She looked up into his handsome face. 'Oh, Stephan, it must! It must go well!'

He took her round a secluded part of the building wall and pulled her into his arms. 'This is goodbye, *lieveling*, till I come for you.' He pointed to a crowd of men pulling long carts. 'Those carts contain the weapons and cannon we'll be needing. I must return with my men to the palace now.'

'Will those men be able to take those vehicles through the jungles?'

'We're using an underground tunnel, which is only high enough to take those carts and men on foot. Meanwhile we who used horses will return via the jungle path.'

Elena could feel her heart ripping to shreds. 'Stephan, can I not go back with you? I know I'm a frail woman but surely every hand is needed now?'

Stephan held her closer, and she could hear the heavy thud of his heart. 'No, my love. You must stay up here.' He kissed her long and hard, then abruptly put her aside and ran to where his horse was tethered.

She leaned back against the wall, the tears blinding her from watching Stephan mount and ride away. What if he were killed? No! They had not discovered this glorious joy for it to be snatched from them after so short a spell. Dragging herself away from the wall, she walked with dejected steps to the building where Aggie and Gertha waited. She glanced towards the spot where Stephan had his horse and saw him still there watching her.

Without thinking she lifted her skirts and ran towards him. 'Stephan!' She raised her hand to touch his, which was resting on the pommel. His eyes dark, his face serious, he gazed down at her. 'Take me with you, Stephan.'

He bent low in the saddle to kiss her hand. 'It will be too dangerous. Have you any idea what your fate would be if you were captured?'

'Whatever the danger I want to share it with you, Stephan. I love you.'

He leaned down, grasped her round the waist and swung her up on the saddle in front of him. 'Perhaps you can make use of your nursing talents if we should have any wounded.' He grinned, and she smiled with happiness at him. He called out to one of the men and sent a message by him to Aggie and Gertha informing them that Elena was returning with him.

'I'll promise to oblige you in any way I can, Stephan.'

He laughed, fondling her breast. 'I certainly hope so, my lady Van Coen.'

There were several riders on the path and much banter and camaraderie abounded among them. Their morale high, they joked that it would be a matter of a few moments before they sent the attackers on their way.

Alas, their good spirits were shortlived. Halfway to the palace a rider came galloping up to them, demanding to speak to Stephan.

'Here I am!' Stephan called, raising his arm.

The islander dismounted from his foaming horse and dashed the sweat from his forehead. Stephan recognised him as his groom.

'What is it, Azim? Why are you here? I thought I told you to go with the other grooms to the hill.'

'*Besar Tuan*, what will I say? I wanted to take care of the horses left in the stables. And I and another were about to lead them into the jungles.' The youth looked deeply distressed.

Stephan frowned and Elena felt her stomach cramp with fear. The other riders remained silent.

'So what happened?'

'*Besar Tuan,*' the youth half sobbed. 'My colleague and I managed to escape with three horses. Alas, the palace has fallen to the enemy and Tuan Fourier has been taken captive.'

CHAPTER FOURTEEN

FOR a few moments stunned silence greeted Azim's information. Then Stephan cleared his throat and spoke in his deep, carrying voice. 'Can everyone hear me?'

There followed a chorus of 'yes's in different tongues.

'Good. What we must do now, my friends, is to make our way through the jungle to the tunnel exit where the carts of weapons will emerge.'

'You mean in the hospital compound, my lord?' someone asked.

'*Ja*. Now let us go.'

Bridles jingled, hoofs stamped, and then the file of riders trotted through the rampant undergrowth, veering in the direction of the hospital. Banter ceased, and a troubled hush fell among the riders. Elena assumed that their gaiety had evolved from the excitement of a battle they were sure of winning. None had dreamed the enemy would have the audacity to actually invade the palace. She did not dare disturb the affronted silence with her insatiable desire to ask questions. A feeling of awe smote her at Stephan's military strategy. Certainly he had taken every precaution to safeguard this island. And why not? He had made it his home and now that she was his wife it had become hers.

Elena rested back against him, trying to convey her comfort, and felt his tense body. If only she could help, but what could a frail woman do?

'I should have taken you to the Prince of Wales Island long ago, *lieveling*. Except you had become a magnificent addiction that I could not rid myself of; did not want to.'

Despite the threatening danger, she smiled with sad joy into the darkness. 'You forget, my lord husband, that I too have fallen prey to you and now I am thankful you did not take me to the East India Company settlement. There is nothing for me to return home to with dear Papa dead. And I was not overly fond of Anthony's parents. Though I do hope they gave him a decent Christian burial and erected a marble monument to him.'

He squeezed her waist, trying to impart his sympathy. 'I'll send enough money to ensure that your wish is respected. I am highly honoured, my love, that you have chosen to stay here with me and I laud your bravery.'

'You are my life, Stephan, I cannot live without you. If you die I shall not wish to survive.'

'I do not deserve you, *lieveling*. My soul is smeared with transgressions. You and I are the prime example of the virgin and the villain.'

She laughed, turning her head to kiss him on his jaw. 'I wouldn't cast you as a villain, darling.'

'No? Then as what?'

'As a man of experience.'

He reacted by chuckling in self-derision, and, kissing her hair, said, 'Now you're making excuses for me, sweetheart.'

For some time the column proceeded at a steady trot, the other riders dropping behind Stephan, automatically putting him in the lead.

Elena's eyes had adapted to the gloom of the forest but it had grown darker, despite the trees having thinned out, as the column had ridden to the outskirts of the jungle. She glanced up and saw that no stars were visible. A gust of warm breeze had risen and then, without warning, the sky split apart, slashed by angry lightning shedding its fearsome illumination across the land, followed by terrifying blasts of thunder which made a mockery of cannonade and forced Elena to wince. The sound echoed, rolling like a hundred boulders down a mountainside.

To her surprise she heard a rumble of laughter coming from Stephan's chest where she rested her head. 'The gods are on our side!' he exulted, increasing the gait of his horse.

Almost immediately the rain precipitated in liquid rods, drumming off the canopy of leaves, pouring down the faces of the riders, partly blinding them and Elena. Yet she sensed Stephan's jubilation. Then suddenly they emerged on to open land. Through the relentless rain she could make out, in the near distance, familiar-looking mounds, and beyond discerned a flat piece of grassland that spread up to low buildings which she recognised as the back of the hospital. The sight of it reminded her of Jan Vans Paul's suspicious death. 'Has anything come to light about Jan's death, Stephan?' She had to shout to be heard above the hammering downpour.

'No. I am still investigating, but have my suspicions, Elena. Meanwhile, priority must be given to the living who are in danger, such as those held in captivity in the palace, which includes one of my senior captains, Alain Fourier.'

'Yes, yes, of course, Stephan. What are you going to do now?'

'Watch!'

The riders rounded the mounds and Stephan dismounted and approached one of them. He felt along the front of it. She brushed the blinding rain from her eyes and strained to see him in the flash of lightning, as he pressed his hand hard on something, then pounded impatiently with his fists. He appeared to be shouting, but Elena could not hear because of the crashing torrent and the periodic cracks and rolls of thunder.

In another streak of brightness she saw that Stephan's vigorous activity was not in vain; the front of the mound yawned wide as camouflaged doors slid open. For a few moments Stephan disappeared into the dark cavern, then he came out and advanced towards his party, standing close enough so everyone could hear him. 'All of you go into the mound and arm yourselves from the carts of weapons inside and follow me to the palace!'

Excitement filled the air as the men dismounted, helped themselves to pistols and muskets, and remounted. Stephan pushed a long-barrelled gun into a leather slot at the side of his saddle, tucked a pistol into his cummerbund, and leaped up behind Elena. Armed men on foot poured out of the cave and ran into the forest.

Stephan did not take the usual road leading from the hospital to the palace, in fact he did not go anywhere near the hospital; instead he led the column back into the forest, and Elena assumed he was making a detour to stage a surprise attack on the enemy in his palace.

There were no signs of the rain easing off. At first it had been a welcome relief from the heat, but now Elena felt uncomfortable in her wet clothes.

Stephan brought the riders to a halt on an incline overlooking the coastal plain with the palace mushrooming from its centre, a glaring target for enemies.

'All right,' he said, sliding off his steed and addressing the group of riders. 'Let us wait for those on foot to join us. We'll leave the horses here and raid the palace on foot. Meantime, let's take a rest.'

Voices rumbled in agreement and the men alighted to lie or sit beneath trees. Stephan lifted Elena down, shrugged off his sodden coat, and laid it on a patch of wet leaves under a tree, the vast spreading branches giving some protection from the rain. 'Sit on that, my love.'

She felt grateful for his solicitude and tried to ignore her discomfort from wet clothes. A chill was now creeping through her which she had not encountered before in the East. Elena supposed that the prolonged wetness of her skin had depleted the natural warmth of her body, for now the rain felt cold. She started shivering and wondered whether the rain was entirely to blame; the trembling could be effected by her knowledge of the forthcoming danger threatening Stephan. She knew beyond doubt that he would never allow her to take part in the raid. While he would be battling down near the palace, risking his life, she would be compelled to remain up here, suffering a million tortures.

Sounds of hacking in bamboo thickets and trampling in the undergrowth heralded the arrival of

Stephan's men on foot. They had probably taken a very short cut because they had arrived almost on the heels of the riders. Stephan greeted them amicably, persuading them to take a rest while he revealed his plan of attack. Elena knew faint pleasure when Stephan returned with a blanket and canvas cape for her. The men on foot had also brought along light, makeshift tents and without hesitation Stephan erected one over Elena, wrapped her in a blanket, and placed the canvas cape for her to sit on. She was already drowsing when she heard him leave her side. From a great distance she heard him speaking to his men...

The deathly quietness woke Elena. She sat bolt upright, throwing off the blanket, which felt hot though she realised it had helped to dry the surplus moisture from her clothes. A second or two passed before she became aware that the rain had stopped and that she could no longer hear the familiar rumble of male voices. Cold fear inched down her back. Cautiously she peered out from the tent flap and felt dismayed that the only people in sight were two island men sleeping across the threshold. Of Stephan's armed contingent there was no sign.

Elena wasted no time in finding out. She woke the men by asking in Malayan, 'Could you please tell me where *Besar Tuan* and his army are?'

The two men shot up with alacrity. 'They have gone on raid to Besar Rumah. *Tuan* asked us to stay here and guard you, and the horses, *mem*.'

Smiling uncertainly, Elena thanked the guards and dropped the flap. She did not know what to do with herself; whether to leave this stifling tent and walk about outside to relieve the restlessness and anxiety in her, or to remain inside and not expose her troubled mind to the guards who might become agitated. She decided on the latter and slumped down on the canvas cape, twisting her hands together and letting out innumerable sighs. What was happening at the palace?

As if in answer to her question a shot rang out, followed by several others. Elena jumped up and ran out to peer down the dark incline at the huge blur of the palace. She became conscious of the two guards just behind her. 'I—I want to go down and see what is happening,' she told them impatiently.

'*Tuan* gave us orders that if he does not return by dawn we are to escort you to the Bay of Porpoises. One of his captains will take you to Pulau Penang, *mem*,' one of the guards told her.

'The Prince of Wales Island? But I do not want to go there. Perhaps we should find our way to the palace and see if there are any wounded people.' Vaguely she heard the guards voicing their objections, her attention caught by the appearance of a light moving away from the palace and heading towards the forest. 'What's that?'

The two men followed her pointing finger and appeared to study the approaching light. One of them said, 'It is someone with a torch. He is coming this way because he may have a message for us, *mem*.'

Yes, it looked like that. What if it were from the enemy? What if they were coming for her? she wondered, swallowing with fright. Yet she made no effort to plan her escape. If Stephan had been taken prisoner then they could take her captive too, she thought, admitting to an air of martyrdom.

She remained where she was, watching the torch bearer rapidly approaching. And then he was climbing the incline, the pool of light from the flame revealing that the image they saw was indeed a man on foot, but he was not the only one; there were more men behind him. At this distance she could not recognise anyone. An instinct of fear compelled her to cower behind the thick trunk of a tree. If these people were strangers, she would keep herself concealed. She glanced round to see her guards, mere shadows in the darkness, hovering behind trees. A little way back were tethered the horses Stephan and his men had left behind.

'Let us stay hidden and watch who comes here, my friends,' she told her guards. 'If they are strangers then it is best that we hide until they are gone.'

'*Mem*, we thought it would be a good idea if we climbed the tree.'

She stared up at the towering limbs. Some of the vast trunks were gnarled and twisted, with plenty of footholds. Would she be able to haul herself up there? She would have to—in fact it would be better to begin climbing now whether the approaching party were enemies or not. 'Yes, a very good idea. Let us start.'

All three ran some distance from the tent and horses, one of the men selecting a tree that he believed would be easiest for Elena to climb. With the agility of monkeys the guards scrambled up first, then leaned down to give her a hand. She disregarded modesty, pulled her skirt between her legs and tucked it into her sash. With all the energy she could summon she hauled herself up with the aid of her guards.

The tree stood quite high, its foliage thick, providing perfect cover for the three of them. They each perched themselves on separate branches, listening and straining to see the advancing men. The section of the incline where they had spotted the torch bearer was now hidden from view, so Elena had no notion whether the party had arrived at her tent. Her range of vision from high up in the branches where she perched made it impossible for her to distinguish in the dark if anything moved down below. Her ears caught the sound of only the drip of water from sodden branches and leaves in the aftermath of the storm. All else was stillness.

Then came the high piercing shrill of a whistle that tightened a coil of terror in her abdomen.

It could be a bird.

It could be an animal.

It could be a man.

She heard rustling from the branch one of her guards occupied. A moment later he had reached her and whispered, '*Mem*, that is *Besar Tuan's* whistle. He said to me that if I hear such, I am to hail him.'

'Then go ahead.'

All three of them called out and next instant the muffled thud of boots could be heard. But Elena cautioned her guards not to descend lest this be a ruse by the enemy.

A torch flared into orange flame and Elena saw her husband. He was squinting up into the branches. 'Where the devil are you, Elena? And you, Sulaiman and Ismail?'

'We're up here, my lord. We took precautions lest you be the foe,' Elena told him in a happy voice.

Looking bedraggled from the rain and perhaps a fight, yet still handsome in a rough way, Stephan threw back his head and roared. His laughter proved infectious; his men, Elena and her guards joined in the hilarity.

After she was helped down, Stephan went into further gales of laughter. But now she detected a different nuance in the sound; mockery laced it. She looked at him, puzzled. 'What the devil have you done to your dress, *mevrouw*?'

She stared down at her skirt pulled up between her legs and felt affected by a fit of mortification. If Stephan had conveyed genuine good humour she would have giggled, but he was deliberately ridiculing her in front of his men. Why?

Hastily she dropped her skirt keeping her eyes lowered, her cheeks stinging with shame and hurt.

Stephan led Elena back to the tent. Here she could not stop herself from asking, 'What happened at the palace?'

For a while he stared through narrowed, speculating eyes which created uneasiness in her. 'Oh, it was all too easy. The crew of two Dutch ships invaded us, but we defeated them. The captains told us they had received information that Pulau Mutiara was a hotbed of pirates.' Stephan eyed her keenly and as she interpreted his look a quiver of fear raked up and down her spine. A chill swept through her face sending the blood running out of it. So that was why he had humiliated her.

'You—you think it is I who betrayed you?'

'Did you?'

Elena gasped in outrage, attempting to rise to her feet and sweep out of the tent. Except Stephan's fingers curled round her slim arm in a grip that felt like steel. 'Did you?'

'How can you think that?' Hot tears of rage stung her eyes. 'If I had known you mistrusted me, I would not have married you, my lord.'

He sighed and rubbed his eyes wearily. 'It's too late to regret what might have been, my lady wife.' He shook her arm a little roughly and she saw his jaws harden, eyes filled with ruthlessness. 'Answer the question!'

She thumped the ground by her side. 'Most certainly I have told nobody about this island! How could I? I had no opportunity to do so. Moreover, if I were a spy, would I have married you?'

'Why not? If I had been taken captive and condemned to hang, you, as my wife, could claim this island and all my riches.'

'Really? What else would I gain by spying on you?'

'Satisfaction of your loyalty to your country and adherence to your so-called principles, madam.'

Daggers pierced and twisted in Elena's heart. Dear God, how could she endure such pain? Even so, she lifted her chin proudly. 'What do you intend to do with me, my lord? Hang me?'

'Nothing can be done to you until I have proof.'

She laughed shakily. 'Oh, you will find plenty of it if you have a mind to. How can I convince you otherwise?'

'Come, it's started to rain. Let us return to the palace, Elena.'

She shared his horse, but now both of them sat stiffly away from each other, and Elena's heart seemed to be breaking into fragments. However, through the blur of pain she had two questions to ask. 'What happened to Captain Fourier? Did the invaders harm him?'

'I fear he will need your nursing talent.' This with a cynicism that increased her anguish.

Elena twisted round to stare up into his face. 'What did they do to him?'

'The law-abiding captains employed by the fine respectable Dutch colonists who function by your principles broke Fourier's arm to force him to reveal where I was and to grab whatever loot they could.'

Elena drew in a sharp breath of horror and covered her mouth with her hand. Slowly she dropped it. 'No!'

He quirked an eyebrow down at her. 'Oh, yes, *mevrouw*. See for yourself what the blackguards did to him and my palace.'

'And—and Captain Fourier?'

'He gave nothing away, *mevrouw*. Now that's what I call true loyalty.'

'I meant, will he be all right?'

'That depends on how skilful your nursing is. I put his arm in a splint and left him in the care of a woman servant and several of my men, till the *hakim* arrives. We have to keep the palace under armed surveillance from now on.'

She felt as if every word he spoke blamed her for the cause and outcome of the invasion. 'If you are suspicious of me, my lord, why are you entrusting your valued friend and captain to my care?'

'Because I know you are fully aware that while you are under suspicion you must do nothing to harm him. And now that the invasion has ended in defeat—most of all for you—you will do all in your power to prove your innocence, do your best to see that Captain Fourier recovers.'

She could feel herself teetering on the sword-edge of despair. She wanted to lay her face on his chest, clasp him to her and beg him to believe her. But pride came to her rescue—or was it to her downfall? She

did not know. Yet to humble herself, to plead with
him, went against her principles. Her lips curled in a
self-mockery. Stephan would certainly find that
amusing; he had always derided her principles.

Elena commended herself for the iron control she
exercised in keeping her tears at bay. She was determined not to experience humiliation by breaking down
in front of him and becoming the butt of his scorn.
So she kept her face a mask of impenetrability.

Nevertheless she knew a pang of relief when they
arrived in the palace. She told herself she would seek
the comfort of her bed; perhaps sleep would ease the
pain that Stephan had so ruthlessly inflicted on her.

As he led her through the familiar arcades she was
appalled at the destruction revealed in the light of the
flaming torch he held aloft. The beautiful filigree gold
lamps that had been suspended on gold chains from
the centre of each scalloped arch had been stolen and
the coloured glass smashed. She had to pick her way
carefully so that shards would not pierce her thin
slippers.

Her hurt deepened when he escorted her to her erst-
while apartment as if their marriage were already over.
On entering her chambers she gasped in horror. 'My
God! Why would they do this here?' She looked at
Stephan and saw that his face was pale with shock.
He did not answer her question.

Slowly, painfully, Elena moved round the once
beautiful entrance chamber. Silken drapes had been
dragged off and unspeakably soiled. Holes had been
dug in the marble-faced walls; perhaps the looters had
been looking for treasure. The tall clock lay on its
side, panels and face broken. Exquisite divans and
chairs had been ripped apart, and their stuffing was

littering the floor. Priceless Indian and Persian rugs had vanished.

With trepidation she entered her bedroom, biting on her lower lip to stop her from crying out at the desecration. Obscene drawings were inked on drapeless walls, the four-poster an unrecognisable heap. 'Why would they do this?' she asked under her breath, more to herself than him.

He gave a bitter laugh that had her whirling round to gape at him. With a smile of contempt he said, 'Perhaps if they had known it was your apartment, *mevrouw*, they would have left it intact.'

'There was no call for that, my lord!'

'Was there not, *mevrouw*?'

She let her head drop back in a tired gesture. 'Where is the use of arguing? Meanwhile, where am I to sleep?'

'Why, *mevrouw*, in my bed—with me.'

'I—I don't think——'

He caught her elbow none too gently and hissed in her ear, 'Ah, but you must, lady wife. This way!' Swinging her around with him, he marched her to his apartment. She resented his ungentlemanly treatment of her, appalled that he was capable of such uncouth behaviour. Or did men become savages when they married? She should not be surprised at him since he already indulged in the nefarious trade of piracy.

Stephan placed the blazing torch in a sconce, pushed open his door, shoved her in and kicked it shut behind him. He swung her up in his arms and carried her to his bedchamber.

She was surprised to see that his apartment had not been touched. All the drapes, furniture and the bed were intact. He dropped her on the four-poster and snarled, 'A Dutch captain commandeered this apartment for his own use.'

Although Elena was angry, she cringed inwardly when she saw in the flickering lamplight the rage in his face and his blazing eyes. He tore off his cravat and began dragging off his coat. 'Strip!'

She raised herself on one elbow, her violet eyes huge and filled with horror. 'What?'

He slammed his coat on the floor and strode to the bed. Bracing his arms on either side of her he grated, 'I said, "strip"!'

'I will do no such thing, sir! How dare you threaten to violate me?' More slowly, hating herself for being afraid, she asked, 'What do you intend to do?'

He straightened and looked derisively down at her. 'You know full well. I intend to do what I am entitled to do.'

'Oh?'

'Claim my conjugal rights, my beautiful, treacherous wife. I'm sure for once you'll agree, that they are not against your principles.'

'But—but, you'll be taking me against my will. That is rape, my lord!'

'Ah, but *lieveling*, this will not be rape,' he said, with sudden gentleness, the fires of rage dying in his eyes, his face softening, his thick gold hair hanging loose and framing it like the mane of one of the majestic lions she had seen in pictures in books she studied. Despite his dishevelled appearance he looked wildly magnificent. Running a long finger down her cheek he went on, 'I will be *making love* to my wife, an alluring woman, not raping her. Come, Elena, take off your clothes.'

'I—I need a bath, my lord.' She plucked at her wrinkled dress and touched her untidy hair.

'We both do. Shall we have one now?'

She looked shocked. 'Together?'

'Naturally! We're married.'

She did not offer any resistance when he undressed both of them and, lifting her into his arms, he carried her into the bathroom. It was similar to hers and, without much ado, he leaped with her into the clear pool. Elena luxuriated in the cool depths, using the essence from the bottles on a ledge above the water. She watched Stephan as he scrubbed himself and splashed about, but neither of them laughed and played. Elena felt distanced from him because he did not trust her, blamed her for the invasion—an abominable accusation. It hurt her deeply, and she was not prepared to forgive and forget so easily. Alas, despite everything, she loved Stephan, found him enticing, alluring and irresistible.

He stepped out of the pool, like a blond Adonis, body slick, hair plastered to his skull. He picked up a towel from a marble bench and vigorously dried himself. Then, as if to give her the privacy she craved, he wrapped the towel round himself and strode into the bedchamber.

Shortly after, Elena emerged from the pool, dried herself quickly and towelled off the surplus moisture from her hair, then, draping the towel round her shoulders, she tentatively entered the chamber.

Stephan lay on the bed, a sheet covering him to below his ribs. One of his muscular arms was flung over his eyes as if he had fallen asleep.

Elena stood beside the four-poster looking down at him, when suddenly he raised his hand and pulled off her towel.

The action was so unexpected and startling that she gasped and took a step backward, but Stephan grabbed her round the waist and pulled her into bed.

There was an urgency in his kiss as his mouth came down hard on hers. His arms tightened round her, neither gently nor painfully, and the strength of them sent the throb of erotic pleasure chasing through her veins. Elena's response was immediate: her mouth opened wider to absorb fully the sensual taste of his tongue.

He blotted out all thoughts of her treachery and concentrated his mind and feelings on this woman who had bewitched him into marriage. Never had he enjoyed a woman as much as he did this one.

His blood sang as she responded to him, her body pliant to his caresses. He rolled her on top of him, lifting her so that her firm breasts were on a level with his mouth, then he drank his fill from them, titillating the nipples till they became hard and swollen. He pulled her down till their mouths met and he kissed her while trailing his fingers down her long damp hair, then gently kneaded her hips, pressing his rigid desire against her centre till he felt her move against him. Yet he held back to give her and himself maximum pleasure. Bringing his hands up her back he lightly pinched the soft flesh. 'If nothing else we have this, *lieveling*,' Stephan murmured against her mouth.

It was a revelation when he discovered how deeply he loved Elena. Whatever she was, whatever she would be, he was willing to accept her for what she was—

no angel. Living with an angel would be boring for him.

The fire in his loins burned for fulfilment. He lifted her to sit astride him and fitted himself to her. Then they were sweating and gasping in a fire dance of erotic ecstasy. He crushed her to him as they rocked in frenzied rhythm that erupted in pure bliss.

In the sated aftermath of pleasure she had not known was physically possible, Elena cradled her head against his wide, hard chest. 'Stephan?'

'Mm?'

'I did not betray you or the islanders. I promise. Ask the Dutch captains.'

'Oh, I shall, *mevrouw*. Now go to sleep. It's dawn.'

CHAPTER FIFTEEN

NEXT morning, after a late breakfast, Elena was driven to the hospital. When she awakened, she had been disappointed to discover that Stephan had already departed the chamber. He had left a note stating that Captain Fourier had been conveyed to hospital and asking her to go there after she had eaten.

She had relished the exotic fare of fruit and flat bread, realising how hungry she was. The two lovely sprays of speckled pink orchids, standing in a vase on the tray, she had decided to give to Captain Fourier. Even so, dejection had set in the moment she stepped into the carriage; she recalled Stephan's mistrust of her and sighed. At least she knew his whereabouts; the woman servant who had served her with breakfast had said, on Elena's enquiry, that the *tuan* was at present at the jetty supervising the disarmament of the invaders on the Dutch ships and making sure they left the shores of Pulau Mutiara.

On her arrival at the hospital, the *hakim* himself conducted her to a single ward where Captain Fourier lay propped up in bed, his broken arm in splints supported by a sling. He looked in a sorry state, his face bruised and swollen, the result of his harsh interrogation. She hesitated in the doorway, not because she found his condition revolting but because, on a wicker chair by his bed, sat Captain Porrot.

'*Bonjour*, Madame Drew!' Fourier greeted her cheerfully despite his appalling condition, and winced as he tried to smile.

'I am——' Elena caught herself up from stating that she was now Madame Van Coen, remembering Stephan had asked her to keep their marriage a secret for a while. Quickly she changed her sentence to, 'I am happy to see you are alive, Captain Fourier. Stephan told me of your ordeal.' She placed the sprays of orchids on a small table at his bedside.

He touched her hand and murmured, '*Merci, madame*, they are very beautiful flowers. I will get the *petite* nurse to put them in a vase, no?' He went on, 'That devil of a Dutchman, he gave me a time most terrible, *madame*. And if it had not been for the good Stephan,' he effected a Gallic shrug with his good shoulder, 'I might have been killed.'

'Good morning, Mrs Drew.' Porrot stood up, grey and sinister even to his grey smile. 'Would you care to be seated?'

Why did this man have to be here? she thought sourly. He made her feel ill at ease and a little afraid. She had hoped to cheer the charming Captain Fourier with a touch of humour, but her dislike of Porrot evoked gloominess that curtailed the idea. 'No, thank you, sir. I came to find out how Captain Fourier was progressing and to enquire if he needed anything. My lord is anxious about his condition.'

Porrot bowed slightly, stiffly, and promptly settled his thin frame back in the chair.

Elena approached the bedside and smiled encouragingly down at Fourier. 'You have a cheerful disposition, Captain, and I feel certain you'll be back to your old self soon. Is there anything you would like?'

He sighed longingly. 'A bottle of cognac would not come amiss, *madame*. It would of a certainty help me to endure the pain, so agonising. Alas, the good *hakim* is not happy about the imbibing of alcohol.'

'With good reason, Captain. But if you promise to make do with a tot twice a day, he'll probably agree. I believe you need more than cognac to keep your mind off the pain.'

'And that is, *madame*?'

'A book, sir. An effective diversion, I do declare.'

'*Madame*,' he said with faint cynicism, 'with my eyes like a frog's with their lids shut, it will not be possible for me to read.'

'Do not trouble yourself on that, Captain. I will read to you. Would you approve?'

'*Mais certainement, madame*. There is one setback. I fear I do not have a book.'

'That can easily be remedied, Captain. I will return to the palace and fetch one from my lord's library. He will surely not mind. I will come back here after lunch and read to you for at least an hour.'

'*Merci, madame*. That is most kind of you.' He licked his bruised lips. 'Erm—perhaps you could persuade the *hakim* to bring me some cognac first, hmm?'

Elena laughed and turned towards the door to do his bidding when Porrot brought her to a halt with, 'Mrs Drew, permit me to escort you to the palace.'

She felt pleased with herself for controlling the shudder of revulsion at the thought of travelling alone with this man whom she abhorred. 'I don't think that will be necessary, Captain.' Please, God, do not let him insist, she prayed.

'It may well be, madam. You never know, there could be some members of the Dutch captains' crews hiding in the shrubbery at the roadside, ready to ambush a passing vehicle and hold its passengers hostage till they receive ample ransom. As it is they have to leave the island empty-handed.'

There appeared no escape for Elena except to be rude and refuse his offer. Somehow she sensed he could prove vindictive enough to cause her harm. Had he not threatened to do so before? Reluctantly she said, 'You have a vivid imagination but it seems logical what you say. Very well, Captain. May I just speak to the *hakim* first about Captain Fourier's cognac?'

'Of course, Mrs Drew. I'll say goodbye to Alain and wait for you at the carriage.'

The *hakim* delayed Elena since he became a little difficult on the matter of supplying Captain Fourier with cognac. 'Our religion forbids us Muslims to drink it, *memsahib*, and I do not encourage others to do so.'

'I'll take the blame for that, Hakim. Please send Captain Fourier's drink by a non-Muslim employee of yours. Then you will be free of blame.' Much against his wishes he agreed. Elena thanked him and made her way to the carriage.

'Ah, madam, what took you so long?' Porrot handed her into the vehicle and it was all she could do to snatch her fingers from his strange stubby ones. The darkness inside the carriage gave the illusion of coolness and she silently commended Porrot for his imaginative foresight in closing the slats of the shutters.

At first she knew relief when he made no attempt at conversation, then as the journey dragged on to long past the time the vehicle was scheduled to arrive at the palace, she experienced foreboding. She stole a glance at him. Porrot sat like a statue sculpted from slate. This grey man, she suspected, was capable of extreme ruthlessness if matters did not proceed to his satisfaction.

A chilling shudder of apprehension attacked Elena's backbone. 'Captain Porrot, I dare say we should have arrived some time past. Would you not say so?'

No answer. His stony eyes looked ahead, his whole body stiff, as if he had not heard her, or chose not to.

'P-perhaps you should speak to the driver, sir.'

Cold panic gripped her. She caught the door-handle, about to open it, when his peculiar thick fingers closed round her wrist like a steel manacle. 'Don't attempt to open the door, madam, or make any sound.'

She swallowed the scream of terror that rose in her throat, at the same time watching malevolence glitter in his eyes and twist his lips.

Lord Stephan Van Coen and his men roared with triumphant laughter as the Dutch ships sailed from the jetty minus their merchandise and under the threat of their own confiscated guns. Both captains had been thoroughly interrogated, not with violence but with ingenious play of words from Stephan. The truth finally emerged that the two vessels were in fact rebel ships, having broken away from the main fleet of Dutch ships—equipped with twenty-pounders—at their colonies of Sumatra and Java, and now resorting to piracy in the Malacca Straits. They had heard that Pulau Mutiara was a nest of buccaneers armed with few and ancient weapons, not from proof but rumour, and, no, it had not come from anyone on the island. They had not suspected that Pulau Mutiara was so heavily protected.

With the menace of the Dutch out of the way, Stephan mounted Bliksem and rode to the hospital in the hopes of finding Elena there and bringing her home to the palace. He needed to apologise for his mistrust of her. His heart contracted with remorse for his callous treatment and he dreaded that she would regret her declaration of love to him. Worse, she might have suffered a change of emotion, and replaced her love for him with contempt.

His pulses quickened when the *hakim* informed him that Elena had already visited Captain Fourier and had promised to return after lunch with a book to read to him. Alas, it was long past that hour and she had not returned yet.

Feeling puzzled and a little uneasy, Stephan visited Fourier. 'Well, my friend, how do you feel?'

'*Bien!* The lovely Madame Drew visited me this morning. Alas, she did not keep her promise to bring a book back from your library to read to me.'

Stephan eyed his captain's battered face which, despite its disfigurement, looked benign and credited it to the cognac Fourier had swallowed, judging from the smell on his breath. 'When did she return to the palace?'

Fourier looked up a little baffled at the concern in Stephan's voice. 'Oh, do not worry about her, Stephan. She probably decided to stay and enjoy Porrot's company.'

Stephan's straight brows lowered in a worried frown. 'What do you mean?'

'Why, *monsieur le capitaine* came here to visit me and so did Madame Drew. He offered to escort her back to the palace. And, *mon ami*, it was natural that she accepted, was it not? Where is the harm?'

'I fear there will be considerable harm done to my... to Mevrouw Drew.'

'You mean she is in danger from Porrot?' Fourier asked with incredulity, but there was no one in the room to answer him.

Stephan raised a furore when he arrived at the palace. He ordered a thorough search of the buildings in the complex when he found no Elena in his library and apartments nor in hers. He himself helped in the search. Unfortunately it proved futile.

A terrible fear gripped Stephan as he returned to his library. He settled on a chair and tried to think calmly. Elena, he knew, would not ask Porrot to help her leave the island; he had sensed her dislike of the captain on the night of the festival. He therefore came to the conclusion that Porrot had kidnapped her. But that letter he'd found in Jan's desk confirmed his suspicions of Porrot's ruthlessness. Where would he take Elena? Unless...

'Captain Porrot, I demand you stop this carriage at once!' Elena resorted to hauteur in the faint hope that it might impress this man. In vain.

'In time, Mrs Drew, in time.' He extracted a snuff box from his waistcoat pocket and took a pinch of snuff, wiping the surplus with a large handkerchief, and put away the box. He sniffed and then blew his long, curved nose. 'Ah, that's better,' he said, tucking away his handkerchief and smiling evilly at her.

'Why have you abducted me, Captain?' She continued to show him a fearless front, but inside she felt terrified.

'Don't profess to ignorance, madam. You know full well why. I have given you enough warnings and now it's time to act.'

'In what way, sir?'

He flicked her a contemptuous glance and drew in a bored breath. 'All right, I'll elucidate. You have without doubt proved yourself to be a spy—don't interrupt with your unconvincing denials. That Dutch invasion was due to you. Oh, yes, the Dutch captains said they had received information that Pulau Mutiara harboured pirates. Only you could have done that.'

'How? I have never left this island.'

'Oh, I'll wager an experienced spy like you can find any number of ways. You could have gone down to the shore with a lantern and signalled.'

'Don't be so ridiculous, Captain.'

'I'm not being ridiculous, woman!' he yelled, and thumped the seat of the carriage, making Elena jump.

This was the first time she had seen him lose control and the terror in her grew. She decided to let him rave on while she maintained a safe silence.

'You had your opportunity to prove your innocence by marrying either Lord Stephan Van Coen, in accordance with Anthony's will, or me.'

Here she chose to interrupt him. 'I have married Lord Stephan.'

For a moment he stared at her, then let out shrills of laughter that set her nerves jangling. 'Now *you* are being ridiculous. Stephan would not marry without consulting all his captains. So do not try any bluff.'

Elena decided on another tactic, to keep this man talking about himself. 'Tell me, Captain Porrot, why are you so averse to women?'

To her surprise he did not hedge but readily vented his dislike. 'Women! Bah! Do you know what? My mother was a village wench who worked as a scullery maid in the Drew household. Yes, Anthony Drew's father's place. She prostituted herself to Mr Drew and became pregnant with me. Of course Mrs Drew had no idea that I was her husband's son—she still does not know. If I had told her I'll wager she would have ill-treated me.'

'How did you come to live with your father?'

'My mother forced me upon him. She left me on the doorstep two days after she gave birth and then disappeared. You might say she did not wish to be branded a scarlet woman and perhaps you're right. She could, however, have taken me to another locale and said she was a widow, like numerous other unmarried mothers do, and reared me herself. Not what she did.' Here he paused and she almost felt sorry for him when she observed the bitter hurt in his eyes. 'She took the vast sum of money my father gave her and disappeared.'

'Perhaps she left you with Mr Drew for your own good.'

'Don't you believe it. It was not me she wanted, it was money. And the only way she could get it was to become pregnant by Mr Drew. Anyway, he took me in and his wife treated me well, thinking I was a foundling. It was she who decided on the surname of Porrot for me. I was not illustrious enough to carry the name of Drew. Then a few years later Anthony was born.'

'How did you come to know who you are?'

'My father told me, just in case I heard it from someone else. But he begged me not to mention it to his wife. I loved him for taking me in and hated my mother for abandoning me. The moment I heard the details from my father, I developed a hatred for all women, even my stepmother. Years later my father told Anthony I was his half-brother, but it made no difference to his affection for me. It was I who persuaded Anthony to join the East India Company.'

She shook her head in wonder. 'I cannot believe that anyone can keep such hatred locked away in their hearts for so many years, allow it to ferment. After all, your father gave you a good life and surely you have learnt that all women are not the same. As there are good and bad among men, so it is with women.'

'Don't imagine, madam, that all your philosophising will impress me. I mistrust you and believe you to be a spy. I should have known that you would try to influence me with your persuasive talk.'

She was about to argue but the carriage came to a sudden halt. 'Come on, Mrs Drew, we have arrived.'

He opened the door and stepped down, but made no attempt to assist her, though he gripped her arm roughly and pushed her along. She struggled to turn round and tell the carriage driver to inform Stephan that she had been kidnapped, only to find him being ordered down by an armed man.

Porrot dragged her forward to a small white house, not unlike her own home in Maldon except that it was on a promontory near a cliff edge. She wondered whether this was where the pearl fishers dived into the Bay of Porpoises.

Elena had no time to take stock of her surroundings as Porrot rapidly unbolted the entrance, hauled her through a dark passage, pushed open a side door, shoved her inside, and shot a couple of bolts.

She did not move till her eyes grew accustomed to the gloomy interior, after which she inspected her new prison. It was probably used as a spare room. Some broken chairs cluttered one corner and a low string bed stood beneath a small barred window which had its outside shutters closed.

There was no doubt in Elena's mind that this man meant to kill her. He was probably waiting for darkness to fall. But why had he not murdered her right away in this room and got rid of her body at night? No, he had other plans for her. It would have to be an accidental death. As the horror of the grim knowledge sank into her mind she experienced the extreme terror of the condemned who despaired of a way to escape. Her stomach cramped; cold sweat dotted her brow, moistening her skin, and fear caused her to tremble violently. Elena hugged herself and marched up and down the small room, her body taut, cold, her mind in turmoil. Oh, Stephan, where are you? Surely we did not make love only to be separated forever perhaps by—by death? God, I love him. You sent me out here to meet and love him, now don't let it end for nothing. She let out a sob. Was this how those on the brink of insanity felt? No, no, keep cool. Clear your mind of panic, Elena. Store your energy, lie down and force yourself to think with serenity and clarity.

Inhaling several deep breaths she found herself growing a little calmer. She curled up on the thin quilt spread on the string bed and forced the trembling out of her body, willing it to relax. It took some time but eventually she succeeded. Stephan would find her here; he knew this island off by heart and he would search everywhere for her. She knew it, she had to know it.

Arranging her thoughts into logical order, she started pondering on the locality. Elena took her mind back to when Porrot led her towards this cottage. In the sunny brightness of mid-afternoon, she had noticed a green sward that spread on three sides of the building to the cliffs. On the fourth side the verdant carpet led to the forest. What was the use of thinking of what lay outside the house? She had to find some implement to help her get out there. To wait for Stephan to find her might be too late; Porrot could be planning to execute her at any time after dusk.

Suddenly an idea struck her. Slowly Elena sat up and stared into the corner of the room.

At the exact time that Elena hit upon her idea, Stephan sprang from his chair and made for the stable. It was growing dark and Bliksem was being rubbed down. He saddled up a black stallion, Midnight Thunder, known for his speed and aggressiveness. 'Come on, boy, you've got to get me to her in time.' He patted the horse's black velvet neck, vaulted into the saddle, and squeezed the animal's flanks with his heels. Blowing and snorting, Midnight Thunder broke into a gallop. And, as if to complement the stallion's temperament, dark clouds gathered on the firmament. Flashes of lightning and ominous growls from the heavens seemed to exhilarate the horse and he sprang forward.

* * *

Elena made for the corner of the room where the broken chairs were heaped. She rummaged around, testing the pieces, and finally settled for a sturdy chair leg which she hoped would prove a worthy weapon. If she could manage to stun Porrot from behind the door when he stepped into the room, she would be able to make some headway in her attempt to escape from here.

It seemed like hours she had been in this room, and now the rolls and echoes of thunder overhead and the hammering of rain would drown out any approaching footsteps. She had better take up her position now even if she had to tarry here for eternity.

She did not have to wait long.

Moreover, above the climatic uproar, her alert ears picked up the sound of the bolts being drawn. Sweat poured freely from Elena as she stood beside the frame at the back of the door, her hand poised, gripping the chair leg, ready to strike. She held her breath as the door opened. A lantern in the passage shed a little light in the room.

'Mrs Drew?' It was Porrot. 'I've brought you some food and drink.'

She remained still.

The gentle clatter of a tray being carefully placed on the floor reached her ears.

Silence.

Then a faint rustle of cloth.

Of a sudden a dark object came flying in and, using all her strength, Elena struck. Too late she realised that Porrot had tricked her by flinging in his coat, and she had fallen for it.

He snatched the leg from her and trounced her over the head with it. The blow was not hard enough to knock her out but it hurt and stunned her sufficiently to render her so helpless that she could not scream for help. He caught her wrist and dragged her out into the driving rain. 'You silly bitch!' he yelled, matching the fury of the storm. 'Did you really think I'd be taken in with that trite trick?'

She stumbled behind him as he dragged her along. Her head hurt, her breath seemed to be robbed by wind, and her sight was blinded by the merciless downpour.

And then suddenly she could hear the roar of the sea. She knew immediately what he intended to do. With her free hand she wiped away the rain and made out the edge of the promontory not far off. She could feel her heart thundering in her breast and knew what he would do—throw her off the promontory to fall below and disappear in the crashing surf and waves. The ideal 'accident'.

Fear gave her strength. She dug in her heels and grasped his wrist, resisting his fierce tugs with all her might. He span round and twisted her arms behind her back and began pushing her in front of him towards the edge of the precipice. She tried to kick him, but he adroitly avoided her. Elena could feel her strength ebbing, her movements becoming more feeble, her head beginning to spin.

A shot rang out in between the claps of thunder, or was it her imagination? Then she felt Porrot's grip relax and heard him swear. Elena wasted no time; she tore free and ran, away from the cliff edge, making for the shelter of the forest. Oh, God, thank heaven she had escaped, but who was the gunman? He might prove just as deadly as Porrot.

Another shot rang out just as she darted behind a tree. She leaned heavily against the trunk, closing her eyes. Then the world seemed to spin round in her head and—blackness.

'Elena! Elena!'

She could not mistake that voice. Of courses, it was a dream.

Porrot had pushed her off the cliff and this roaring in her ears was the sea. Was it not?

'Elena! Where the devil are you?'

She opened her eyes.

That voice was no dream.

It was reality!

Exhilaration surged in her breast. Stephan! Stephan! She pushed herself to her feet and peered round the trunk. Not a few yards from her stood horse and rider silhouetted in the faint light of a lantern the latter held. 'Stephan!' she shouted, but it came out between a squeak and a croak. Stepping out from behind the tree, she swayed towards him. 'Stephan!'

He heard her at last—she saw him swing his black steed round and urge him in her direction. They were both soaked to the skin, as they had been the other night. Sobbing and laughing, she tottered towards him.

Stephan swept her up in front of his saddle and hugged her close. 'Oh, God, *lieveling* I—I—thought... I love you, Elena. I didn't know how much till today!'

CHAPTER SIXTEEN

'How did you know where Captain Porrot would take me?' Elena asked. She and Stephan lay in his bed ensconced in each others' arms, on the night following her ordeal with Porrot.

'I knew he had a lodge there because he was interested in pearl diving himself. It was no secret place. He took you there to throw you off the cliff edge because he thought no one cared enough to trouble what happened to you, since we all suspected you of spying. Even so, he had to make it look like an accident because he knew I was against murder.'

'Why did he not kill me in the house and then throw me over the cliff?'

'He did not want to leave any tell-tale marks on you that would point to murder. Besides, he had to set the scene first. He probably drugged the carriage driver and the man who had held him prisoner, pushed the two men into the vehicle and drove it at full speed to the edge of the cliff then jumped off before horses and carriage tumbled over. He then hoped to push you off at the same spot to make it look as if the horses had bolted in the storm, with you, the driver, and his mate in the vehicle. An ingenious accident.'

'But how did you know all this?'

'Because, unknown to Porrot, the two men he drugged were pearl divers. They cannot pursue their profession during the monsoons so they take up other work. As soon as they hit the water the men revived and managed to swim out of the carriage because the door flew open as it went over. They told us what happened.'

'Porrot must have hated me.' Elena nestled closer to him. 'Did—did you shoot him, Stephan?'

'No, he backed off the cliff. That was a genuine accident, I fear.'

'I'm sorry, Stephan. I know you valued your captains.'

'Don't apologise, *lieveling*—he was a murderer. He also pushed Lucy into the sea and poisoned Jan.'

Elena gasped and curved her head back to stare up at him. His face looked grim in the dim lamplight. 'How did you find out?'

'We discovered a letter in Jan's escritoire, addressed to me, when we were searching the place after the Dutch invasion. Jan must have told Porrot he suspected him of Lucy's death and threatened to report it to me, but didn't mention he'd written a letter and so...'

'Why did Porrot kill Lucy?'

'He probably was present when Jan and Lucy were quarrelling on deck, she begging her husband to take her home. Jan must have refused and stalked away leaving Lucy and Porrot alone on deck. As you know, Porrot was adamant that no one left the island. I don't think I need to tell you more.' He rubbed his cheek against her hair. 'I'm sorry I mistrusted you, sweetheart, I should have known better. But that did not make me love you any less, Elena.'

She smiled and caressed him. 'I forgive you, darling. Just one more thing, Stephan. I expect Porrot slipped poison into Jan's drink?'

'*Ja.* He probably thought Jan's death would be put down as another casualty of malaria.' For a while silence reigned as they thought about the dead people.

'But enough of gloomy thoughts, *lieveling.* Your finger will be fitted with a new wedding-ring—mine! I cannot permit you to wear Anthony's. Then, later in the week, celebrations will be held. I hope Aggie will be reconciled to living on the island.'

'Oh, yes, Aggie is happy to do so. She was over-joyed when I mentioned that you and I are now married. I hope you don't mind my telling her.'

'Not at all!'

She lapsed into silence. And, sensing something wrong, he asked, 'What is troubling you, Elena?'

'Will you continue with your—er—your profession?'

He laughed. 'No, my love, we held a conference today to the effect that we will engage ourselves in honest trade through our newfound company, The Oriental Pearl. We have also agreed to recruit an army from among our people to defend this island. No more being taken by surprise. But enough of talk. I think, Lady Van Coen, you and I need to engage ourselves in more enjoyable practices. Nothing against your principles, I promise you!'

And as she laughed his mouth came down on hers.

DEAR REBEL

Mary Nichols

Like many men in his position, Lord Carthorne was
more concerned to protect his property, the lovely
manor of Waterlea in the Fens of East Anglia, than to
take sides in the escalating war between Charles I
and his Parliament.
So he had no hesitation about using the childhood
betrothal between his daughter Alys and
Cromwell's captain, Sir Garret Hartswood, to get out
of trouble. This was an enormous shock to Alys, who
had forgotten the betrothal, and was a fervent
Cavalier to boot! There seemed to be no escape
from Garret's relentless intention to honour the
agreement . . .

TWO HISTORICAL ROMANCES & TWO FREE GIFTS!

Masquerade historical romances bring the past alive with splendour, excitement and romance. We will send you a cuddly teddy bear and a special MYSTERY GIFT. Then, if you choose, you can go on to enjoy 4 more exciting Masquerades every two months, for just £1.75 each! Send the coupon below at once to – Reader Service, FREEPOST, PO Box 236, Croydon, Surrey CR9 9EL.

- - - — — — — — — NO STAMP REQUIRED — — — — — ✂